HAUNT

my

HEART

LISA MEDLEY

Haunt My Heart © 2015 Lisa Medley.

ISBN: 978-0-9908856-1-0

Cover and formatting by Sweet 'N Spicy Designs
http://sweetnspicydesigns.com

This book is a work of fiction. While reference might be made to actual historical events or existing locations, the names, characters, places and incidents are either the product of the author's imagination or are used fictitiously, and any resemblance to actual persons, living or dead, business establishments, events, or locales is entirely coincidental.

Published in the United States of America

Lisa Medley
http://www.lisa-medley.com

DEDICATION

To Alexandra Chauran, professional psychic and fortune
teller, for tirelessly answering my every question
regarding hexes, curses and magic. Visit her
at http://earthshod.com/

CHAPTER ONE

"Hurry up, Sarah. We're going to miss the ghost!"

Sarah Knight rolled her eyes in the cold December darkness, but trotted after Ellie's bouncing flashlight beam. Sarah's heels crunched through the frozen topsoil as she crossed the lawn, and she worried about the damage being done to her only pair of sensible work shoes. Ellie had failed to mention this would be an outdoor excursion.

Ellie had been dragging her out on girls' nights against her better judgment since they graduated from college. Last month, they'd gone to a mixed martial arts fight, complete with blood, screaming and more than one missing tooth. And that had been the spectators.

It was only in the car on the way over that Sarah had learned tonight's adventure would be a ghost hunt. Ellie had a strange idea of fun.

Sarah and Ellie caught up to the tour group as the leader, a tall dark-haired man in his mid-forties, wrapped up his ghost-hunting protocol explanation. She'd missed the rules. Ellie wouldn't care about missing that part. She hated following the rules, but Sarah was a little miffed. If she was going ghost hunting, she wanted to know exactly what the boundaries were.

"Great," Sarah whispered. "We missed the rules."

"At least we didn't miss the ghost," Ellie pointed out. "And they haven't doled out the equipment yet." Ellie's mouth split into a mischievous smile, and she angled up closer to the group leader.

"Again, my name is Allen, if you have any questions during the tour. Since we have such a large group tonight, we'll split into two teams. Carla will take this half." Allen sliced an imaginary line through the group of twenty or so ghost-hunters. "And the rest of you will go with me."

Relieved she and Ellie were on the same side of the line, Sarah snuggled up closer to her friend and surveyed the rest of their team. A middle-aged couple, a grandmotherly woman, and a group of ten sorority girls—exactly the type of girls she'd avoided in college—made up Team Allen. The girls sported matching Greek-lettered sweatshirts, scarves and mittens and tittered incessantly. Sarah was fairly sure their chance of seeing a ghost with this group was nil. Fine with her. Ellie was the one who went for the paranormal stuff.

"We'll walk the path where the Lady in White has typically been spotted. Carla's team will cover the grounds around the house," Allen said. He nodded to Carla, and she gave him a little salute, then led her team around to the side of the building. Allen's group stayed put in the doorway.

"First, I'll need a couple of volunteers," Allen announced.

Ellie's hand shot up before Sarah could register what was happening. "We'll do it."

Classic Ellie, leaping before she looked. She didn't even know what she was volunteering for. It could be anything. If Allen wanted virgins to sacrifice, however, he was out of luck.

Allen pulled two little handheld meter devices out of his messenger bag. His brows lowered a bit as he studied Ellie, cast his eyes around the group, then settled back to her. Ellie's enthusiasm won out and Allen handed one device to her and the other to Sarah.

"This is the Anomaly Detector," Allen said with all the reverence of presenting the sword Excalibur. "It measures EMP and temperature. If these lights change, it's your job to let us know. I'll be taking photos and interacting with the ghost, trying to draw her out. I can't keep my eyes on all of the devices at once. Can you manage this?"

"Absolutely," Ellie squealed.

Sarah resisted rolling her eyes again. She accepted the detector and did her best to reduce her scowl.

"It's okay to be skeptical," Allen said. "It makes it all the more exciting when we convert you to a believer." His smile warmed and Sarah realized he was actually handsome. Old, but handsome. What an otherwise normal and attractive man—who was way old enough to know better—was doing leading a bunch of ghost hunters, she had no idea. People were strange. She supposed she'd have to include herself in that judgment, considering she now held a ghost detector.

"Let's get started." Allen took off down the trail along the terrace with an enthusiastic tail of college girls behind him. The middle-aged couple and the grandmotherly woman fell into step behind the girls. Ellie and Sarah followed.

A few feet down the trail, Allen stopped and addressed the darkness. "The spirit we seek tonight is known in the lore as a Lady in White, a common sort of spirit ghost found in many cultures. This particular lady, however, we know a bit about. Typically, our Lady has only been viewed once every seven years, on the anniversary of her death, which occurred on June 21, 1790. But a friend who works on the grounds called me and said she'd smelled lily of the valley twice this week while making her nightly rounds *and* saw a white cloud of smoke appear in absolute darkness as she walked to her car."

"Nice," Ellie said.

"For whatever reason, the ghost has been active. We were lucky to get permission to check things out. Park administrators usually only allow a hunt once a year on the anniversary. It's become a real tourist draw for them."

"How did she die?" Sorority Girl Number One asked.

Allen came to a stop and turned to address the group. "We don't know for sure, but natural causes from all known accounts. It wasn't her death that made her spirit restless. A lost love is the cause of that. On her deathbed, she swore she'd search for her true love here on the Chatham Manor grounds until she found him again. She was an English woman who fell in love with an English man well beneath her social status. Her father sent her across the ocean to Chatham in the hopes of finding a more suitable match. But her lover followed her here, and they made plans to elope. They were foiled by George Washington, of all people. Our Lady returned to England and her lover was arrested. The two were never to meet again. She still searches for him."

"What a great love story," Sorority Girl Number Two said.

"Not really. It sort of sucks," countered Sorority Girl Number Three. "She spent her life without her true love, and now her death too? What's great about that?"

"It's great for ghost hunting." Allen smiled. "Ladies, let me power up those detectors, and let's get to work."

Allen fidgeted with the gadget and the lights flamed to life on Sarah's device. The Anomaly Detector cycled through its setup. One green light remained steady after the flashing settled.

Allen pointed to the device. "It's normal for one or even two green lights to fluctuate a bit, but if the yellow, and certainly if the red lights up, we may have something."

"Have you tracked her before?" Sarah asked.

"Many times," Allen answered.

"Any luck?" Sarah pressed.

"Nothing we could document empirically, but I've sensed a presence," Allen said.

Sarah cut her eyes to Ellie, silently transmitting her growing sarcasm.

He sensed a presence?

What a bunch of hooey. It was going to be a long hour.

Allen led them down the darkening path, away from the ground's lighting, and the rest of the team fell into a silent parade behind him. Even the sorority girls quieted down with only the pinprick beams from their flashlights to alleviate their fears. Everything seemed peachy in the light, but a chill ran down Sarah's back, one that had nothing to do with the early December cold. She shivered, trying to fling off the odd feeling like a dog shakes off water. Her imagination was acting up. Nothing else.

Ellie walked a few feet ahead of Sarah with her head down. She looked determined, but seemingly oblivious to anything other than her ghost gadget.

"Departed spirit, we mean you no harm this evening. Will you show yourself to us? Will you visit us for a while?" Receiving no response, Allen tried again. "We know your story. We know how you search for your lover. Friends have smelled your flowers this week. What is it you are trying to communicate?"

Allen snapped photos left and right, then stopped when one of the girls laughed.

He gave her a sharp look. Sarah felt bad for him. At least she'd managed to keep her own sarcasm contained thus far. The other girls were clearly less reserved.

"Sorry," the girl said.

Sarah looked down at her detector. "Um, what does this mean?" The lights held steady all the way to the red zone for several seconds. Long enough for Allen to get a good look at the readings.

"We know you are present," Allen said. "Please show yourself. We mean you no harm."

Ellie scooted in close to Sarah and frowned, shaking her own detector. "I wonder why mine didn't go off."

"Please don't agitate the meter. It's very sensitive," Allen said.

"So you say. Why didn't mine go off?" Ellie gave the detector another shake.

Allen continued to snap photos, turning in a circle. *Snap. Snap. Snap.*

Sarah didn't see anything, but the college girls were getting restless, and when her meter lit red again, one of them screamed.

"What? Did you see her?" Allen asked, spinning a tight circle.

An icy breeze blew past them, creating a tiny dust devil of leaves. Sarah's temperature light blinked in warning and registered a ten degree drop.

"Um."

"I see it," Allen said, watching her detector.

"Seriously. What is wrong with this thing?" Ellie slapped her meter against her leg hard enough to leave a bruise, checked its reading, and then repeated the meter abuse.

"I think I see something," Sorority Girl One said, her face going even paler in the glow of her flashlight as she pointed at something behind Sarah.

"Where? I don't see anything." Ellie followed the girl's beam, and Sarah tried to clear her own night vision after several more flashlights temporarily blinded her.

The *Eurythmics'* "Sweet Dreams" split the night and Sarah jumped. She searched her coat for her phone to silence it.

Allen glared at her. "Your phone is on?"

"Yes. Sorry." Sarah hit decline and silenced it, stuffing it back into her pocket.

Allen's shoulders dropped and he closed his eyes, pinching the bridge of his nose. "Is anyone else's phone still on?"

"You told us to turn them off," Sorority Girl Number Three offered in all her helpful glory.

"Yes. I did." Allen reached for Sarah's meter. "Every time your phone updates, gets a notification, searches for a signal, it sends out electronic pulses. This"—Allen held the meter inches from her face— "measures electromagnetic signals. Do you understand what that means?"

Sarah's face grew hot, and she was thankful for the cold air. Now if only a hole would appear under her feet, all would be well.

"She didn't know. You should have warned us," Ellie said, coming to her rescue.

"I did. It was the first thing I told you all." Allen shook his head. He held out his hand for Ellie's meter, but she snatched it back in defiance.

"I don't even have a phone, Ghostbuster dude. No rules violation here. I am still the Keymaster," Ellie said, gripping the meter.

The middle-aged couple laughed and this time, Allen's face grew red. Sarah had no idea what Ellie was talking about. She'd already managed to make herself as invisible as possible and tried to fade to the back of the line.

Allen relented, hanging his head, eyes closing briefly as he steeled his patience, most likely deciding any further disturbance of his ghost hunt wasn't worth it. He handed Sarah's detector to the grandma. "Before we continue, does anyone else have *any* devices still powered on? Of any kind? Phone? iPod? He gave Grandma a second look. "Pacemakers?"

Grandma shook her head no, and no one else fessed up to any rule violations. Embarrassed, Sarah wanted to leave. But by the way Ellie coveted her Anomaly Detector like it was the One Ring, she knew there would be no bailing. She'd have to ride this night out to its bitter end.

Allen gave Sarah one more disappointed look and turned around, shaking his head and heading back down the trail. Sarah waited as the other team members, still huddled around her, dispersed and followed Grandma and Allen.

"Don't worry about him," Ellie said, not taking her eyes off her meter. "He should have told you about the phone thing."

Sarah opened her mouth to argue several points— that if they hadn't been late in the first place, hadn't missed the rules talk at the beginning, if Ellie hadn't volunteered them, it wouldn't have mattered. No use arguing the obvious with Ellie when she was in the zone, however. Instead, she resigned herself and tagged after Ellie like the sidekick she was.

Had always been.

Only fifty more minutes of humiliation, and another girls' night would be history. She couldn't wait.

CHAPTER TWO

Ellie opened the driver's side door, and Sarah waited for her to crawl across the seat of the old Mustang and pop the passenger-side lock. The broken power locks were one of many deficiencies in the classic car. Sarah retrieved her betraying phone from her pocket and powered it up as Ellie shuffled about inside the car.

As she checked her phone display, a glint of light on the ground to her right caught her eye. Aiming her screen at the ground like a flashlight, she bent low and searched for the source of the flash. Just as she began investigating, though, she heard the lock pop, and Ellie pushed the door open. The door hit Sarah in the head, knocking her to the cold, hard ground.

"Sorry," Ellie said, scrambling to catch the door before it slammed closed again.

Sarah mumbled a few choice obscenities and rubbed her head. She reached down and ran her finger over something half-buried in the ground.

"What is that?" Ellie was hanging out the car, her body stretched across the seats.

"I don't know." Sarah turned the flashlight of her phone up to full beam and picked at the object in the frozen turf. "Do you have a pen or something?"

Ellie scuffled around inside the dark, rolling landfill that was her car—the interior lights long burned out—and produced a screwdriver instead. "Will this work?"

Sarah took the offered screwdriver and dug at the buried treasure. After breaking it free from its cold grave, she examined it by the light of her cell phone. "It's a ring."

"Let me see."

Ellie scrambled back into the driver's seat. Sarah joined her in the car, then shut the door against the cold.

"Hold the light," Sarah said, digging a Kleenex from her coat pocket to clear as much of the mud from the ring as possible.

The ring remained caked with mud, which filled the engraved edges, but the stone cleaned off easily enough. The set, a square cut black onyx, glinted. The cold metal of the band warmed in her hand.

"You know what that is, right?" Ellie asked.

"A ring?" Sarah couldn't keep the sarcasm from her voice, not after the night she'd had.

"An artifact."

"No. Someone just lost a class ring. Like one of the sorority girls."

"Does that look like a woman's ring? No. *No* is the answer. That is a man's ring. An officer's ring or something. That could be a real-life, true-blue Civil War artifact."

"I doubt it. And if it is, we'll return it. This is a national park. There are rules."

"I say finders keepers. Let me see it better."

Sarah handed the ring to Ellie, who examined it like a jeweler, squinty-eyed and mouth turned up in one corner. She held it up to the light of Sarah's phone and dug at the dirt in the engravings with her fingernail.

"Interesting," Ellie said.

"Enough. Let's get home." Sarah snatched back the ring. She had experienced all the fun she could stand for one night. The park offices were long closed and Ellie's was the last car in the parking lot. "I'll bring it back tomorrow and turn it in to Lost and Found."

"You're such a goody two-shoes."

"No. Thanks to you, I'm a rule breaker. Or did you not notice the entire ghost-hunting debacle tonight? Oh, wait. You probably didn't notice because you got to *keep* your Anomaly Detector. Your eyes were glued to it the entire night. When you weren't kissing Allen's ass, that is."

"Fat lot of good it did. After you turned off your phone, neither of them went off the rest of the night. Turned out to be a cold walk through the park, not a ghost hunt. Although…Allen was kind of hot, right?"

"He was old." Sarah gripped the ring and stared into the dark parking lot.

"He wasn't *that* old. You need to broaden your horizons. There are a lot of fish out there, you know. You don't have to keep the barracuda you currently have."

"Jason isn't a barracuda. He's…complicated."

Ellie snorted. "He's an asshole. Nothing complicated about that. He's a smarmy real estate agent with his face on twelve billboards in Fredericksburg. Like everyone in town doesn't already know him. He's in a bar every night. He's a drunk, Sarah. A mean one and you can't fix him. He's unfixable. You can't fix asshole."

Sarah fidgeted. "He takes out clients. It's part of his job."

11

"He takes out people who are looking for homes? To *bars*? Is that what he tells you? You're smarter than that."

"Thank you for the insightful psychological analysis."

"All right, but admit it. Allen was hot in that Captain Mal sort of way." Ellie poked Sarah in the shoulder for emphasis and smiled.

"Captain who? Speaking of hot. How about some heat in here?"

"You had better be kidding me. Captain Malcom Reynolds? *Firefly*? Best show in the history of television, prematurely canceled after its first season? Mal? That's so not shiny." Ellie turned the key in the ignition. When the motor didn't turn over immediately, Sarah sighed.

"Seriously? When are you going to get this thing worked on?" Sarah asked.

"When I have the money. Where's that screwdriver?"

Sarah handed the tool to her. Ellie hopped out of the car again and said, "Give her some gas when I tell you."

Sarah straddled the console and put her left foot on the gas pedal as Ellie popped the hood and fiddled around with the motor.

"Turn the key and give it a tap of gas."

Sarah did as told and the car roared to life. Ellie slammed down the hood, then climbed back in as Sarah repositioned herself.

"Sometimes the carburetor gets stuck," Ellie said, ducking her head. "My brother showed me what to do when it won't start."

"Can we just get home now? We both have to work tomorrow, and it's already after midnight."

"As you wish."

Sarah couldn't wait to get the ring home and cleaned up to see what it really looked like. She clutched her find, then jumped as something jolted against her skin.

Probably more electrical problems with Ellie's car.

That girl was going to be the death of her. Sarah waited in expectant silence for the car to burst into flames on their ride home.

* * *

"See you at work tomorrow?" Ellie asked as Sarah stepped onto the bricked sidewalk in front of her apartment building.

"Bright and way too early," Sarah said.

"I'm sorry about tonight. I appreciate you being such a good sport." Ellie smiled, her eyes dropping briefly. Then that same old mischievous smile broke across her face. "At least you got a souvenir."

Sarah rubbed the goose egg on her head and offered a scowl back. "Yeah, a concussion and a public chastisement from a Ghostbuster. Great souvenirs."

"The ring, dork. See you tomorrow."

"Good night, Ellie." Sarah shut the car door, and Ellie drove away.

God only knew what she would come up with for next month's girls' night.

Sarah searched her pockets for the key. After finding it, she pulled out both it and the ring. She opened the shared entrance door and made her way up the narrow flight of stairs. Her apartment was a primo loft directly over Greysmith's Book Shop & Coffee Bar. The rental was small but surprisingly affordable due to the effusion of noise from the espresso machine and constant drift of music from below. Both wafted through the floor from six a.m. to midnight daily. Sarah could sleep through anything, though, and the disclosure wasn't a deterrent. What she wanted was a place of her own close to work.

Considering she and Ellie barely made forty thousand as web site developers, affordable was good, and she'd snatched the opportunity to rent the loft a few months ago. A little noise seemed a small price to pay for the ambiance and personal space. Jason had tried to get her to move out to the sticks in a rental he'd found, but she liked being in the midst of things, not secluded.

Most storefronts on Princess Anne Street had apartment lofts above them, thanks to the Fredericksburg Chamber of Commerce's revitalization efforts to bring back business and life to the downtown area.

Sarah entered her apartment, shut the door and leaned back against it with a sigh. *What a night.* She kicked off her shoes at the doorway. Her yellow tabby weaved between her legs.

"I know. I'm late. I should have stayed home with you, Bitly." She bent to scratch behind the cat's ears, then started to the bathroom, shedding her clothes as she went.

Showering was foremost on her agenda, and then bed. But the muddy ring in her hand beckoned her. She started the shower, then dug around under her bathroom cabinet for an old toothbrush while the water heater worked its magic.

Surely if the ring had survived being buried, a little gentle scrubbing wouldn't hurt. She turned on the faucet and held the ring under the water, then went to work with the toothbrush. Gentle scrubbing soon gave way to more vigorous efforts as the dark engravings along the sides of the setting were revealed. The bathroom steamed up as she worked. Flecks of mud plugged up around the sink stopper, pooling the water.

An image appeared as the mud and grit sloughed out from the ring's indentations. A head, wings, and a tail of a dragon took form. Engraved flames licked behind the beast, circling both sides of the band and meeting in the back center. The dragon image was mirrored on the opposite side.

With the ring free of mud, Sarah retrieved a tube of toothpaste, squeezed a line along the toothbrush bristles, then applied the same vigor to her task, scrubbing and polishing the silver band until it gleamed. She rubbed the stone with a soft cloth. The onyx was now so clean she could almost see her reflection in it.

Not quite a diamond ring, but still a very pretty stone.

She slid the ring on her finger. Even on her thumb, the ring was far too big. She would lose it in ten minutes. She removed it and set it on the countertop.

Shower. Bed. Do it.

Ten minutes later, Sarah was warm, snuggly and tucked into her bed. Bitly curled by her side. After setting the alarm, Sarah placed her phone on her nightstand beside her new treasure. The ring turned out to be the only good thing about the night. She noticed six missed calls from Jason. She'd had the phone off after the ghost-hunting debacle, and then in the ring excitement, hadn't noticed her missed calls. He hadn't left a message. Typical. He had made her chase him since college.

Well, she wasn't going to chase him tonight. It was much too late to call him back. Turning over, she tried not to replay the night's humiliation in her head, but it was no use. She loved Ellie, but sometimes…

Bitly purred as Sarah scratched his head. One thing about living downtown was that it never grew truly dark. Between the street lights below and the floor-to-ceiling windows on the street side of her loft, nights were more like dusk than dark. She'd looked into purchasing blinds or curtains, but couldn't afford a custom job. Instead, she grabbed the sleep mask from under her pillow, slid it over her eyes, and slipped off to sleep.

CHAPTER THREE

Tanner woke screaming.

Anger, not fear, set him off. The question was what had awakened him in the first place? And after all this time. At least it had seemed like a long time. Being dead made it hard to keep track. He'd counted sunrises for months after he'd died, but even that became too taxing after a while. And when he'd finally been crushed into the ground and damned to the darkness, he'd lost all hope.

His life energy had begun to wane immediately upon his death and his semi-corporeal form—his ghost self—had dissipated a few days after his men removed his body from the battlefield. Not that it would have mattered anyway. No one could see him. He'd tried to make contact as the soldiers crossed by him: screaming, begging, anything to get their attention. To tell them he wasn't dead. Not really. When he noticed the soldiers could also pass *through* him without so much as a shiver, he'd given up.

Despair filled him as he realized Sylvia had achieved exactly what she'd promised. He was a stupid man. Maybe he could have loved her. Maybe…

God, what a witch.

No. It would never have worked. He'd have been damned either way. At least he'd saved soldiers' lives, his own good men, with his decision at Chatham. He'd done the right thing, even if it had cost his life.

He surveyed the room as best he could from his prison.

Clearly he'd traveled from the grounds where he'd lingered for…decades? He wished he knew. Pent-up frustration filled him. Tanner could see energy emanating from something, just out of his reach. A glow—the signature of a living soul. An entity he hadn't seen for a very long time. The aura, bright and strong, *almost* reached his prison cell, but not quite.

So close.

Something had sparked him to life. But what?

He startled when a face appeared before him. A non-human face. The face of some creature filled the mirrored prism of his cell.

What fresh hell was this?

The next thing he knew he was falling, falling, falling. The clatter when he landed nearly deafened him. His stomach roiled as if he'd leaped from a great height.

"Bitly. Stop it."

A voice? A female voice?

Sylvia? Could she still be in possession of him?

Dear God.

"Bad kitty."

His stomach lurched again as he was returned to his previous perch; the view was exactly the same, except the face that stared into his for the briefest moment was different. A woman's face.

A woman most assuredly not Sylvia.

Relief flooded him. Of course Sylvia was long dead. *Of course.*

And she wouldn't have followed him into the afterlife. She'd never loved him that much. Not enough to spend eternity with him. Only enough to damn his soul for it.

* * *

Sarah untangled herself from her bed coverings and snapped on the lamp. Bitly batted at the ring he'd managed to swat under her bed after knocking it from the nightstand in his late-night wanderings. Anything new in the house automatically piqued the cat's interest. Clearly, the beast didn't know the cautionary tale of curiosity and the cat.

Scrambling under the bed, she searched and finally retrieved the ring. A small shock passed through her hand as she clutched it. She couldn't blame Ellie's car this time. Maybe onyx was a conductor of some sort, or the silver band?

Weird.

She placed the ring back on the nightstand and crawled underneath her covers.

"Bad kitty," she repeated. Bitly seemed less than repentant and turned his head away, having already lost interest in the potential toy. Light glinted off the newly polished stone, and Sarah was proud of the restoration job she'd done.

She'd return it tomorrow. Maybe she'd even get a reward or finder's fee of some sort. God knew she could use the money. At this rate, she would never be able to afford curtains.

Ugh. 2:45 a.m.

She would be worthless tomorrow. Rolling over, she punched the *on* button of her electric blanket and slid the eye mask over her face, willing herself back to sleep.

* * *

Tanner felt the jolt down to his bones. Metaphorically speaking, of course—his physical bones were long disintegrated. As should have been his soul. Yet here he was. Honestly, he had no idea how to describe his current state of spiritual flux. His vocabulary and knowledge of the occult had been extensive before he found himself in this predicament. But now? His own semi-existence was beyond comprehension. Seeing the supernatural imposed on others was one thing. Experiencing it in a very personal and permanent way was another. He was certain there were words to put to his condition, but even they would be inadequate to accurately portray the horror of his current existence.

Between this spark and the first, his awareness peaked, full and intact. He'd been awakened—thoughts, memories, emotions, longings, fears. Everything about him was as it should be except for his physical body. And the fact he remained trapped inside an onyx stone.

Bloody witch.

Anger boiled within him. Neither his Major General nor his Masonic Brotherhood, the Brothers of Peril, had been any help against the witch's hex. They'd been playing with fire. All of them. But it was he, Lieutenant James "Tanner" Dawson, who'd been burned. *One for one thousand.* That had been the bargain after Tanner refused Sylvia's overt sexual advances. She'd been after him for weeks, but he had not time nor inclination to pursue her. Something was off about the woman. That, and she was a bona fide witch.

Tanner had been assigned as liaison to the witch when the Major General, Tanner, and a handful of others had been sent ahead to Fredericksburg to secure Chatham Manor as headquarters. The Major General had insisted upon employing a seer to ensure military success in the upcoming battles. After the fiasco at Bull Run, he was taking no more chances. The Brothers of Peril had been invoked. Confederate forces began forming across the river days later, upping the ante for them all.

Tanner closed his eyes, overcome by the flood of memories and regret.

"Sylvia. I'm sorry. You are by all accounts, and by my own eye, a beautiful woman. However, I find that I am simply not interested in you in that manner."

She'd grabbed his hand, her eyes filled with faux sorrow as she twisted his ring around his finger.

Momentarily distracted by her odd behavior, Tanner laughed. "The prediction, Sylvia. The General waits."

"You avail yourself of my spiritual talents but refuse my physical gifts when freely offered?" She lowered her gaze to his hand.

"Again, I—"

"All for one? Or one for all?" Sylvia asked him, her eyes red with rage as she lifted her gaze to his. He attempted to pull away from her but she held on tight. Not wanting to be rude, he let her.

"All for one? Or one for all? The Lieutenant's choice shall determine the fall.

Lead the charge and win the day, or be the coward and run away.

Upon the Earth, his soul shall stay forever more and then a day.

Lest true love fill his spirit shell, his body rot while soul's in cell.

Upon this mortal coil may stay, if somehow love does find a way."

A sharp pain sliced across his palm and Tanner tore his hand free from her hold, all pretense of civility gone. The woman was clearly insane.

"You cut me?" Blood seeped from the fresh wound. "What are you doing?" Tanner backed away toward the door. "Do you have a prediction for the Major General or not?"

"His success depends on yours. You have my last word on the matter."

Confounded, Tanner turned to the door and peeled back the tent flap. The afternoon sun streamed in, and he shielded his eyes against the harsh light. When he looked back, a fiery glow surrounded Sylvia. Dust motes danced about her like sparks as she smiled.

An icy shiver crawled up his spine, and he stepped from the tent.

It was only later as his wound was being treated that he realized she'd stolen his ring during their exchange.

He shook his head, trying to erase the memory. Of course, that one would stick most solidly in his psyche. It was the most oft played of all his days thus far. He hadn't wanted to take her seriously, but her previous predictions had all proven to be accurate. The Major General had orchestrated a plethora of tests before accepting her advice. She had passed them all. Sylvia DeWitt, a direct descendant of a long line of witches stretching back to the dark days of Salem, was not a woman to be trifled with. Her ancestors had moved to Virginia from Salem, but still many had perished in the early days of witch hunting paranoia. It seemed the Puritans were right to have been paranoid.

A lesson Tanner would have done well to learn before he'd accepted the task of witch liaison.

Despite his efforts, he couldn't stay the unpleasant reverie of that faithful day.

"Lieutenant Dawson, we need our orders." Captain Newcomb stood in the open flap of Tanner's tent. The Confederate threat had escalated. Waiting for the reinforcement battalion on its way from Richmond was no longer an option.

"I'll deliver them myself. I'll be there in a moment," Tanner replied.

The tent flap closed and Tanner paced. If only he knew what those orders would be. He'd lay awake all of the long night struggling for a decision. Replaying the prediction in his mind, puzzling out Sylvia's riddle, he'd realized it was much more than a mere prediction. He was sure it was a hex. And if his determination of Sylvia's hex was correct, and he led the charge...he would die. If he didn't lead the charge, the entire battalion of one thousand soldiers would die. It was a ridiculous predicament with only one solution.

His hope was the witch was bluffing. The slow burn in his gut told him she wasn't. The hex had been elaborate and detailed, and the words singed his consciousness like a demonic embroidery sampler.

The entirety of the ramifications of the successfully executed hex were not at first apparent. Only later—much later—did he come to full realization concerning the last part and its improbability.

Tanner closed his eyes and resigned himself to his next action, if not his fate. He'd lead the charge. It was the only thing he could do. He'd leave his future to whatever the fates had in store for him, but he wouldn't be reckless. He'd do his job. He would not, however, walk in front of a bullet on purpose. Suicide was for lesser men than he.

This wasn't his first battle.

He hoped it would not be his last.

Determined, he threw open his tent flap and crossed the threshold, then stopped. A small box lay at his doorway. He cast his search about the grounds, wondering if the Captain had noticed the box, or perhaps left it for him. Confounded, he bent to retrieve the small pine box and lifted the lid. Inside lay his ring, entwined with red and black threads, the colors of the shawl Sylvia wore.

Tanner hesitated. Perhaps it was an apology—a peace offering from her. Her words echoed through his mind, but the ring was important to him. He didn't have time for her nonsense. He was relieved to have his ring returned. Cursing under his breath, he unraveled the strands of thread, tossed them to the ground, and pushed the ring onto his hand. He was finished dealing with the witch. After today, the Major General could appoint a new lackey. Even if it meant he was transferred. Or disciplined. Although, he doubted it would come to that. The Major General would not be keen for anyone outside the Brotherhood to discover he'd solicited the services of a witch. And as far as Tanner was concerned, the farther away he was from the witch, the better.

With long, swift strides, he made his way to the gathering of soldiers to address the men. Major General was nowhere to be seen. Per usual for him. A twinge of fear coursed through Tanner, but he straightened his spine and fixed his gaze on the men. His men.

"We'll line the front lawn of Chatham with our artillery. Move cannons there and there." He pointed out the positions. "We'll hold our high ground. Let them cross the river. We have the numbers and this bluff on our side. No man in our battalion needs die today. Prepare to fight."

Tanner turned on his heel and walked toward the ridge. He stared across the river at the town. He knew every inch of the Chatham grounds. As his men marched, he did indeed lead them. As they arrived from the tent encampment behind the grounds, he made his way forward moving toward the edge. He knew exactly how close he could get to the Chatham boundaries before he'd be visible from the ravine below where the Confederate forces hid amongst the trees and overgrowth. He hugged the edge, flanked by his men. He had no intention of crossing that invisible barrier just yet. For all intents and purposes, he was living up to the letter of the hex. He led the charge.

The witch hadn't specified how far he had to lead it.

The line filled in to his left and right—a hundred men on either side of him, and layer upon layer behind him. The ridge curved around in a perfect geographical bowl. His frontline soldiers belly-crawled to the edge of the woods for a better look, and stopped before the land sloped off into the ravine. The first crack of gunfire startled Tanner as it came from his right side and very nearby.

Had one of his own men fired without order?

The second shot caught him in the chest, and he fell to his knees on the hard ground.

His immediate thought was he should have written a note.

Should have left something for his mother in New York. But he'd been consumed with his predicament, and he'd left nothing now but a body. Reaching to his chest, he pressed his palm against the wound as warm blood pulsed free. Melee commenced around him. With each beat of his heart, he watched his lifeblood pump out from him. Shots hit the dirt beside him. His ears filled with the sounds of his own demise. He drew his hand away to look at his life on his palm. A mortal wound. No doubt. He counted the labored thuds of his failing heart. One. Two. Three.

He slid the ring from his finger and gripped it tightly in his bloody hand. Maybe his men would notice it this way and think to send it home to his mother. The ring was all he had left and the culmination of his time on Earth embodied in one piece of jewelry. It was the symbol of his service to the Brotherhood and his country.

A solider scurried to his aid, but it was no use.

His vision faltered first and then his hearing. Everything grew silent, and his body crumbled beneath him. He fell to the ground, face first before the soldier could catch his fresh corpse. Confused, he floated up and then out from his body. He stood beside it. He caught the flow of a white gown from the corner of his eye and turned to face Sylvia. Across the lawn behind him on the steps of Chatham, she appeared to float toward him, ethereal in the hazy veil he now inhabited. The wind picked up her hair, which licked like flames about her head. She touched her palm to her lips and blew him a kiss.

The kiss of death, *Tanner thought.*

And then she vanished.

Tanner shook himself from his unwelcomed recollection.

Get hold of yourself, man.

He opened his eyes again and took full measure of his surroundings, desperate to reunite with the here and now, to ground himself. Energy filled his desiccated essence, reigniting forces that were beyond his meager understanding. It wasn't more than a spark, and not nearly enough, but it was a start. And the closest he'd been to another living person in years.

Concentrating, he let the energy gather, and a great roiling ball of light surrounded him inside his onyx cell. The witch had trapped his soul inside the Brotherhood ring. Bound him with her words and string to the one possession he'd cherished most. When they'd removed his body from the field, instead of collecting the ring as he'd hoped, it had slipped from his cold, dead hand. The soldiers he'd spared from death had unknowingly trampled his treasure into the muddy soil.

Body and soul buried but separately, he'd spent every second for the first few months testing his prison boundaries. It hadn't taken long to realize the depths of his despair. His was a fate far worse than death—a living Hell.

A soft glow from beside his cell caught his attention. The woman. Her aura emanated around her body in a bright pink fog, waves of light rising and falling with her breathing, pulling him toward her energy like a moth to flame.

Tanner's essence stretched and strained inside his cell, reaching toward the light. A shadow passed over his window, and he found himself hurtling through space once again. A glimpse of the yellow beast filled him with horror. He came to a soft landing on the bed and inside the glow of the woman's aura.

Pink light filled his confine, and he was drawn through the black onyx stone in a cyclone of magic and power. Stunned, Tanner reformed beside the bed of his liberator.

He was freed.

The ginger tabby cat hissed from the nightstand, arching his back and baring his teeth.

Tanner startled, leaped back from the bed, and looked about the room to determine the source of the beast's distress. A low growl rumbled from the animal's chest as Tanner took a tentative step toward the cat.

"Easy now." He reached his hand out in an effort of friendship.

The creature fled, racing off into another room. Rattled, Tanner took inventory of his situation as he basked in the glow of the aura beside him. For the first time, he got a clear view of the aura's source.

The woman's dark brown hair lay across her pillow, not like a fan, but in a jumble more resembling a bird's nest—tangled and wild. With her face half-covered in some sort of mask and her blankets wrapped around her like a death shroud, it was impossible to determine her visage.

Still, to Tanner, she was the most beautiful creature he'd ever seen. His liberator. His heroine.

Whatever magic had befallen him, previously or current, he was freed from the ring. Freed from Purgatory. Tears dampened his face as joy surged within him. A soft sigh escaped his deliverer's lips, and he noticed his ring lying against her back. The cat, having knocked the ring from the nightstand and into her aura, could also be credited in his rescue.

He owed the beast his eternal debt of gratitude. Clearly, the direct contact had released him from his confinement. Tanner fell to his knees beside the bed and pressed his forehead against the cool sheet, his hands clutched in prayer.

"Dearest Lord, you have not forsaken me. Thank you for delivering me to this kind woman and her clever beast. Show me the way to redemption." He sobbed his prayer in great gasps of relief.

Whatever fates befell him from this point forward, he was free, and he had no intention of returning to his onyx cell. With each passing moment that he remained within the glow of her energy, he grew stronger and more alive.

A new spark flared within him.

CHAPTER FOUR

Sarah hit the snooze on her phone for the third time. Exhausted from her night with Ellie and plagued by odd dreams, she finally rolled over and glanced at the display.

Nine a.m.?

Dear God, late again!

She groaned into her pillow and pushed herself to a sitting position. Bitly growled from above her head. Perched on her headboard, he stared into the ray of sunshine as it cast a warm rectangle on her wood floor.

"What's your problem? I'm the one who's going to get fired."

She untangled herself from her blankets and swung her feet over the side. Something flew from the coverings and clanged across the floor and into the light.

"You couldn't leave it alone could you, Bitly?"

Sarah picked up the ring and examined it. What a night. Her dreams had been filled with the craziest nonsense. Most of it starring a Civil War soldier...and blood. A lot of blood. Exactly what one would expect after a midnight ghost hunt on a battlefield. Her imagination had been on overdrive, and today she'd pay the price.

Late and exhausted. A perfect start to her day.

"Thanks for that, Ellie."

The cat meowed.

"All right, already, I'm on it."

After dressing in record time, she filled Bitly's food and water bowls and gave him a quick scratch behind the ears, despite his poor attitude this morning. If anyone should be upset, it was Sarah. Bitly had spent half the night batting around that stupid ring. Thinking of the ring, she retrieved it from the nightstand and dropped it in her purse, then thought again. She'd never remember to return it if it was in there. She had the memory of a gnat these days. Rummaging through her jewelry box, she found a silver chain, threaded it through the ring, then fastened it around her neck. She tucked the ring inside the collar, pulled on her coat, and threw a knitted scarf around her neck.

She walked four blocks to work every day. Since her car was parked in the multi-garage four blocks in the opposite direction, walking was actually faster than driving.

Sarah hustled down the stairs and past Greysmith's, ignoring the rumble in her belly. The smell of fresh brewed coffee and the fantastic little pastries they served nearly did her in. Stalwartly, she pressed on and broke into a trot after she hit the bricked sidewalk and the winter sunshine.

A half hour late. Maybe not that big a deal, but it wasn't the first time.

It was the seventh.

In two months.

She hated being late. Since the web developers could technically work from home, it shouldn't have been a big deal. But her boss, Candace Day, seemed to have a vendetta against her from the beginning. Sarah was very good at her job, but Candace was sleeping—*working*—her way to upper management. Sarah's success should have been an asset to Candace, but instead she was a threat. Candace had taken credit for Sarah's work more than once. Not wanting to make waves, Sarah hadn't said anything. Instead, she'd put in tons of face time in the office to try to demonstrate her commitment to the job. A job she desperately needed to keep unless she wanted to move back home to Georgia, which she most assuredly did not.

Sarah didn't break rules, and she didn't make waves. She had this one, tiny problem with being on time. And it had haunted her for twenty-three years.

She needed a break.

A lucky one.

* * *

Tanner was slightly less thrilled with his new state of being the second he realized he was still bound to the damned ring. And noncorporeal. While he was no longer caged, he was far from free of its hold. His one consolation was the ring remained within the woman's aura, which meant he could at least receive a constant infusion of life-renewing energy. As he tested his new boundaries, it didn't take long to discover his tether seemed to stretch a paltry hundred feet. Maybe less. Distance was difficult to accurately measure as the woman rushed ahead of him, dragging him through the streets of the futuristic metropolis. Every few seconds, he'd forget himself and be snapped from his goggling back into her sphere of energy like a leashed dog.

It was infuriating. And terrifying.

Hell, indeed.

He'd never seen the manner of conveyance, dress and color along these streets—the same streets he himself had once traveled. This new version of Fredericksburg was barely recognizable. He'd never seen anything like it in all twenty- nine years of his short life. Not even in New York. And the noise...

Horseless transports raced by near the sidewalk they hurried along. Every storefront held colorful signs and banners proclaiming wares and services for sale. Gone was the simplicity of livery, bar, church, school, hardware, and staples. In its place was pawn, jewelry, antiques, hair supply, an entire store below her home dedicated to coffee and books alone.

Dear Lord.

They traveled by foot for what might have been a mile before she entered a building, then a metal box, which shot them straight up in vertical transport lift of some sort with no visible ropes or pulleys. Before he could determine the witchery behind such a thing, they were out and into a large office area of some sort three stories above the street. The hustle and bustle reminded him of the Major General's war room at Chatham Manor, but the configuration confounded him. Across the top floor of the building they'd entered, each employee seemed allotted an approximate six foot by six foot, half-walled work space. A desk covered with all manner of contraptions resided in the center of the three padded walls.

His liberator entered one of the cubes, tossed her shoulder bag under the desk, then unloaded the oversized satchel she'd lugged from her home. A name plate on her wall read SARAH KNIGHT.

Finally, the name of his savior.

* * *

"You're late," Ellie whispered, crouching beside the chair in Sarah's cubby.

"It's your fault. I had nightmares all night, thanks to our little outing."

Ellie patted her thigh. "Don't sweat it. Candace has been in a closed door meeting all morning. No one even noticed. Besides, you're salaried. She's lucky you're even in the office."

"What's going on with the closed door thing?" Sarah plugged in her laptop and booted it up.

"I don't know. But she lost her flash drive this morning with some big presentation on it. I thought she was going to cry. Can you imagine? The Ice Queen crying?"

"Not in this life."

Ellie rose and perched on the edge of Sarah's desk. "Did you bring the ring? I'd love to get a good look at it in the daylight."

Sarah reached under her hair and undid the clasp of the chain, then pulled the ring from beneath her sweater and dangled it for Ellie's inspection.

"Aw, you're going steady." Ellie snatched the ring from her hand.

She held it toward the skylight and the onyx stone glinted. Sarah seized Ellie's elbow and pulled her arm below the cubicle wall.

"Contraband here. Let's not advertise it, please."

"Sorry. It's not like its micro-chipped or something." She turned the ring to examine the dragon design. "You really got it cleaned up well. That must have taken forever."

"Another reason I'm so exhausted today. Seriously, no more weeknight adventures. I'm too old for this stuff."

Ellie snorted. "We're the same age. So no, you're not too old. You're beaten down because of that loser boyfriend of yours."

"Oh, no." Sarah remembered Jason's missed calls. He'd be angry she'd waited so long to call him back, but he'd have to deal. If it were an emergency, he could have at least left a message. She checked her phone. Three more missed calls since she'd gone to bed last night. Her heart sank.

"What is it?" Ellie looked over her shoulder at her phone. "He'll live. It's good for him to wonder where you are. Know you aren't at his beck and call. That you have a life beyond his selfish needs."

"He's not selfish."

"He's the definition of selfish. You've just been blinded by his demonic charms."

"Enough, please."

"All right. All right." Ellie strung the chain around Sarah's neck and fastened the clasp. She smoothed out Sarah's hair. "It is a pretty stone. What do you think the ring is worth?"

"I have no idea. It doesn't matter anyway. I'm taking it back at lunch."

"Too bad. It might be the only piece of jewelry you ever get at this rate. I mean, it's been five years. If he were worth marrying, it would have already happened. Something to think about."

"Ellie!"

"I'm going. I'm going."

Ellie skipped away, and Sarah watched her bounce along the cubby farm, her head bobbing as if disembodied before she vanished into her own cube. That girl had hated Jason from day one. Sarah had attributed it to jealousy at first, but after five years, she knew it was genuine love and concern. Ellie had been her champion since grade school. The past few months, she'd been not so subtly nudging Sarah into situations where she might meet someone new. Someone of the male persuasion.

Jason was erratic and non-committal. That much was true. But he was still building his career. Realtors were on call 24/7, and he was one of the top three in Fredericksburg at only twenty-three. He'd gone to real estate school straight out of high school and built his sales quickly with his charming smile and smooth talking. Nothing wrong with using your assets to get ahead.

Candace appeared in her doorway, crushing her *using-your-assets-to-get-ahead* theory. Her eyes pinched at the corners and her mouth thinned into a grim line.

"You were late. Again."

"I know. I'm sorry."

Candace stared a hole through Sarah's soul. Her arms crossed under her visible cleavage, pushing up her breasts in case one was sight impaired and perhaps hadn't yet noticed them. She tapped her Manolo shoe in an uncharacteristically nervous gesture.

"I just got out of a meeting with corporate. Apparently, they got a call from Zymetron. They love your website revamp and their sales doubled last month. They insisted you receive a bonus for your work and sent over a check in your name for one thousand dollars." Candace uncurled a damp, crumpled check from her well-manicured fist, and tossed it onto Sarah's desk.

With shaky hands, Sarah smoothed out the check. Sure enough, one thousand dollars. Her mind raced and her cheeks heated with pride. Curtains would soon be hers.

"Don't be late again." Candace spun on her pointy heel and clicked across the antique grade wooden floor back to her office.

Ellie reappeared seconds later. "What was that all about?"

Sarah held up the check, dancing it around and wiggling in her chair.

"A grand? A bonus? God, that had to have *killed* her," Ellie said. "We need to celebrate tonight."

"No thanks. I need curtains. Celebration is for the weekends. Didn't we have this talk not ten minutes ago?" Sarah folded the check and tucked it into her wallet.

"Do not tell Jason you got that bonus check. Do you hear me, Sarah Elizabeth Knight? He has no need to know about it. The man made six figures last year and all he's given you is grief. And possibly some yet to be determined disease."

"I do not have a disease!" Sarah pushed back from Ellie and glared at her. "You are harshing my high over here."

Ellie's lip quivered in an exaggerated faux pout. "I'm sorry. Saturday then. We go curtain shopping, and *then* celebrate. Promise."

"Much more reasonable. Promise."

* * *

Tanner learned a lot in the three hours he spent tagging along with Sarah at her place of work. But every new development only led to more questions. The sheer number of women working side-by-side with men in the building was confounding to him. Who was looking after the women's families? He collected knowledge like the soldier he was and began to piece together an amazing tapestry of impossibly curious facts.

The most curious of which he still could not adequately process. The calendar on the lighted box sitting on her desk professed the date to be Dec. 5, 2014.

TWENTY-FOURTEEN?

Incredulous, he tried to absorb the fact. Clearly, the world had continued while he lay dormant for the past one hundred fifty years. It was much as the story he'd once read of Rip Van Winkle. Well, perhaps not *much* as the story. Still, the apt parts most assuredly applied. Unexpectedly, he too found himself a stranger in a strange land. And no one knew it.

Refusing to become downtrodden, he reminded himself his current condition was much improved from only a day earlier. Despite his confusion and sudden thrust into this brave new world, he was thankful beyond measure to be out of the ring. If he must be slave to a mistress, he could have fared far worse than this Miss Sarah Knight.

A verse from Shakespeare's *The Tempest* came to mind.

"How many goodly creatures are there here!
How beauteous mankind is! O brave new world,
That has such people in't."

Indeed.

Sarah was on the move again, and Tanner continued behind her, arriving at a canteen of some sort. The smell of rich, dark coffee staggered him, nearly bringing him to his knees. He reached for the countertop for support on instinct, but his hand passed directly through it. The aroma was the first true sensory experience, other than sight, he'd encountered since his energy had extinguished and his faculties faded to nothing. While he could sense and feel his awareness on a metaphysical level and he continued about as if all were well, his physical body remained mere spirit. Inhaling deeply, he marveled at the ebony wonder of life-affirming liquid Sarah proceeded to ruin with copious amounts of cream and sugar, turning the delicious, dark delicacy to a pale beige color.

Dear Lord.

Once awakened, his olfactory sense was overwhelmed with a barrage of all manner of unrecognizable scents. Despite the heinous desecration of her cup of coffee, Tanner reveled in the gift of its bouquet and its complete lack of coffee grounds floating about.

People scurried about the canteen. Sarah sliced, then dropped a biscuit of some sort into a contraption. The device immediately began to glow inside with hot coils that appeared to heat the bread. A few seconds later, much to his surprise, the bun popped up, steamy and toasted. She slathered white frosting containing what appeared to be blueberries—very much out of season—across its toasted face. The knife she used to spread the frosting slipped from her grip and skittered under the cabinet.

Sarah bent to retrieve it and returned with not only the knife, but also what looked to be a small tool.

"Holy cow." Sarah looked around the canteen and scooped up her bread and coffee.

She scurried across the office and stopped in front of a door, which led to a room where sat a person he assumed was her superior. She was the same unpleasant woman who had reluctantly brought some good news to Sarah earlier.

"Candace. Is this yours?" Sarah stood in the doorway.

Candace looked up from her spread of paperwork and glared at Sarah over the rims of a pair of glasses. She leaped up from her chair and crossed to the door in two quick strides, her gait surprisingly agile despite her torturous footwear.

Eyeing the flash drive, Candace snatched it from Sarah's hand. She gripped Sarah's elbow and pulled her into her office, then shut the glass door behind them.

"Where did you find this flash drive?"

"In the break room, under the cabinet. You must have dropped it when you went for coffee."

"How did you know it was mine? Did you open it?" Candace's face reddened and a vein in her neck pulsed visibly.

"Of course not. I heard you had lost a flash drive. When I found this one, I thought the chances were good it was yours."

"You're sure you didn't view it?"

"Positive."

Candace's shoulders lowered in apparent relief. She smoothed her hand down Sarah's sweatered arm, practically petting her. Her eyes lingered on Sarah's necklace.

"What is that? Are you going steady? A little old to be wearing a class ring, aren't you?"

Sarah grasped the ring and tucked it under her collar, out of sight. "It was a gift."

"Very well. Thank you for returning my flash. I was going crazy trying to recreate everything on it. It seems you've saved the day." The look on Candace's face said otherwise.

That woman was not to be trusted. Tanner hoped Sarah recognized the underlying hatred emanating from her tone and wished she could see the mustard colored aura surrounding her boss. A talent he himself had only acquired in death.

Then again, it didn't require a Samuel Morse to understand the message her superior telegraphed.

CHAPTER FIVE

Sarah collected her purse and phone and headed out to lunch. Her original intention had been to go straight to Chatham Manor and turn in the ring. Being late to work today and without her car made it impossible to complete the task during her lunch hour. Basically, she'd accomplished nothing since arriving at the office. She had a lot of ground to make up this afternoon. Her growling stomach finally got the best of her, and she left for Deaton's, the little sandwich shop down the street. Ellie was working through lunch so Sarah decided to bring her something since she was currently flush with cash, thanks to her unexpected windfall. Or at least she would be as soon as she deposited it at the bank, which was also along her route of travel.

She buttoned her bright pink peacoat, then plugged in her ear buds and tuned into WZRK in time for the Ladies of the 80s lunch show. No one need know her secret indulgence, especially Jason, who would only make fun of her. She stepped out into the cold sunshine of Caroline Street to Katrina and the Waves singing *Walking on Sunshine,* and smiled at the appropriateness.

Living and working downtown was fantastic most days, and this was one of them. The bank was a block away and Deaton's was too, which meant she could enjoy the added perk of window shopping along her way. Thursdays in downtown Fredericksburg were typically pretty quiet and today was no exception. Lunch crowd regulars hustled by to their favorite spots, but the tourists were mercifully scarce. Tomorrow night would be a different story. First Friday Art Walk brought out entire families. The bars, galleries, and restaurants would be hopping with locals, who were happy to get out of the house and enjoy some culture and fellowship.

Ellie and Sarah rarely missed a First Friday.

After depositing her check, she headed to Deaton's just as the radio station began the Out to Lunch trivia segment.

"What 80s rocker should have been born in Fredericksburg, with hits including 'Love Is a Battlefield' and 'Hit Me With Your Best Shot'? First caller gets lunch for twenty from Papa Paul's for their office tomorrow and four free concert tickets to WZRK's Rockin' New Year's Eve Extravaganza. And go."

Sarah tore off her gloves and hit speed dial on her phone. Always too slow, she still tried every chance she got. She stepped away from the ATM and leaned against the bank window front, bouncing excitedly when her call rang through.

"Come on. Come on."

"WZRK. You're on air and caller number one. For the win, what 80s rocker should have been born in Fredericksburg with hits including 'Love Is a Battlefield' and 'Hit Me With Your Best Shot'?"

"Pat Benatar."

"You got it! Who's calling and where are we sending lunch tomorrow?"

"Sarah Knight and lunch goes to Rappahannock Reveals Web Arts."

"Stay on the line, Sarah, and we'll get the deets. Now for you Ladies of Lunch listeners, some Pat Benatar to get you through the lunch hour, because some days love really is a battlefield."

Sarah's heart pounded as she finished up with the radio station on her walk to Deaton's. *What a crazy day.* Glancing at her phone, Sarah saw the little red notification circle on her app boasted an impressive eleven missed calls, taunting her and filling her with guilt. Another missed call from Jason just now as she waited in line at Deaton's for her sandwich order. Her heart sank. Still no message, just Jason's name filling her recent calls list.

He wouldn't be excited about the New Year's Eve bash. For one, he hated all things 80s, and two, he wouldn't be caught dead at the Masonic Mosque, where the bash was held. Frequenting the downtown venue was not the image he strove for.

Ellie would go with her in a heartbeat, but there would be hell to pay for missing New Year's with Jason. Which to go with—girlfriend or boyfriend? That was the question. Her excitement mixed with anxiety as she ordered her sandwiches. Her stomach did weird little flip flops when she walked back out onto Caroline Street.

She refused to call Jason back now and let him ruin her day. Despite a rocky start, this was one of the best days she could remember. A bonus, finding Candace's flash drive, lunch for her coworkers tomorrow *and* free New Year's Eve tickets? Tempting fate for sure. Besides, if he really needed her, he could leave a freaking message.

The cold wind picked up as she left Deaton's. She scrolled through her emails one-handed while she walked back to work. The wind snapped a shop flag from the doorway beside her head. Startled, she looked up from her phone, and realized she stood in front of Caroline Creations, a jewelry store she'd only ever considered by window. She couldn't afford expensive jewelry, and Jason had made no mentions of an engagement, despite the fact they'd been together five years.

Five years.

Ellie wasn't entirely wrong about Jason. He wasn't an asshole, but he was passionate about his career. Sometimes, it seemed he cared more about his work than her.

A necklace in the window caught Sarah's eye. She pulled the ring out from underneath her sweater, debating whether to go in.

She still had some time remaining in her lunch hour, and it wouldn't take more than five minutes to make the walk back. No one had to know where the ring had actually come from. She was very curious as to its value if any and even the history behind it. Clutching her sandwich bag, she walked into the shop. A tiny bell rang out announcing her arrival.

"May I help you?" A gray-headed man emerged from a small office behind the counter, holding a sandwich of his own.

"Sorry to disturb your lunch."

"No. No. Happy to help you." He set the sandwich on a napkin on the display case and smiled. "What are you interested in seeing today?"

Sarah examined the case in front of her, which was labeled with a glossy sign. *Custom Designs for all Occasions*. She set her own lunch sack on the case, then reached behind her neck to unclasp her necklace.

"I'm curious about this ring."

"Oh?" The jeweler took the ring to examine it and slid on a pair of thick glasses. After a long moment, he cut his gaze back to Sarah and raised an eyebrow, his mouth quirking into a half smile. "Funny, you don't look like a Civil War Mason."

Sarah felt a warm blush creep up her neck, which she hoped didn't make it to her face.

"It was a gift from my ex."

"Well, it's quite a gift. There were many Masons active during the Civil War here in Virginia, but there was one sect in particular rumored to have dealt in—let's say, some blacker magic. This ring is of the Brothers of Peril, a fringe group of the Masons. The dragon and the black onyx stone give it away. Of course, this is the first I've actually seen of one in real life. The number of membership was never known."

"Black magic? What did the Brothers of Peril do exactly?"

The jeweler twisted the stone in the light. "They supposedly cavorted with local witches, trying to affect and predict the results of battles. Onyx was once thought to be the manifestation of demons who would awaken in the night and spread nightmares to anyone within range. Considering that the stone is formed from volcanic lava, you can see where early folks might think it came from Hell. Later, onyx was used for protection and even defense against black magic. Major General, right here at Chatham Manor for a bit, was supposedly a member of the Brothers of Peril. Although that's mostly urban legend. Where did you say this ring came from?"

"My ex-boyfriend got it off eBay." The lies slipped out so easily, Sarah felt herself blush again. "Is it worth anything? He's so cheap I'm sure he didn't spend much on it, but the stone is so pretty. And since we broke up recently, I thought maybe…"

"Maybe you'd sell it?" The jeweler's eyes lit up.

"I'm not sure. Just curious." Even though she fully intended to return the ring, there might still be a reward or a finder's fee. Although she wouldn't be that lucky, a girl could hope.

"The stone isn't worth much by itself and the price of silver is even less right now. If the band had been gold, you might have a few hundred dollars. Without any provenance to go with it, and only urban legend to substantiate it, there are some collectors who would still pay maybe a few hundred dollars for it. But it would take a while and a lot of legwork to track them down. If you want to sell it now, I'll give you two hundred for it."

The gleam in his eye told Sarah he'd double, and maybe triple, his offer.

"How much to turn the stone into a proper necklace instead?" Sarah asked.

"Considering you already have the cut stone, and depending on how you want it set, etcetera, it would run anywhere from fifty dollars to the sky's-the-limit, my dear. I would hate for you to defile such a potential artifact, however. Of course, it's your choice."

He handed the ring and chain back to her. She restrung it, then clasped it behind her neck before tucking it back beneath her sweater.

"I'll think about it. Thanks so much." She smiled, grabbed her lunch and returned to Caroline Street. The Fredericksburg town clock bell sounded one time and fear stabbed through Sarah's heart.

Late. Again.

Breaking into a trot, then a full-out run, she raced the remaining three blocks and took the excruciatingly slow elevator back to the top floor offices. She slid sideways into her cubicle—thanking the gods for reminding her to wear sensible shoes today—at five past one.

Sparing a stealthy glance in her vanity mirror hanging in the corner of her cube, she saw Candace's office was still dark. No one counted the boss's lunch hour. And really, being on salary technically meant no one was supposed to be counting Sarah's lunch minutes, either. Still, probably better not to press her luck, even though today had been exceptional so far.

She unpacked her sandwich and emailed Ellie to come and retrieve hers.

Seconds later, Ellie's chair rolled around the corner of Sarah's cubby. Arms crossed, she settled in. "Do you have a death wish?"

"I don't know what you're talking about." Sarah bit into her chicken salad croissant.

"You know exactly what I'm talking about. I thought you were the responsible one in this relationship. You are falling apart, girlfriend." Ellie unwrapped her Reuben, closed her eyes and smiled. "You are a lucky girl."

"You have no idea." Sarah recounted her radio station win and her visit to Caroline Creations.

"So now what? Are you still going to return the ring to Chatham? I mean, it's pretty clear it's a lucky talisman, right? Have you ever had a day this lucky? Wait. No. The answer is no. I've known you since kindergarten. You are keeping that ring."

"The jeweler said there could be a demon in the stone," Sarah teased.

"He was trying to get you to sell it to him. I'm pretty sure onyx has lots of magical and healing properties. And if it is a talisman, it would have had to be charged with magic. Alex would know."

"I'm not taking it to your psychic." Sarah pointed at her own chest. "The practical one, remember?"

"Responsible one. Practical is a whole different thing. Although after last night, I probably shouldn't contest that assessment, either."

Sarah rolled her eyes. "The jeweler's appraisal is enough for me. It's a rock. A pretty rock, but a rock nonetheless. As for a lucky talisman? I'm not going to argue that it's been a great day. The only thing that could possibly make it better is if I could actually get some work finished."

"All right. All right. Thanks for lunch today." Ellie pushed away from Sarah's imaginary doorway, sandwich in hand. "And tomorrow. You'll be the heroine of the office. First Friday tomorrow night?"

"Absolutely. Right after work. Now go."

* * *

Tanner breathed a sigh of relief. For a moment, he'd feared Sarah would sell the ring. God only knew what would become of him if that happened. While he wasn't sure what the time frame or even the process for his impending resurrection might be, he was certain Sarah had a vital role in it.

The jeweler's knowledge of the Brothers of Peril was disturbing. Tanner found himself extremely curious to learn more regarding the outcome of the war. He couldn't imagine how the true mission of the Brothers of Peril had ever been disclosed. Something had to have gone horribly wrong. But that was more than one hundred fifty years ago. For now, he had more urgent matters to attend to. Sarah had to keep the ring at all costs.

While he had no control over the lucky events she'd ascribed to his ring, nothing would surprise him. One man's prison could as easily be another's paradise. He had no doubt of the depth of Sylvia's diabolical machinations.

He wandered about the office, as far as his metaphysical tether would allow, while Sarah pecked away at what he had determined was a futuristic letterpress or telegraph machine. With no hope of understanding how the contraption worked, he quickly grew bored and stared out the third floor windows onto the street below.

How many times had he crossed those same bricks? Gazing out the window, he could see the steeple of St. George's Church and knew that the Masonic Cemetery was only a block away. Chances were high his body was interred there. Not that it mattered.

Many of the buildings they'd passed on Sarah's lunchtime trek were still recognizable but with new names and purposes. From the windows of her office, he could see the Rappahannock River, from which he'd filled his belly with the sweetest oysters he'd ever known. And beyond the river were the bluffs of Chatham.

Fredericksburg hadn't been all bad. But it was no New York.

So many questions plagued him, threatening to overcome him. Some way, he had to make contact with his unlikely savior. Sarah Knight was his one chance to break the hex.

He didn't let himself consider the alternative.

CHAPTER SIX

Sarah declined the invitation to join Ellie and her coworkers at happy hour at the Ale House. She was beat. Being up late last night, the combined anxiety/excitement of the day, and hours of staring at her computer screen had left her depleted. Her happy hour would consist of ice cream for dinner and maybe an hour of television.

It was nearly seven p.m. when she got home. Greysmith's was hopping for a Thursday night. Poetry reading, from the chalked sign out front. That might have been fun if she had any energy left.

She made her way up the stairs and tried to readjust her laptop bag as it continued to slide off her slumped shoulders. At the top of the stairs stood Jason in front of her apartment door. For once, she was glad she hadn't gotten around to having a key made for him. Not that he liked to stay at her apartment, anyway. Too noisy. Too Bohemian. Too Sarah and not enough Jason. But it felt great to have something all her own. Like a proper adult.

"Where have you been?" The scowl on Jason's face set the tone before she could even utter her greeting.

"Hello to you too, Jason. I was at work. Is everything okay? You look upset."

Jason pushed away from the wall, his hands opening and closing at his sides. His loosened tie hung askew and the front tail of his shirt, partially pulled free from his dress pants, sagged below his expensive suit jacket. *Disheveled* was the word that came to mind. She continued toward him, her smile faltering when a wave of scotch drifted to her. Jason had already enjoyed his happy hour.

"You didn't return my calls. Any of them."

"I know. I'm sorry. I went out with Ellie last night, and I had to turn my phone off. I forgot to turn it back on. Then when I got home and saw your missed calls it was so late, I didn't want to wake you."

He tilted his head back and looked at the ceiling tiles. "And this morning? Lunch? This afternoon? I called you a dozen times."

"Eleven," Sarah whispered, her reply sounding meek even to her.

"Twelve. Still no reply. Do you know what would happen if I didn't call people back? I'd be out of a job. It's disrespectful to not return a call. How disrespectful is it to ignore a *dozen* calls?"

When she didn't reply, he raised his volume. "Answer me."

"You didn't leave a message. If it were that important, couldn't you have left a message?"

"I bought that smart phone for you and put you on my plan because you couldn't afford it. Also so I could get a hold of you when I needed to. If your phone is off, or if you don't respond in a courteous manner, then it's a useless piece of shit. Don't you agree? Maybe you don't even need a phone since you can't manage to use it."

Sarah reached into her purse, digging for her door key. She closed her hand around it when she found it, not sure she wanted Jason inside her apartment in his current state.

"Give me your phone."

"Jason, I need my phone. If you don't want to pay for it anymore, then I'll get my own plan tomorrow."

"Oh, suddenly you can afford a cell phone? Aren't you moving up in the world? This slumlord apartment *and* a cell phone. Did you win the lottery and I missed the news report? God knows you didn't call me back to tell me about it."

"I got a little bonus today. That's all. It's okay. I don't want to be a burden to you. Thanks for your help so far. It was very kind."

Jason took another step toward her. The scotch reeked from him with each breath. "That's me. Kind." He grasped her shoulders and held her briefly. Then he rubbed up and down her arms, gentle strokes at first, but then his grip tightened. His fingers bit through her peacoat and he pushed her back against the door. Sarah's heartbeat picked up.

She didn't like him when he drank. All of the qualities Ellie hated about him were magnified with alcohol. Sarah wasn't blind to his flaws, but most of the time, he was kind. Most of the time. No kindness shone in his eyes tonight.

He bent down and pressed his mouth to hers so hard it made it difficult to breathe. The force of his kiss turned her adrenaline up a notch. It was suffocating, not erotic. His hands slid down her shoulders, trapping her arms. Her laptop strap slipped to the crook of her elbow. When she tried to turn away, he bit her neck, holding her in place, and pushed his knee between her legs, lifting her off the floor an inch or so.

"Jason! Stop it." She twisted in an effort to get free of him, but he was too strong. Her purse dropped to the floor, the contents scattering around their feet. The door key remained clutched in her right hand. She didn't want to hurt him, but he scared her.

Jason released her arm and yanked her sweater hard, stretching the neck off her shoulder. Seeing the chain, he pulled it from under her sweater until the ring became visible.

"What's this?"

"Nothing."

"*Whose* is this? Are you cheating on me?"

"It's no one's. I found it last night. It's not a big deal. I'm going to return it to the lost and found."

"Open the door and let me in."

"No."

"No? Are you fucking kidding me? I don't see you for more than twenty-four hours, you refuse to return my calls, and now you get me all hot and bothered in the hallway and won't invite me in?"

His volume continued to rise. She didn't know many of her neighbors. Not really. Had only met them in passing. She didn't know what to do. No way was he coming into her apartment, this drunk and agitated.

"I'm sorry. I said no. You're drunk, and you're scaring me."

Jason's body vibrated with anger, and she stood still, trying to make herself invisible. He wound the chain around his hand and tore it from her neck. The broken chain dangled through his fingers as he squeezed the ring in his closed fist.

"What the hell?" He opened his hand and the ring glowed red hot against his palm. He threw it against her door and stared at the dragon imprint seared into his hand, his face colored with fury. The ring bounced off the door, left a little charred spot, and rolled across the floor.

"Open. The fucking. Door. Or I'll kick it in. Do you want to pay for that?"

She tried to skirt past him. To run. Somewhere. But he caught her arm and wrenched her back to him.

"Jason, no! You're hurting me."

"Good. Then we're even."

Her neighbor, Adam Something, stepped into the hallway. Sarah had never been so happy to see another living person.

"What's going on out here?"

"Nothing. Just a disagreement," Jason said, his charming business smile covering his red face before he turned to Adam. "We're good."

"She doesn't look good. How about you leave her alone?"

Jason laughed and gave Adam the once over, clearly sizing him up. Jason wasn't much of a fighter. At least, Sarah had never witnessed him in a fight, but he did work out and was in good shape. Adam was in a little better shape.

And not drunk.

Jason glared at Sarah. "I'll see you tomorrow night. Check your voicemail later. I'll be sure to leave you a message."

She started to remind him that tomorrow night was First Friday with Ellie, but bit her tongue. No need adding fuel to his fire. He gave the ring a kick and sent Adam a mock salute on his way toward the stairs. Sarah held her breath until she heard the street door click behind him.

Relief flooded through her, and she bent to retrieve the ring and broken chain. Adam moved to her side in a flash and picked up her computer bag. Carefully, he leaned it against her door. They both gathered the contents of her spilled purse.

She avoided Adam's eyes as he helped. Her embarrassment grew as she realized what her new neighbor must be thinking. Domestic disturbance came to mind, but that didn't seem right. Whatever it was, she was glad Jason went home before things got ugly…er.

"Thanks."

"Is he always like that?" Adam stuffed her wallet, a brush and a compact into her purse, kindly ignoring the other unmentionables lying at his feet.

"No."

"Does he have a key?"

"No. Why do you ask?"

"I just wanted to know if I need to keep an ear to the door tonight in case he comes back."

Abashed, Sarah shook her head. "No. He doesn't have a key. I still haven't had time to have one made for him."

"Probably a good thing. New boyfriend?"

"Not exactly."

"Old boyfriend?"

"Five years."

"Huh." Adam scooped up some gum, errant Tylenol caplets, and a roll of mints. "Maybe you should consider a new boyfriend."

"You sound like Ellie."

"Is that the girl who visits you all of the time?" Adam smiled.

"Yes," Sarah said, happy to change the subject.

"She's cute. Is she available?"

"Very."

Adam stood and Sarah stared down at his bare feet. "Well then," she said.

"Right. I'm just going to run downstairs and make sure he's really gone, if you don't mind." Adam gave her a good once over.

"That would be great. Thanks again."

"You're welcome. You should know though, next time, I'll call the police. Guys like that don't usually get better."

Sarah sighed. "You definitely need to meet Ellie. Good night."

"Night."

* * *

Tanner raged as he followed Sarah into her apartment. The fact that ne'er-do-well Jason had laid hands on her and that Tanner himself was helpless to come to her aid was only eclipsed by this Adam character who *had* come to her aid. Not that he seemed a bad sort. Mostly, Tanner directed his anger to the situation, not her neighbor.

No man had the right to lay hands on a woman.

Images of Sylvia flashed through his mind. Sylvia was in a completely different category. For her, he would have made an exception. But Jason had no reason for his outburst other than his own underlying poor character.

Jason's boorish behavior was beyond his comprehension. Although this was his first encounter with the scoundrel, he shuddered to think Sarah had endured five years of such treatment.

Her hands trembled as she arranged her belongings on the top of her small banquet table causing her to drop her phone completely. It landed face-up on the floor, saved from destruction by its protective case. Another wonder of this future. A handheld communication device? With no visible power or connections? He'd heard rumors the government had been experimenting with such a thing while he served, but this was amazing. And this device? Voice and photographs? Some of them in motion? It was miraculous.

This new world was filled with distractions. And distraction was his enemy. He needed to direct his full and utter attention and energy to his topmost priority. Making himself known to Sarah before it was too late.

Sarah sat heavily in an overstuffed chair in the stylish architectural curve of her living area window. Staring down at the traffic along Princess Anne and William Streets, Sarah's tears glistened, shiny from the street light illuminating her face. She drew a fuzzy blanket around herself and burrowed into it, pulling her knees to her chest. Moments later, her soft sobs morphed into more labored gasps. Tanner couldn't blame her reaction after her recent exchange.

Her cat sent a baleful stare his way, then jumped onto the back of the chair, pawing at her hair while she wept.

Tanner's heart ached for her. Wanting to comfort her, stranger that she was, he stood behind her and lay his hands upon her shoulders. After she had no visible response to his touch, he simply stayed near, maintaining his connection and hoping his intentions conveyed what his physical presence could not. Her normally pink aura stained to a muddy gray. Tanner strained to resist drawing in her energy. Not because he feared the results for himself, but because she was clearly exhausted from the exchange with Jason. She needed all the light she could manifest.

Eventually, she fell asleep in the chair, and Tanner used the time to investigate her apartment. A small mechanical fireplace against the hall-side wall ignited seemingly of its own accord. Flames licked at the glass enclosure, warming the smallish room, and Tanner spent a good half hour sleuthing out the source behind its magic. To even imagine heat at a moment's notice? Impossible.

Photographs lined the mantle directly above the fireplace, filled with color and a glossy finish the likes of which he'd never seen. Sarah and Ellie cavorted in a variety of strange poses and locations. They both appeared in their underthings on a beach in one photograph. A scandalous display of tanned flesh and...

He continued across the mantle.

One photo of Sarah and Jason together at some gala. She was dressed, mercifully, in fashionable finery. Sarah's ball gown was a deep green, which accented her chocolate brown hair and green eyes. Her smile radiated at the camera. Jason's gaze drifted off to the side, unaware the photograph was being taken, it seemed. If Tanner hadn't disliked Jason already, he would have from this one photograph alone. How could any man look away with a beauty like Sarah by his side?

He tried not to return to the beach picture—an image which would never leave his mind, anyway. No need to stare at it profusely. He had to remind himself several times as he continued about the apartment.

Tanner studied every visible possession and read the bits of notes and paper he found, trying to glean as much as possible of the workings of her life. Bitly continued to watch Tanner. The cat transmitted his evil-eyed message and Tanner understood the intent clearly as the beast guarded his mistress.

He could view the entirety of the apartment from the fireplace. The abode was one large open room with a high ornate plaster-tiled ceiling. A tiny kitchen area resided in a corner nook, which consisted of one top and bottom cabinet, a cooking appliance of some sort and an icebox. A desk sat in the center of the room where she'd deposited her bag and a large, overstuffed divan sat before the fireplace. The only other room was a small bathroom, currently closed off by a door. Sarah slept in the chair by the bank of three floor-to-ceiling windows overlooking the street below.

Two wide bookcases stood like good soldiers against the back wall on either side of her bed. They were filled with glossy spines, some of which were brightly colored where others were dark and foreboding. He canted his head to the side to read their titles.

Fifty Shades of Grey? Clearly a Civil War tome discussing the merits and meanings of Confederate uniforms.

The rest seemed to be love stories and the like.

A confounding number of works on web development? Spinning or weaving perhaps? He saw no evidence of such work around her apartment.

He longed to pull the books from their place of rest and open their pages, as he'd always enjoyed reading, having consumed the majority of published offerings at Chatham House as the war efforts ramped up. He'd read all of Paine's work on revolutionary politics and Hawthorne's fiction—none of which he found represented on these two overflowing shelves. What he did find of common interest were the works of Ms. Jane Austen. Every volume he'd known of sat on her shelf, as well as one tome which was new to him. Perhaps *Pride and Prejudice and Zombies* was an annotated edition of some sort, which left him with a burning curiosity.

As Sarah rested, he continued to absorb as much knowledge of her personality and existence as possible, reconnoitering for his upcoming plan of battle.

A battle for his life.

CHAPTER SEVEN

The Eurythmics' "Sweet Dreams" blared from her phone, awakening Sarah around ten that night as her phone sang from across the room. She tangled in the blanket as she struggled to leap from the chair. Finally free, she scrambled across the slick wood floor, desperate to reach it before it went to voicemail. She was sure it was Jason, calling to apologize.

It took her a few seconds to gather her wits when Ellie's voice started mid-conversation instead.

"I'm sorry. What?" Sarah asked.

"I said I'm outside your door. I've been knocking for ten minutes. I know you're in there because your neighbor, Adam—cute, cute, Adam—came out to see what the ruckus was and told me. Open up."

"Coming."

Sarah hung her head and shuffled to the door. Good chance Adam had already spilled the beans about Jason. Guess there was no need to introduce Ellie to him now. She ran her fingers through her tangled hair, and rubbed a thumb under both eyes, hoping her mascara hadn't smeared too much. Then she opened the door.

Ellie stood statue still. Appraising. "You look like hell."

Sarah stepped aside and swept her arm wide, motioning her to come in.

"Were you in bed?"

"No. The chair."

"Crying yourself to sleep, from the looks of your face."

"I guess my good luck ran out." Sarah offered a weak smile.

"Uh huh." Ellie flipped on the overhead lights and cast a glance around the apartment—looking for signs of a disturbance, Sarah was sure. "So, he didn't get in? Are you hurt?"

"Of course not. He was just a little drunk. You know how he gets when he's tipsy. And the fact I hadn't called him back pissed him off. It's not that big a deal."

"Adam said he attacked you in the hallway and was cursing at you when he came out. Is that true?"

She didn't want to answer. It was true. *Attack* was a bit of an exaggeration, but from Adam's viewpoint, it could have seemed that way. A cold wave of fear passed through her chest and goose bumps covered her arms. Remembering how he'd had her trapped against the wall, his knee between her legs, brought the experience back into focus. What if he'd gotten her into her apartment?

She didn't want to think about it. He was her boyfriend. They'd had sex lots and lots of times in the past five years, and it had never, ever been even remotely scary or upsetting. He was a strong, confident man. Nothing more.

"Sarah?" Ellie pressed.

"He was upset. I'm sure he's fine now."

Ellie picked up the ring from the table and examined the broken chain. "How did this happen?"

"It was an accident."

Ellie crossed the room and wrapped her arms around Sarah. Her comfort was more than she could take, and Sarah lost it, snuffling into Ellie's fleecy jacket. Sarah was thankful the interrogation had ceased. The last thing she wanted was to continue to revisit her evening.

Wiping her eyes again, she brushed at the mascara smears on Ellie's jacket. "Sorry."

"Don't worry about it." Ellie smiled.

"What brought you by?"

"We hung out at the Ale House a bit past happy hour. I thought I'd stop by to see if you were still watching TV. Thought I'd join you. I brought snacks." Ellie pulled a greasy bag of chicken tenders from her purse, and Sarah's stomach growled. She'd missed dinner.

"I don't know how good of company I'll be, but I am hungry. You're the best, Ellie."

"Uh huh. Remember that tomorrow night when I'm recounting all the reasons you need to dump Jason."

Sarah cringed.

"What now?"

"He's forgotten about First Friday. He said he'd call later and leave me a message. He has something tomorrow night he wants me to go to, I think."

"Girl…"

"I know. I'm going with you. He can take someone else."

"Now that's the reasonable girl I know and love." Ellie grabbed the remote, tossed the tenders onto the table and settled onto Sarah's loveseat. "I'll find something to cheer you up."

* * *

Tanner was happy to see Sarah's aura return to its former pink glow. He'd even managed to recharge a bit from Ellie's energy as they watched some insipid display on the box hanging on the wall above her mantle. He was captivated and disgusted.

"If *Supernatural* doesn't cheer you up, nothing can. Mmm, Dean," Ellie said.

It was like a nightmare come to life through a portal on the wall.

They watched for more than an hour before Sarah began to doze off again, her head in Ellie's lap. Her friend stroked her hair, comforting her as Tanner could not and his heart thawed a bit toward the girl and her late-night invasion. Ellie was unconventional for a lady in her speech and behavior, but he admired that she continued to be a strong advocate on Sarah's behalf. Her friendship pleased him, while tonight's overlong visit did not. Sarah needed rest if she was to aid him in his plan.

He was more than relieved when she finally terminated the display and said her goodbyes.

"See you at work," Ellie said, leaving.

"Bright and early."

"And hey, free lunch."

Sarah smiled and closed the door behind her.

"Deadbolt." Ellie prodded from the hallway.

Sarah slid the deadbolt across the frame.

A few short minutes later, Sarah undressed and retreated to the bathroom. Tanner attempted to look away and let her maintain her illusion of privacy, but *dear Lord*. If the beach photograph had been seared into his brain, this new image would sustain him the remainder of his days.

Her slim body was smooth and well-toned, but with curves in all the right places. He'd only glanced before looking away. Years of gentlemanly training demanded his discretion, but other urges, more primal, had his manhood standing at attention. Of course that would be one of the first human reactions to return.

That and his desire for food.

The aroma of the coffee today and the continued onslaught on his olfactory senses from the shop below them were heavenly. Being a wispy apparition—spirit alone—he had no mechanism or corporeal vessel yet to partake of such luxuries. For all intents and purposes, the energy he'd consumed since being released from the ring had restored him completely on a physical and mental level. His handicap was that he remained on the wrong side of the veil and entirely invisible to Sarah or the world at large. The uncertainty of his condition and corporeal existence drove him to near madness. To be so close to his goal and not know how to realize it was…exasperating.

He paced outside her lavatory door, waiting for her to reappear. He missed the warmth of her aura and felt his own energy waning. It was becoming clear to him, however, he'd have to be careful not to leech more light from her than necessary. In her overly emotional state, he saw that she was depleted. With no inkling how long the process of his resurrection might take, he'd have to bide his time, despite the gnawing urge in his gut to accelerate things.

The bathroom door opened and warm steam oozed from the tiny room. Sarah emerged, clothed in a fuzzy button-up, long-sleeved top and drawers, both boasting a leopard print, which would have been considered the height of scandal in his day. Ne'er had he seen even one woman in attire remotely resembling the fashion of his time. In fact, the only aspects of this new existence that remained the same were many of the buildings they'd passed. A small comfort, but it was something to cling to. And cling to it he did.

Sarah picked up her phone and carried it to bed with her. She pulled the bedding up and around her neck until only her hands and head peeked out of the downy nest. Once again, she examined the display. Frowning, she placed the device on her bedside table, attached a cord to it and rolled over. Moments later, she flung off the covers and sat up in bed. She rose, then crossed the room to retrieve the ring.

With great gratification, Tanner watched as she returned to bed. After settling once again into her nest, Sarah slipped the ring onto her finger. It was much too large, but she curled her hand into a fist and gripped her pillow tight as she drifted off to sleep. Her pink aura glowed intensely, even through the blankets.

Tanner reclined beside her. Facing her on the oversized bed, he studied her features as her face relaxed in sleep, her sweet, minty breath drifting past him. Cocooned in her aura, he luxuriated in its warmth for several hours, careful not to take more than she could spare, and drawing away when the color faded.

He even managed to drift off inadvertently. Having been dormant so long, he feared sleep, worried he would fall back into the dark trance in which he'd been long imprisoned.

The same dreams haunted his repose. Sylvia's curse and the day of his death replayed over and over, a relentless reminder of his troubles. Then and now. In retrospect, he saw the pieces of the hex fall into place and wished he'd had the intuition then to believe what she was truly capable of. He'd been skeptical at best and arrogant at worst, never expecting his refusal to elicit such a dramatic response. Why any woman would desire him so fiercely, he had no conception.

He'd had his share of romantic interludes, but discreetly and only after long-term relationships, never catting about like many of the soldiers. As for love, no one had captivated him while he was in New York, and once he arrived in Fredericksburg, his attention had been demanded by the Major General and the imminent war.

All of that was behind him now. History, one which he had no inclination to repeat. He reached out to Sarah and traced his finger along her hairline to no effect but his own satisfaction.

He'd known Sarah Knight for one day. One day, which he'd spent in silent observation, that seemed like a lifetime.

He owed her everything.

And needed her more than she could ever know.

CHAPTER EIGHT

First Friday dawned cold and dreary as ice pellets clinked against Sarah's windows. The weather didn't dampen her relief when her alarm went off seconds after she'd already awakened, and she realized she wouldn't be late for work.

Nightmares had plagued her dreams. Again. And the same ones as the night before. A dark-haired Union soldier, shot in the chest and dying on the grounds of Chatham. That part had been clear and detailed. Other confusing bits played randomly through the night, but she couldn't remember the specifics in the light of day.

It was First Friday, a new day, and all of her coworkers would have lunch on her.

She flipped back the blankets and made a beeline to the bathroom and the warmth of her little space heater. The gas fireplace flamed valiantly, but it couldn't keep ahead of the bitter cold, which seeped through her windows. The building was old. Revolutionary old. While much had been retrofitted, electrical, plumbing, and gas lines, an old building was hard to keep warm in the winter and cool in the summer. The character and ambiance drew people to historic architecture, not the climate control.

Wrapping her fleece robe over her fleece pajamas helped some, but her feet were freezing on the icy floor. One would think the warmth of the coffee shop downstairs would waft up through the wooden slats as easily as the sound of brewing grounds and the aroma of baking pastries. One would be wrong.

She slid her feet into her knitted, cat-faced house slippers, and pulled a brush through her hair, trying to tame her locks into submission. Bitly stared after her with disdain, refusing to leave the one warm spot on the floor, which was directly in front of the fireplace.

Twenty minutes later, she was dressed and ready to go. She filled Bitly's water and food bowls, and then pulled on her coat. After gathering her laptop and purse, she disconnected her phone from the charger. She wrapped a scarf around her neck, then searched in her coat pocket for her gloves and put them on. She poked the ring into her front jeans pocket. First Friday was also casual Friday—Candace's once-a-month concession to the minions. Best day of the month, as far as she was concerned. She checked her phone before she opened the door. No voicemails.

Her heart did a little flip flop, unsure whether she wanted a message from Jason or not. He could put her at ease or fill her with anxiety with just a few words. After high school, he'd been kind and attentive, just as excited for her college courses and career opportunities as his own. But as he made more money and gained more respect in his field, his priorities had changed. He used to mention marriage and their future together a lot. But lately, he'd barely talked about anything with her other than his demanding social schedule. She felt more like an adornment than a partner and, despite the rosy outlook she projected to Ellie, she was concerned.

More so in the past few days than ever before.

Even with his neglect and growing bossiness, she'd never seriously considered life without him. He was a part of her. The very thought of not having him in her life after all this time made her twitch with anxiety. But after last night? She was beginning to believe mere history wasn't enough to justify staying with him.

As she opened the door, something on the floor caught her eye. A long, black velvet box wrapped with a red bow sat in the center of her doorway. She glanced down the hallway. No secret admirers lurked about.

With effort, she bent to pick it up, stiff and sore from her encounter last night. She pulled the ribbon free and lifted the lid. A platinum chain lay inside with a matching letter *J* pendant dangling from its center. No note accompanied the gift, but the letter *J* made it clear who it was from.

J for Jason.

Of course, he'd brand her with his initial instead of her own.

Unexpected anger built inside her as she considered the necklace. The offering felt more like a bribe than an apology.

It was still only 8:45. How he'd managed to buy a platinum necklace before nine a.m., she had no idea. Perhaps his networking efforts had paid off. She hesitated, then pulled off her gloves and retrieved the ring from her jeans pocket. Allowing the letter pendant to slide from the chain, she dropped it inside the box, and then strung the ring onto the chain instead. She tossed the box and wrapping inside, then clasped the chain behind her neck. Pulling the door closed behind her, she smiled.

Bitly would have a field day with that ribbon.

She pounded down the stairs and into Greysmith's for a café mocha to go. The last vestiges of her nightmares evaporated like the steam of her coffee as she made her way to work. Compulsively, she checked her phone again. No missed calls and no messages.

The necklace was her apology. He couldn't even manage to verbalize it. Instead, he'd given her a five-hundred dollar necklace to replace the one he'd broken last night in his childish blowup.

For the first time, she felt less than forgiving toward him. She did deserve better. At lunch, she'd go to AT&T and set up her own cell account. Oh, she'd keep the chain. It was a gift, after all. And the least he owed her for supporting him emotionally and attending his functions these past five years. She wasn't ready to call it quits completely. Change was scary. But she was stronger than the fear. Stronger than change. Getting her own phone was the first step to laying the ground work and disentangling herself from being so needy for his approval.

It was a start.

* * *

Sarah worked through most of the morning without incident, chasing her fatigue with cup after cup of coffee. She'd lost track of the exact amount, but five cups wouldn't be an overestimate. A call from the pizza delivery guy broke her from her coding coma around lunchtime, and she gathered Ellie to help carry up the food and drinks.

"That's a lot of food. They know there are only twelve of us, right?" Ellie asked.

"I told them," the pizza boy said, handing stacks of boxes to each of the girls. "They said to share it around the building if there were leftovers. We like to over deliver."

"Are those coupons taped onto the boxes?" Ellie asked as they made their way up the elevator.

"Papa Paul's sweepstakes scratchers," the pizza boy replied. "The franchise is giving away a Ford Fusion. Of course, there are twelve hundred stores in the U.S. so the odds…"

"I so need that," Ellie said, tearing off one of the cards, then hesitating. "Here, you scratch them, Sarah. It's your prize and with the luck you've been having? Who knows?"

Ellie tore the scratcher cards from the remaining boxes.

They returned, pizza guy in tow, to cheers from the cube farm. Candace even managed to slide out of her office and make an appearance. Sarah ate quickly and deflected much of the admiration and gratitude, but couldn't deny her heart was full. It felt good to be able to do something for someone else. To be appreciated.

She placed the untouched scratcher cards in her desk drawer and used the remainder of her lunch hour to complete her AT&T run, still high on the results of her good fortune. Sliding the ring absently across her new chain, she wondered about it. Maybe it *was* a lucky talisman. And possibly more. Last night, something had happened to Jason's hand and her door after contact with the ring. She'd felt it warm and spark oddly beneath her own touch. Neither had escaped her notice. Since she'd had no similar experience with the ring anywhere close to that intensity, she guessed it was perhaps some sort of chemical reaction. There was most likely a perfectly logical explanation for it all. She had no idea what it might be.

Regardless, the ring had certainly gotten Jason's attention. So much so that he wanted to replace it. A fact that made her suddenly determined to keep it rather than turn it in as she had planned.

Lucky talisman or not. The ring was hers, and it would stay.

Jason was another story.

Forty-five minutes later, she was the proud owner of her very own cell phone and account. She hoped there would be enough left over for curtains after using her bonus to pay in advance for the next six months service. She dropped her old phone into her purse, intending to return it to Jason, though she doubted he'd want it. The phone would be a bone of contention with him. He'd be angry when he discovered that her account had been terminated. He didn't have her new number, and she debated whether to give it to him.

Finally back to the office, she crashed from her carb lunch letdown and searched through her desk drawer for something chocolate.

The scratcher cards caught her eye. She rummaged through the bottom of her purse for a quarter to reveal them with.

Twelve cards in all. It took a while to get through them. A pile of gooey, silver shaving grew on her desktop. Hands shaking, she held the final scratched off card. A winner, clear as day.

WINNER!! 2015 FORD FUSION

She flipped the card over to read the fine print on the back, sure it was a mistake. That there must be some caveat. "Takes three cards to win" or "not valid in Virginia."

No such disclaimer existed.

She emailed Ellie, subject-line reading *COME NOW!* with no text in the body. Seconds later, her friend slid, breathless, into her cube.

"What? Are you on fire?" she asked with faux concern, searching the cube for danger.

Sarah handed the card to Ellie.

Ellie took the card and studied it for several long moments. She flipped the card to read the back just as Sarah had, then settled against the corner of Sarah's desk for support.

"You won?" Ellie asked, her eyes round with awe. "You won a freakin' car?"

Sarah nodded. "I think so. I mean, I haven't called the number on the back yet, but am I reading it wrong?"

Ellie picked up Sarah's desk phone, handed her the receiver and started punching numbers on the keypad. "We're going to find out."

The call rang through. "Papa Paul's Corporate Office, how can I direct your call?" the Papa Paul's receptionist said.

"Um, I have a contest card from you I just scratched and, um…I think I might have won the car."

"Congratulations. Do you have the card in your possession now?"

"Yes."

"Can you take a picture of yourself holding the card, then send it to me via email or text so I can verify it before we proceed?"

"As a matter of fact, I can," Sarah said.

Sarah handed Ellie her new phone. "Take my picture. We have to send it to her of me holding the card."

Ellie did as instructed. Seconds later, the Papa Paul's Corporate Office received it.

"Congratulations. That is definitely the winning ticket. It's for the 2015 Ford Fusion, which will be available after the first of the year. I'm going to transfer you to our legal department and then to marketing. You'll need to take the ticket to your local franchise office, and they'll send it by certified mail to our offices here in New Jersey. Congratulations again."

Sarah felt all the color blanch from her face as she hung up the phone.

"Well?" Ellie vibrated with energy in front of her.

"They'll deliver the car sometime before the end of January."

"Are you still wearing that ring?"

Sarah pulled it from beneath her sweater and smiled.

"Holy shit. You have got to keep that thing."

"I think you might be right."

* * *

Tanner didn't know what a Ford Fusion was but Sarah's excitement was contagious, and he'd fed his fill from the overabundance of energy she manifested for the hours following the phone exchange with Ellie and the Papa Paul's Corporate Office. Sarah's pink aura glowed with a pale yellow tinge, which he attributed to the light and airy happiness that radiated from her the rest of the afternoon.

While in the office, Sarah tapped away on the contraption that he'd deciphered was called a computer. The device's workings and purpose remained a mystery, but the fact that she seemed to manipulate it so deftly was impressive. Quite by accident, when one of her coworkers passed through him on her way through the cubical hallway, Tanner discovered he could tap into the energy of her coworkers as well, and made the rounds as Sarah worked. By the time Sarah's work day ended, he felt like Hercules. Strong and ready for battle.

Reclining against her desk, he admired the way the dying winter light from the west-facing windows played across her hair, bringing out shades of red hidden in her chocolate brown tresses. Someone in her family line had been a full-on redhead, no doubt. Her green eyes and fair porcelain complexion betrayed her lineage, even if her hair did not. Irish. He was sure of it.

His own British/Scottish lineage held similar characteristics, and as the cultures mixed, so did each country's physical features and traits. Sarah Knight was the most pleasant blending he'd ever had the fortune to meet.

She'd spent a long and laborious afternoon fidgeting and presumably working at the computer, clearly distracted. He was relieved when Ellie came to collect her.

"First Friday. It's on like Donkey Kong, girlfriend. Pack that laptop up and let's go. We have some celebrating to do."

Sarah closed the lid of her computer and packed her belongings as instructed. Tanner followed the twittering pair onto the street. Street lamps illuminated their walk, first to Sarah's to change clothes before they traveled to a pub on Caroline Street. Tanner did his best to give Sarah her privacy, and Ellie rambled on relentlessly as they planned their evening.

He watched the busy Friday night foot traffic pass below her window. The cold, dark winter evening seemed to drive even more business to the coffee shop and bookstore. It had not escaped his notice that the marquee board outside the store proclaimed to hold an extensive Civil War collection. A fine place for study if ever he were in the situation again. He longed for the smell and feel of a book, especially after coveting several of Sarah's. The smell he could manage, barely. The physical feeling, however, eluded him.

Although, he realized, he had yet to actually try. And after his infusion of energy today? Perhaps he could test it?

A pile of paperwork lying on Sarah's table caught his eye. Post and such littered the small dining table, which he had yet to see set for a proper meal. The poor girl seemed to exist on dining out and nothing more.

A single sheet of thin parchment rested askew atop the pile, hanging ever so slightly off the edge at a precarious pitch. A strong breath could have dislodged it. He bent to study it, a notice of payment due to Fredericksburg Gas and Light for the impossible sum of $49.15—an amount that made him fear for her future fiscal solvency.

Reaching out, he grasped at the corner of the sheet and his heart sank as he watched his hand pass through without so much as a twitch. If he couldn't manipulate a thin piece of parchment, what would it take to become corporeal again? Filled with rage, he swiped at the paper once again and watched with awe as it swept from the table and floated to the floor. Bitly arched his back, rising from his cozy reverie in front of the fireplace and hissed his disapproval.

Tanner froze, unsure of whether or not he was actually visible. Bitly had seemed to take notice of him before, but this was so blatant and in direct response to his actions, there was no doubt the cat had sensed him, if not actually seen him.

Sarah peeked her head from the lavatory. "Bitly, you are getting pissy in your old age."

The cat yawned and curled again in the warm glow of the fire, his message delivered and received.

Unaffected, the girls continued chatting. Tanner squatted near the fallen paper and pushed his finger at its edge, thrilled when it slid the smallest fraction to the right. With full and utter concentration, he pushed at the parchment again, and it moved an eighth of an inch farther. Before he could test his powers further, Sarah emerged from the lavatory dressed in a shockingly short black dress with neither corset nor bustle visibly employed. Her shapely legs were covered with thin black hosiery, and she teetered precariously upon sharp heeled footwear, which looked more like a weapon than a mode of travel.

"I'm ready," Sarah said.

Ellie clapped the back of her hand to her forehead in a faux swoon. "You're going to be a hit tonight. You're going to freeze your ass off, but you look great."

Sarah blushed. "If you say so. Let's go."

"Um, not that I want to throw cold water on things, but have you heard from Jason today?"

"Not exactly." She reached up and pinched the chain between her fingers, spinning it around her neck in a nervous gesture.

"He hasn't called to apologize after last night? Beg your forgiveness? Sent you expensive presents?

The pink aura around Sarah morphed to dark blue. "He apologized with this chain."

"I thought that was new. It's platinum, you know."

"I do."

"Well, good then. Just because he gives you an expensive gift doesn't mean you owe him. He can't buy his way out of being an asshole."

"I'm beginning to agree with you."

"Fantastic. This day keeps getting better. Let's get down to the Ale House and eat before Art Walk starts."

Tanner followed, a silent sentry behind the girls as they made their way to the Ale House. The building beside their destination was one he recognized, but it had been a two story structure last he'd visited. Now it appeared the second floor of the tavern had been removed, leaving only the street level. His Fredericksburg dealings on behalf of the Major General had led him to the adjacent building a few times in the past. The now far past.

Well before he'd died.

CHAPTER NINE

The cacophony of the packed Ale House pounded inside Sarah's head. Instead of casing the patrons, as Ellie surely hoped she'd do, curiosity got the better of Sarah, and she mined her old phone from the bottom of her purse and checked it while Ellie retrieved two beers from the bar. Even though she'd requested the service to be terminated, the phone still showed a signal. She'd nuked it on her walk back during lunch and reset it to its factory settings, clearing all of her personal information. Jason could even sell it and recoup some of his money if he wanted to.

There were no missed calls or messages, but the uneasy feeling in her stomach wouldn't let up. He'd promised—threatened, if she wanted to be realistic—that he'd contact her. While she dreaded the imminent confrontation, she was also ready to get it over with, knowing the likely result would be the end of the one and only long-term relationship she'd ever had.

Over the course of the day, she'd begun to come to terms with that idea. She didn't need a man to make her life complete. She could do this. It would be a change for the good. A change for her future.

She had a great apartment, a job she was good at and great friends. Not to mention a cat who loved her. Even though the past couple of days, Bitly had acted oddly. Maybe he was lonely? Maybe a friend to keep him company during the day would help? A thought she quickly quashed. Two cats in a five hundred square foot apartment brought her one step too close to becoming the neighborhood cat lady.

Bitly could just get over whatever was bothering him.

Sarah dropped the phone back into her purse and hung the bag on the chair beside her, before Ellie returned to chastise her for checking it again.

"Raspberry Pale Ale for you." Ellie handed her a beer. "And tall, blond and handsome for me." Her eyes strayed to something behind Sarah. "Isn't that your neighbor in the corner?"

Sarah turned around and glanced. Sure enough, Adam stood with a group of guys hanging around a tall bar table full of Happy Hour tumblers. "Looks like it."

"Let's go talk to him," Ellie said, lasering in on her quarry.

After his embarrassing intervention last night, Sarah couldn't quite face him. Buy him a drink maybe, but certainly not face him. "You go ahead. I, um, my feet are killing me already. I'm going to run home and change shoes. I'll be right back. Promise."

Ellie eyed her suspiciously and cast an appraising look at her shoes. "I was surprised you went with those. They look great, but I figured they'd be torture. Ten minutes. Don't make me hunt you down."

"Don't worry."

Relieved, Sarah handed her beer back to Ellie as collateral and spun around to make her way out of the already-overcrowded bar. By ten o'clock, the place would be unbearable. The art galleries drew her to First Friday. Not the bars.

Her lie to Ellie had only been by half—her feet really were killing her already and walking along the uneven bricks was an exercise in fashion precision she was barely capable of performing. Removing the shoes and walking barefoot, however, wasn't an option. The freezing temperatures had her rethinking her entire wardrobe choice. She might have to add pants instead of tights to her ensemble as well.

She'd only walked a few feet when a red car caught her eye as it zipped into the handicap spot to her right. A Mercedes. Jason's Mercedes. He was out of the car with his hands around her neck, his icy fingers pulling at her platinum chain before she could process why he parked in a handicap spot and his car was still running.

"I see you got the gift all right, but couldn't manage to call and thank me?" His warm fingers tugged at the chain.

Sarah cringed. "Thank you. I'm sorry. I…"

Jason pulled the chain free and his face reddened when he saw the ring. "Are you kidding me? You put this piece of shit on an eight hundred dollar chain?"

Sarah's heart sped up and blood pounded in her ears, embarrassed as people passed them. "Jason, you're being ridiculous."

"Get in the car," he said, tugging at her elbow. "We have a dinner to attend."

"No. I'm out with Ellie. You never called, and I assumed you made other plans. How did you find me anyway?" She tried to jerk her elbow free, but his fingers dug in through her coat.

"I tracked your phone. Let's go."

He tracked my phone?

Sarah finally tore her arm free. "Speaking of phones, you can have yours back. I got a new one today." She reached for her purse and realized she didn't have it.

"The car. Now."

Jason grabbed both of her shoulders and pushed her toward the Mercedes. Her heel caught between the bricks, and she fell to the sidewalk, tearing both stockings and bloodying her knees.

"It's okay. She tripped. She's fine," Jason told some well-meaning passersby as he opened his passenger car door for her.

Tears filled her eyes, and Sarah was one second away from screaming for help when she felt Jason's looming presence lift from behind her. Ellie squatted beside her, eyes full of fury.

"She'll be going with us, thanks," Adam said.

Jason's hands balled into fists at his side and a crowd began to gather. More than one spectator had his cell phone out, snapping or recording.

Jason smoothed his jacket, then bent to help Sarah up from the sidewalk. Ellie already tended to her knees as best she could with a Kleenex from Sarah's purse.

"She fell. We were going to dinner, and she twisted her ankle is all," Jason told Adam, his explanation aimed more at the crowd than her friends. He didn't want his business reputation damaged with the truth.

"Liar," Ellie spat.

"My purse?" Sarah asked.

"You left it in the bar. We were trying to catch you, 'cause I knew you'd need your keys for your apartment."

On trembling legs, Sarah rummaged through her purse for the phone.

"There." Sarah threw the phone on the passenger seat of his car and tried to walk away, but the broken heel of her shoe brought her to a halt.

"Let me drive you home at least," Jason cajoled.

"No." Sarah slipped off her shoes and stood on the freezing pavement, trying to decide what to do next, desperate to be away from Jason and away from prying eyes.

"We'll take care of her from here. I think you've done enough," Adam said, dialing on his own cell.

"Who are you calling?" Jason asked.

"Depends on how long it takes for you to get into your car and leave. A cab if you leave now. The police if you don't."

Jason raised his hands in acquiescence. "Whatever. I don't need this shit." He directed his glare at Sarah. "Not any of it."

He slammed the passenger door and walked around the front of his car. Seconds later, he peeled out onto Caroline Street at a ridiculously high speed for the busy pedestrian traffic. Street debris rooster-tailed behind his car.

"Asshole!" Ellie called after him.

"So a cab would be good," Sarah said, all the adrenaline leeching from her and leaving her exhausted.

"No way. It's only a couple of blocks. I'll carry you," Adam said and smiled.

"Um...I don't know." Sarah had had all of the attention she wanted for one night.

"My hero," Ellie said and stretched up to kiss his cheek.

Adam shook his head. "I don't know about that, but I think I can manage a block or two."

He scooped her up before she could protest and a few minutes later, she stood inside the foyer of the shared entrance.

"I can make it from here. Thanks," Sarah said, struggling to make eye contact.

"Oh don't you worry. I'll be around later to thank you properly," Ellie cooed at Adam, then turned her attention to Sarah. "Now, let's get you upstairs and cleaned up."

"I really think you should file a report against your boyfriend, Sarah. Next time, one of us might not be around to help," Adam said.

"I know. I'll think about it."

"Think hard." Adam nodded at Ellie and slipped out the door, presumably back to his friends.

"He's just so wonderful," Ellie said dreamily, watching him walk away. Turning back to Sarah, she fixed her gaze on her. "This is it. You have got to be done with him. What's it going to take, Sarah? What if he'd gotten you into that car? In his mood? This is more than me not liking him. He's become dangerous. No more kidding around."

"I was scared," Sarah admitted.

"You should have been. Let's get upstairs."

* * *

Tanner paced, agitated beyond measure. Being a spectator while Sarah was in peril was nearly more than he could bear. The mere manipulation of a piece of paper or small object was far from an adequate weapon. While he'd tried to intervene, his efforts had made no impact. He was virtually helpless to come to her aid. And why no passersby offered assistance on the street, he couldn't explain. Strangers passed within feet of their exchange but only gawked, then walked away, whispering heatedly to their friends or ignoring the situation completely. His previous misgivings concerning Ellie and even Sarah's neighbor Adam vanished in light of their continual support and friendship.

Jason, however, was a different sort all together.

Many such men had made up the ranks of his battalion. Men like Jason were drawn to battle for the rush of power and the mere pleasure of violence, hand-to-hand combat specifically. Again, his consideration turned back to Sylvia but she was in fact no sort of lady.

He watched with concern for some time as Ellie tended to Sarah and her wounded knees. His heart ached to ease hers, wishing there was something—anything—he could do for her. She'd taken steps in the right direction today. Cutting the tie to Jason's phone—her own personal tether, it seemed—was one such step.

Sarah was a much stronger woman than she seemed to realize, and he credited Ellie with advising her correctly that Jason had to go. The sooner the better. Tanner feared for her safety and wished Adam had, indeed, contacted the authorities.

"Your knees are really going to be sore, girl. We got all of the brick dust and dirt out of them, but clothes are going to hurt them for a few days. I'm so sorry that happened." Ellie squirted some ointment onto both knees. "You might want to spread this around. Probably hurt less if you do it."

Sarah tried to hold it together, but tears welled in her eyes. She blinked them back and worked the ointment across the wounds, turning it pink with her blood.

Ellie pressed a large bandage across each knee. "Better?"

"Yes. Thank you, Ellie. You're always there for me. I don't know how I can ever repay your friendship."

Ellie smiled conspiratorially. "Oh, let's see... Break up with Jason for good. Give me your new car. Um, I'm sure there are more opportunities."

Sarah laughed and Tanner's heart leaped at the sound.

"Done."

"Oh? Which part?" Ellie laughed.

"Both. I'll send Jason an email. I don't want him to have my new number. And when the car comes in January, it's yours."

"Um, no. I mean, yes on the Jason bit. Stellar plan that one. But I was kidding about the car. That's the Tylenol talking. That's a major prize, and you're keeping it. You won it, fair and square. Well, sort of fair—you have that whole lucky talisman thing going on."

"It wasn't feeling so lucky tonight with Jason, or last night either, come to think of it."

"Are you kidding me? Last night Adam was Johnny-on-the-spot. And tonight? You got both of us. I'd call that plenty lucky. You need a clear perspective."

"You're right, of course."

Ellie stood and gathered up the leftovers and trash from her triage work. "So, looks like a Friday night in. I'm cool with that. How about I run out for some takeout, and we watch some television? *Supernatural* season one? You really need to be schooled."

"That would be great. You're the best."

"I am, aren't I? Back in a jiffy."

Ellie gathered her purse to leave, and Sarah hobbled behind her to close the door.

Before she made it back to her sofa, Ellie called out through the door. "Deadbolt."

"Got it." Sarah clicked the lock into place.

Gingerly, Sarah settled into the couch, obviously trying to find a position that didn't bring pain to her fresh injuries. She pointed a handheld device at what he'd learned was called a television and the box flared to life. The differences between it and the computer eluded him, other than the lack of a lettered typing board. Tanner sat beside her and lay his arm across the back of the couch. She readjusted again and stretched her body out, unknowingly laying her head in his lap. The unintentional intimacy so surprised him, he froze in place, daring not disturb her from her position. His heart raced, thumping so loudly in his chest he fancied she might even hear its treacherous gallop.

No such acknowledgement ensued from her repositioning, however, and his hopes were quickly dashed. The only one who seemed to notice him at all was the cat. Bitly jumped up into an arch and stared straight at him with a baleful glare. After a bit, the cat settled again and curled against Sarah's stomach, clearly choosing to ignore him. Certainly an improvement over the beast's previous displays. Maybe he was growing on the old cat.

Ellie would return soon and who knew how late she would stay. The only bright point in an otherwise devastating evening was that he was home alone with Sarah. At least for the interim. He hoped Ellie would eat and then take her leave. Already he had come to appreciate spending time with Sarah, even if Bitly was less than impressed with him.

They watched the images flicker across the television, and he tried to follow the storyline. Distracted by Sarah's slow breathing and proximity, he was mostly at a loss, but from what he could gather, a group of scantily clad vacationers had been stranded together and were slowly voting one another off the island. Occasionally, they had strange competitions and received an idol of protection. It was the most bizarre situation he'd ever encountered. Next to his own.

A soft sigh hissed from Sarah, and he realized she'd fallen asleep. He couldn't resist reaching out and stroking the hair along the side of her face. When it fluttered at his touch, he froze again.

The sheet of paper had been one thing, but the thought that he could touch her—really touch her—filled him with hope. Under duress earlier during Jason's attack, he hadn't been able to manifest so much as a breeze. Now he focused with all of his concentration and hooked his finger beneath a lock of hair, then pulled it back and away from her face. Excited, he tried again. Another strand realigned according to his ministrations.

Tanner placed the back of his trembling hand to Sarah's cheek and drew it across her face. She shifted beneath him at his touch, and Bitly took exception this time, sending him a warning hiss.

A rapid series of knocks at the door woke her, and she sat up with a start.

"I'm back. Open up," Ellie called.

Sarah opened the door, and Ellie set a brown paper bag full of food on the long, low rectangular table in front of her couch. The food smelled delicious, although it was nothing he recognized. Ellie moved to sit on the couch, exactly where he currently reclined. She passed through him as he rose and tried to get out of her way.

"Do you feel that?" Ellie asked.

"What? Are you cold?"

"No. It's something else. A vibration almost. Weird." Unknowingly, Ellie stared right at Tanner, making him uncomfortable with her strange appraisal.

"It's probably the grinders downstairs. Sometimes you can almost feel it through the floor when they grind the coffee beans," Sarah said.

"Maybe."

He quickly scooted out of the way and walked to the windows to watch the revelers pass.

His mind raced as he considered the possibilities. If he could manipulate a piece of paper and a lock of hair, even the slightest of physical touch—how much longer before he was corporeal once again?

All of his hope was pinned to the promise of a cryptic hex.

"Lest true love fill his spirit shell, his body rot while soul's in cell.

Upon this mortal coil may stay, if somehow love does find a way."

How could Sarah or anyone ever love him if he remained a spirit shell only? And what was the definition of love? A feeling? A proclamation? What would it take to bring him back?

He prayed for answers.

CHAPTER TEN

Sarah couldn't keep her eyes open any longer. The adrenaline dump had abandoned her hours ago, leaving her weak and shaky. While she appreciated the food and Ellie's attempts to cheer her up, she was more than ready for a good night's sleep and a long weekend of hibernation. Right now, the farthest she planned on venturing was downstairs for coffee and a pastry in the morning. Then she'd curl up in her chair by the front windows and read the weekend away.

Yeah, that was a plan.

Her silent go-home-please vibes finally made their way to Ellie and she frowned. "Okay, I'm going already. Far be it from me to keep you from bed, Grandma."

"I'm sorry."

"Quit apologizing. I'm kidding you. I can't believe you made it this long." Ellie gathered up the trash. "I'll dump this downstairs so it doesn't stink the place up any more than it already has."

"That would be awesome. Thanks again. For...everything."

Ellie slipped past the door and turned to give her a motherly look. "Dead—"

"Bolt," Sarah finished.

* * *

Hours later, Tanner made sport of testing his newly acquired abilities, pushing papers around the desk, nudging toiletries across the vanity, rearranging the framed photographs along the mantle. Each manipulation was a small victory and one step closer to his goal. Just past three in the morning, he struck upon an idea.

He managed to retrieve a fresh piece of paper from a stack upon Sarah's desk and then worked until he could deploy a writing utensil into an upright position. He found no jars of ink, but had watched Sarah utilize a similar tool for writing at her office. After several awkward attempts, he began to get the flow of the instrument, and began again.

It would take the utmost care for his plan to come even close to fruition. Even then, the chances were slim at best. He'd once been considered something of a wordsmith, but he'd never had to write for his very life. His real skills of persuasion worked better in the flesh, man to man—an admirable trait that had led him to become involved with the Brothers of Peril, and then straight into his position as the Major General's supernatural liaison. A few good negotiations and one poor one led to his downfall.

Tanner wrote the greeting of his missive and then agonized over the first sentence for the next hour, pacing, deliberating and finally committing to a course of action. Much later, as the sunrise began to lighten the sky overtop the buildings across the street, with great effort, he managed to fold the paper in half and push it onto the floor. Little by little, he shuffled the letter to her doorway, and slid it underneath so that it lay halfway into the hallway.

Bitly leaped from Sarah's bed to investigate his offering, sniffing at it and giving it a halfhearted paw. Finding it of little interest, he mercifully abandoned the effort all together. Tanner's stomach churned at the thought of Sarah discovering it, and then even more abhorrently, reading it. If he frightened her away before he even had a chance to convince her, all would be lost.

For the first time since his reawakening, he was thankful he was not with body or appetite, for surely if he were he would find himself sick with the worry that roiled within him. He offered the only other weapon he had—prayer. And he sat heavily into the overstuffed chair by the window and waited.

* * *

Sarah woke, forgetting her injured knees. An over enthusiastic stretch reminded her with alarming sharpness as the now-scabbed skin pulled at its new seams. Flipping the covers back, she struggled to readjust slowly enough not to reopen the wounds. She hunched and hobbled her way into the bathroom to relieve herself.

Her apartment filled with light, belying the severe cold that blew outside and howled down Princess Anne Street. She was thankful she wouldn't have to experience the weather at all when she popped downstairs for a hot coffee and pastry.

Once again, she'd passed a fitful night of dreams and it had her curious to research a bit more of Chatham Manor's role in the Civil War. Images of the

Lieutenant—a rank she knew only from the concerned calls of his men when blood bloomed across his chest—had haunted her since her trip to Chatham. Why that particular soldier starred in her mental reel, she had no idea. She'd never scanned as much as a brochure of the battlefield or the war all the past few months she'd lived in Fredericksburg. History was less than exciting to her. *Boring* was the word that came to mind.

The only other explanation she could think of was that the Ale House walls were filled with Civil War photos, postcards and memorabilia. Perhaps she'd seen him there and subconsciously ascribed him to her dream soldier. Nothing else made sense. She couldn't have conjured him from thin air.

She dressed and pulled on a soft, oversized fleece top against the impending cold of the hall and stairway, then grabbed her wallet. Maybe she'd find a book downstairs to ease her troubled mind. Greysmith's purported quite an expansive Civil War and History section, or so their sign proclaimed, and while it wasn't a library, the staff often let her borrow books if she wanted. She'd mostly perused the romance section and had bought several, as was evident from her overflowing to-be-read collection on her bookcases.

She kicked something protruding from under her doorway. Curious, she retrieved it and unfolded a letter, written in a large and looping hand. The script wandered across the page at an increasingly precarious slant until the closing barely fit on the page.

Sarah opened the door and peered into the hallway but saw no evidence of who might have left it. It was signed *Tanner*. She didn't know anyone named Tanner. Puzzled, she kept the letter to read with her coffee downstairs. It would take some time to decipher the script, if she even could. Good thing she liked working puzzles.

Of course, the current puzzle was how to navigate the stairs without falling or bleeding to death from her wounds. She'd worn her yoga pants, the most comfortable and loosest fitting pants she owned. Still, the stairs presented a challenge. Hanging onto the rail for dear life, she staggered down at the pace of an eighty-year-old. Each step a reminder of why she needed to send that breakup email later.

Greysmith's bustled with what she recognized as several Saturday morning regulars. She knew them only by sight and hadn't struck up conversation with any of them. Still, they often nodded or acknowledged her as a same-said regular. It was comforting to be a regular somewhere, and she appreciated the security of routine. Of course, the staff all knew her by name. Living so close, the temptation to stop was nearly impossible to ignore most mornings. The smell of coffee had her stomach demanding attention, so she ordered a café mocha and a raspberry pastry, then settled into a back corner chair by the gas fireplace. She had no desire to be on display up front, exposed to passersby, on the remote chance Jason wandered in, looking for her.

Finally finding a comfortable position, she sipped her drink and unfolded the letter to begin her translation efforts. It had been so long since she'd read an actual physical letter from someone—let alone one written in cursive—that doing so would be quite the trial.

Dearest Sarah,

After much consideration, I now endeavor to humbly and with utmost trepidation, reach out to you and profess my new, although deserved, smitten state. I came to notice you many days ago in the coffee shop below and have not been able to occupy my busy mind with much else since. Please do not be alarmed with my forthrightness. I begged a servant of the store for your name and nothing more and then contracted for his utmost discretion and secrecy. It was only later, as we were both taking our leave, that I realized you lived upstairs.

Not that I have anything to hide, I only wanted to assure you that I mean you no harm nor would I ever intrude upon your safe abode. It's only that I'm in the coffee shop nearly every evening and have already developed a habit of hoping to spy you there as well. I knew no other way to contact you, and so I resorted to the one way I do know. The written word.

I'm sure it shall fail miserably in conveying my delight in discovering you, a bright light in an otherwise dark winter. You see, I'm quite new here and everything seems to overwhelm me as of late, but when I saw you with a smile so lustrous and a way so obviously kind, I said to myself, there is one to know!

Perhaps we have little in common? I do love to read, mostly of the nineteenth century. I've not dabbled in anything of this century. Is that much too odd? Seeing that you live directly above a bookshop, I must conjecture you might also enjoy the same pastime? How could you not? Is there any author in particular who might strike a chord?

Please tell me more about yourself. What leisure activities do you most enjoy? Where, if anywhere, have you traveled? To New York, ever? I am from there myself, although I'm sure it has changed much since my absence. Do you have family near? Mine have all passed away, long ago and as of late I find I miss them dearly. I have lost much and now hope to—not regain what was lost, which is entirely impossible—but to live for what is possible.

I yearn to learn more about you. I feel... I feel a heavy weight on my heart as I write this and hope that we might somehow cut through this thin veil of our separate existences and make contact of a substantial sort. In time, perhaps we may even... no I dare not dream it.

Yet...

It is simply that I have discovered, as many before me, that life is invariably short. A fact I've come to appreciate in alarming clarity these past few years, months, and days especially. I have determined to act upon and participate in Horace's age old admonition to pluck the day. A philosophy from henceforth I intend to employ with gusto.

It is with this course of action in mind that I pluck up the courage to write to you in the hopes that you are of a similar mind, at least as far as discourse shall go. I have found in my life that sometimes the best way to get to know a person is through their written words. While it's true that action speaks more than words...thoughtful and careful words have launched entire civilizations. Surely, you and I could take a chance at launching a friendship?

If you are so inclined as to respond in kind, I would greatly enjoy getting to know you better, which is to say, at all. To be so bold as to say my heart leaped the very first time I laid eyes on you would be too much, I'm sure. But it is the very truth.

I shall peek up your stairway to see if a reply appears under your door for me tomorrow. If so, we shall begin this journey. If not... I shall suffer indeed.

Yours truly,

Tanner

Sarah immediately cast about the coffee shop, scrutinizing its patrons, wondering if Tanner sat here, in the coffee shop with her, right now.

His letter!

She took a sip of her coffee and looked into her mug, startled it had grown cold so quickly. Then she checked her phone. Eleven thirty. It had taken her an hour to decipher the letter. And then reread it. It was as if she'd time traveled back to Pemberley and her own Mr. Darcy had taken a fancy to her.

After her disastrous First Friday outing and even with Ellie's indulgence, her heart had sat like a heavy stone in her chest, impossible to breathe around its burden. But now? Someone *liked* her?

The fact that he obviously knew where she lived maybe should have set off a few mental alarms, but what was the difference? If she'd met him in a bar or online, chances were he'd make his way here to pick her up for a date eventually anyway. Besides, she had the Adam security override system now. Between him and Ellie, she felt confident that after the last few encounters with Jason, one of them would have the police here if so much as a heavy footfall neared her door.

Ironic that it was the man she knew and had loved who set off all of her internal alarms now. It had certainly taken long enough.

Five years too long.

She was embarrassed to even think about the time and tears she'd wasted on him. Ellie was right. He wasn't going to change. No, he *had* changed. He'd gotten worse. There was no use kidding herself any longer. The Jason she'd seen in the past few days— months even, if she were honest—was not the man she'd loved. Not the man who'd encouraged her to leave Georgia and make a life away from factory work. Not the man who'd made her romantic playlists, sent her flowers at random and picked her up from her late night classes so she'd be safe on campus.

Those days had been gone for some time. Ellie had seen it. But Sarah hadn't. Her and Jason's relationship had slipped into something comfortable, then convenient—for Jason—and for the past year or so, controlling.

Still, she hadn't considered leaving. But now? With his exaggerated displays the past few days she realized she had options and with this letter in her hand she also realized...

She had prospects.

Any man who could write such a beautiful letter couldn't possibly have a heart like Jason's. For the slightest moment, she let the possibility that Adam might have written the letter play across her mind, but quashed it. He was interested in Ellie. And Ellie was more than interested in him. No. This was someone new. Secret. An admirer.

The mere thought of it sent a blush to her cheeks, and she felt her face grow hot. Out of habit now, she slid the ring along the platinum chain, lost in thought. Another lucky break. On the day she decided to break up for good with Jason, she met—okay, sort of met—a new man. What were the chances of that?

Slim and none.

This ring *was* a lucky talisman. And she was keeping it.

Determined, she gathered her coffee mug and plate, and carried them to the counter for a to-go cup and a sack.

She couldn't wait to get back upstairs and write her reply.

CHAPTER ELEVEN

Writing a letter by hand was hard. *Physically hard.* Sarah's hand cramped, and began to resemble that of an arthritic old woman. First her injured knees, and now this? It was a concurrence she didn't want to ponder too closely.

For God's sake, she was only halfway down the page.

It had been ages since she'd written more than a grocery list by hand. Even that she usually composed on her iPhone.

How did people do this in the old days?

And a love letter? No, not a love letter. A what? A pen pal letter seemed too childish. So what was this? Good old fashioned correspondence. That was all. Like online dating for the nineteenth century.

Arg!

She'd started and stopped a dozen times already. It was worse than helping Ellie write her eHarmony profile for real online dating. Code was her first language.

English was second. Even with a hoard of devoured romance novels under her belt, putting together words as lovely as Tanner's nearly proved impossible.

Finally, she buckled down and started writing, determined she wouldn't stop until the page was filled. She was who she was, and if her rambling scared him away, so be it. She was tired of being the girl someone else expected her to be. Which reminded her—she still hadn't sent Jason's email.

As soon as she finished, she would. Tanner was right—she needed to pluck the day and this day was quickly getting away from her.

What to say? He already knew what she looked like, which gave him a clear advantage. She liked to think of herself as open-minded, and surely someone who wrote so beautifully and hung out at bookstores wouldn't turn out to be a troll, but the possibility remained.

Oh, for the love of all things sparkly, it's one letter.

Sarah read through what she had so far.

Dear Tanner,

Thank you for your beautiful letter. I appreciate your kind words. Things have been complicated here lately and your letter was a wonderful pick-me-up this morning. I can't help but wonder which of the coffee shop staff was so susceptible to your charms, but I can hardly blame them. You have quite a way with words.

I'm afraid you have me at a disadvantage, having already seen me when I have no idea what you look like.

As I read, I couldn't help but think of one of my favorite books. Can you guess the one? You're correct in guessing that I love to read. Although, the fact I live above a book and coffee store was merely serendipity. No one else could stand the noise, ha.

I read mostly romance novels, but have read a few classics as well, including the one I alluded to above.

I spend most of my time at work. I do web design and development. For fun, I mostly hang out with my girlfriend, Ellie. She's constantly planning some sort of crazy adventure or another.

As for travel, I've not been to New York nor had the opportunity to travel much, but I would love to one day. My family is scattered around Georgia, none more than a few hours away. I'm sorry to hear that yours has mostly passed. It makes me very curious about your age and/or the circumstances of their passing.

It sounds as though something life-changing has happened to you very recently. I've had a bit of that myself. In fact, today, as soon as I finish this letter I will break up with my long-time boyfriend. Five years we've been together and last night was the final straw. I'm embarrassed to say I've allowed him to treat me badly for some time, but last night he actually scared me.

I tell you this so your eyes will be wide open if you wish to continue corresponding. While I love your letter, I would like to meet you in person before we continue much further. Honestly, I don't want to lead you on if we have no chemistry. You seem like a very nice person. I'm interested, and I have to say your timing is impeccable.

Hope to hear from you soon.

Sarah

She folded the letter in half and set it on the edge of her desk. She'd leave it under her door, and then go downstairs to quiz the bookstore staff to see who might have met her admirer. Someone had spoken to him, and she was determined to find out who. Tanner had said he'd *contracted for his utmost discretion and secrecy.* That left four possibilities: Drew, Samuel, Thomas and Kevin. One of them would fess up.

Well played, Tanner. I don't even know your last name.

I would know more about you if we'd met in a bar.

Taking a deep breath, she booted up her laptop. This had turned into a day for letters. The only good thing about the next one was it would be short and sweet. She wasn't wasting one more minute on Jason than was absolutely necessary. Emailing him was a cowardly way out, but there was no way she was prepared to do it in person. Not after last night.

Jason,

I know you're going to find this difficult to understand, but I am officially breaking up with you. Last night was more than I can bear. I'm sure with your considerable talents you'll be able to find someone better matched for you in the long run. I'll miss you. Five years is a long time to be together. But honestly, we hadn't been together, really together, for a very long time. Please do not contact me. I need time alone, and I do not want to see you for a while. I hope you'll respect my wishes.

Sincerely,

Sarah

She hit send before she could chicken out, and then immediately regretted it. Her heart pounded in her ears and her vision tunneled to black for a split second. Closing her eyes, she concentrated on slowing her heart and breathing calmly until she didn't feel like throwing up anymore.

Had she made a mistake?

No. It was the right thing to do. It was.

She needed to keep repeating that mantra until she believed it. It was just after lunchtime, and she still hadn't eaten. Unwrapping her pastry again, she sat on the couch and debated whether to read or watch television when she noticed the framed photographs on her mantle.

Odd.

Curious, she rose, cringing at abrasion of her pants scraping against her wounded knees, and went over to investigate. Dusting was not one of her favorite housekeeping tasks. The clean tracks and frame footprints left clear evidence that the photos had been moved recently. Had Ellie moved them? And if so, why?

She startled when her phone rang and jerked quickly toward the sound, the skin along her wounds pinching in reminder.

"Hello?"

"Sarah, it's Ellie. Are you sitting down?"

"That question never ends well. What's up?"

"Three guesses who went to jail last night."

Sarah could hear Ellie bouncing on the other end of the line. "Don't make me guess. Just tell me."

"Jason."

"What? Why? How do you know that?" Sarah's palm grew damp around the phone with nervous sweat.

"My brother called me last night. Mike's friend Carl works at the sheriff's office. He said Jason got pulled over for speeding, asked to walk the line, and then booked for a DWI. And if that's not enough, Jason got all belligerent with the arresting officer and spent the night in jail!"

"He's going to be so upset. This could ruin his career," Sarah said, pacing in front of her windows.

"Nothing he doesn't deserve. He's been on this track for a while now."

"Still. Oh, Ellie, I just sent a breakup email too. He's going to go off the rails."

Ellie laughed. "Well, if he does he'll land right back in jail."

"He's out already?"

"Of course. He made bond no problem. But he'll have to be on his best behavior. If he shows up, you call the police. Promise me, Sarah. You should go down to the station and get a restraining order against him too."

"I don't need a restraining order. He's got enough problems right now. I don't want to ruin him. I just don't want to see him anymore. Besides…"

"Besides what?" Ellie asked.

"I met someone."

Ellie's scream blared through the phone, and Sarah yanked it away from her ear but could still hear her just fine. "Who? When? Are you still wearing that damned ring? You are officially the luckiest girl in the universe. I'm coming over. I want all of the details."

"No! There are no details. Someone left me a sweet letter and wants to get to know me better. I don't even know what he looks like. He's probably a troll. Or old. Or I don't even know. I feel foolish even telling you about it but you're my best friend. It's practically the law!"

"You'd better believe it is. Rule number one of the girlfriend code. Are you sure you don't want me to come over? I mean, Adam might be wandering about the hallways or something too."

"You've got it bad for him." Sarah smiled into the phone.

"Excuse me? Have you seen the man? If you hadn't been so blinded by all of the Jason nonsense lately, you'd have beaten me to him. So what are you going to do tonight then?"

"I'm staying in and reading. I don't feel like going out."

"What about the curtain shopping?" Ellie asked.

"I'll browse online. Maybe I'll find something there. I'm…"

"What? Is something else going on?"

Sarah hesitated a moment too long before answering. "No."

"Liar. What happened?"

"Did you rearrange my mantle pictures?"

Ellie paused. "No. Are they rearranged?"

"Just a few. Maybe. Seriously, it's probably Bitly moving things around."

"Framed pictures? Your cat is an interior decorator now? Are you even listening to this gibberish?"

"It's nothing. I'm stressed, which is exactly why I need to stay in and relax. Quit worrying."

A long silence filled the phone.

"Ellie? Are you still there?"

"I'm here. Just thinking. If anything else weird happens. I want to know."

"Nothing else is going to happen." Her gaze drifted back to the photos.

"Promise you'll tell me if it does. Even if it seems like a silly thing. Okay?"

"What are you worried about, Ellie?"

"Probably nothing. Just promise."

"I promise."

* * *

Tanner was torn. His need to communicate with Sarah was strong but if he wasn't careful, he'd frighten her away before he had a chance to make her understand what was at stake. He'd been surprised she'd even noticed the photos. So thrilled had he been at being able to influence them at all, the thought hadn't occurred to him she might notice they were slightly out of place. Whether by the necessity of his circumstance or the mere proximity and whimsy of fate, he really was developing feelings for her. More so than for any other woman he'd ever courted. A list that was quite short, as it was. Love at first sight was a fairytale best left to young girls to muse upon. With the little stab of fear piercing his heart at the thought of losing Sarah already, however, he couldn't help but wonder if love at first sight was at least a possibility.

Sarah put on her shoes and grabbed her wallet again. He followed, and she slipped her letter under the door on her way out.

Down the stairs they trekked, once again to the bookstore below, his heart picking up its pace. He'd read her reply letter over her shoulder as she composed it and was encouraged that her efforts in communicating to a stranger were almost as taxing as his own.

If she meant to quiz the shop staff, she'd get no answers, which worked in his favor. He wouldn't be able to quell her curiosity forever, but as long as she held the ring, and he was less than corporeal, this exchange would have to do. He feared laying all of his cards on the table, as it was, would only frighten her away before he could win her over. Still, his plan was risky.

She went straight to the counter as he'd expected her to.

"Hey, Sarah. Twice in one day?" the attendant asked.

"What can I say, Drew? You tempt me all day with your sweets." Sarah smiled.

"What can I get for you then?"

"A black coffee would be great, whatever you have brewed." She glanced behind the counter. "You all by yourself this afternoon?"

"Yeah, Samuel comes in at six."

"Would you know if anyone has been asking about me? Like my name or anything? Maybe even a regular?"

Drew poured black coffee into a white logo mug for her. "Not that I know of. Why?"

"Someone left me a letter, and I want to know who it was. He said his name is Tanner and that one of the staff told him my name. Ring any bells?"

Drew shook his head. "None of us would do that, Sarah. And no one's been asking about you. I'll check with the other guys, but I'm absolutely sure they would protect your privacy."

"I'm not mad. Just curious."

"You should be mad if someone did that. You're too trusting. I'll keep an eye out though."

"You're sweet. I think he's harmless. Thanks."

Sarah took the mug and walked around the stacks to the back corner once again. This time instead of lounging, she stood before the Civil War and History section, perusing titles. She collected four from the shelf, cradled them in her free arm, then settled into the chair with her coffee.

The 10 Biggest Civil War Battles: Gettysburg, Chickamauga, Spotsylvania Court House, Chancellorsville, The Wilderness, Stones River, Shiloh, Antietam, Second Bull Run, and Fredericksburg

Fredericksburg! Fredericksburg! (Civil War America)

The Fredericksburg Campaign: Winter War on the Rappahannock

The entire wall bookcase was filled with similar titles, floor to ceiling, and Tanner longed to hold each book and devour its pages. His tether would reach this far without a doubt, and coming down here would help to pass the long nights while Sarah slept. In the meantime, he scanned as quickly as he could while she flipped through the pages. His attention riveted on one book in particular, filled with battle photos and soldier portraits. His breath caught in his throat as she paused on a page dedicated to Chatham Manor. His Major General's portrait sat alongside the accompanying text.

The witch had tricked him.

If the text was accurate, the battle that had cost him his life had been lost after all. Fury filled him, and he struck out at the bookcase behind him in anger. Sarah jumped up when three books fell from the shelves behind her, and she spilled coffee down her white shirt. Her books slid to the floor from her lap as she set her mug on the small reading table. Reaching inside her collar, she retrieved the ring from beneath her blouse and held it, her eyes wide with wonder.

The ring glowed and an orange light radiated from it.

Tanner wondered if he was the only one who could see it, but Sarah's reaction made him think she saw it too.

She glanced around, then bent with effort and picked up the fallen books. One by one, she placed them back on the shelf. With trepidation, she sat again and scanned the bookshop once more before resuming her reading. Tanner spent the next few hours alternately plugging into the free energy supply of the bookshop patrons while Sarah read and stopping back by to see what other treasures she'd discovered.

He'd take his fill of history later and at his leisure. He could study the books more thoroughly after the shop closed.

Lost in her own reading, Sarah rarely even looked up until a store employee interrupted her long after dark.

"Sarah?" the employee asked.

"Hey, Samuel. Wait, is it six already?"

"Yeah, Drew said you had some questions about some guy who's harassing you?"

"Not harassing. Only asking about me. Did someone named Tanner or anyone at all ask about me?"

"No. Drew's right. We wouldn't share any information with some random guy, anyway. You're like our coffee bar little sister. We'd have to kick his ass, not give out your name," Samuel said, stuffing his hands into his jeans pockets.

"No ass kicking necessary. Good to know though." Sarah smiled. "Hey, do you mind if I take a few of these upstairs with me for a couple of days?"

"Civil War nonfiction? Not your usual. Got a hankering for history? Fredericksburg has a way of wearing you down like that with all the old buildings and stuff. I've read a few of these myself."

"Really? Do you recommend any—especially on Chatham Manor and any battles there?"

"Looks like you found the ones I would have recommended. If you really want to know about Chatham, you need to go out to the national park and spend some time. They have a ton of stuff out there. They'll even give you a tour of the grounds."

Sarah blushed again. "No thanks. I've seen enough of the grounds. I would like to know more though. Thanks."

"You bet. If this Tanner guy bothers you or you need anything while we're here, you bang on the floor. One of us will be up in a jiffy."

"Thanks, Sam."

Tanner grew more than a little worried about the sudden number of gentlemen indicating interest in Sarah. Her kindness seemed to draw them like bees to honey. Her naiveté made her absolutely oblivious to their underlying intentions. *Little sister, indeed*. He didn't like this Samuel. Not at all. Suddenly, he was not nearly as pleased about these lads' proximity—all of the coffee shop staff's proximity—and their daily interactions with her.

He was the one who should be looking out for her.

Dear Lord. Was he jealous?

His emotions were all over the map.

Sarah gathered her collection of books, adding two more to the stack, and set her long empty coffee mug on the small bussing bar. She walked extra slowly out of the shop, surveying the window crowd as she left, perhaps silently willing her secret admirer to manifest.

If she only knew, she already had him under her spell.

CHAPTER TWELVE

Over the next week, Sarah and Tanner exchanged daily letters, and still she hadn't caught him. She'd tried to stay awake all night Sunday, despite knowing she had work the next day, waiting for his reply to appear under her door, but had lost the battle and fallen to sleep. The coffee and bookshop staff insisted no one had inquired about her, and she believed them, which meant that Tanner had lied for some reason. Maybe he worried his methods would seem too stalkery.

Whatever the reason, it didn't matter. She'd learned a lot about him over the course of the week. He'd been a soldier in the war—which war, he hadn't specified. Maybe he had PTSD and had trouble interacting with strangers? That might explain his reluctance to meet, but his writing still surprised her. Each letter was more eloquent than the last. Her replies paled in comparison, and she was actually surprised he remained interested, although he assured her he was.

They'd talked about books, Fredericksburg, New York, everything and nothing under the sun. He didn't watch television or listen to modern music and seemed to have no pop culture knowledge at all, which made her wonder how his spent his days. He also claimed to be retired from the military, a fact which made her even more curious about his age. She continued to press for a meeting at the coffee shop, but Tanner held firm. It was too soon for that, he said. He needed more time.

Meanwhile, nothing from Jason since she'd sent her email.

It was Friday evening, and Ellie would settle for nothing less than a night out, but Sarah had other ideas. Ellie tapped her foot in the doorway of Sarah's cubicle as Sarah shut down her laptop.

"Come on. Adam is waiting for us at the Ale House, and he has a friend."

Sarah froze. "What friend?"

"A guy friend. Does it matter? I told him it would be okay. Just a drink. You don't have to sleep with him. Just, you know, hang out for a while. It's time you meet some new people."

"Ellie, it's only been a week since I broke up with Jason."

"Don't make a big deal out of this. It's just for fun."

"I don't want to go." Sarah swung her laptop case over her shoulder and grabbed her purse. "Besides, I have met someone and you know it."

"Um, writing letters to one another like junior high is not 'meeting someone.' Your secret admirer is more like the invisible man. It's getting a little ridiculous, actually. You need to date a real boy, not someone hiding behind a bunch of letters."

Sarah shrugged. "I like this guy."

"Of course you do. He's perfect. Writes like Darcy, is as handsome as your imagination can conjure, never says the wrong thing—thanks to the magic of editing—and doesn't leave the toilet seat up. He's a literary boyfriend fantasy. You know what they say about things that are too good to be true, right?"

"I'm not going. I'm sorry. Thanks for trying, but no. I'm going to the mall to look for curtains. If you want to come with me, great. If not, I totally understand. Go. Have a date. Or two. I'm not upset. Just not in the mood for whatever this is."

Ellie pouted, arms crossed and forehead creased. "Well hell. I'm not going without you. I'll call him on the way. We can take my car to the mall. I'm parked out back."

"You're not mad?"

"No. But you have to buy me one of those giant cookies at the mall. If I'm not getting lucky tonight, at least I'm getting chocolate."

"Done."

* * *

A half hour later, Tanner followed Sarah and Ellie through the "mall"—an amazing indoor marketplace with a dizzying array of people and products. The atmosphere was charged with the energy of hundreds of shoppers, and Tanner took full advantage of his opportunity to binge on this astounding and seemingly unlimited resource. With each passing contact, Tanner felt himself grow stronger. So strong, in fact, he marveled he didn't cast a reflection or take corporeal form.

The hex was clear. True love would break the curse. How would he ever win true love if he couldn't even manage visibility? It was the cruelest of jokes, and only a matter of time before Sarah tired of his excuses for not meeting her in person. He didn't blame her. He had to take a bold leap of faith and reach out to her before it was too late.

"These are perfect," Sarah said, running her hands along thick burgundy velvet drapes.

"They look like stage curtains," Ellie said. "They *are* perfect."

"But expensive." Sarah turned the tag so Ellie could see it. "This would take every bit of the bonus I have left for enough panels to do all of the windows."

"Do it. That was your lucky money. You deserve something nice. Me? I'd spend it on something much less practical than curtains. Like backstage tickets to Kings of Leon. Now *that* would be awesome."

Sarah laughed. "It would be awesome, but that would last an hour." She ran her hand along the soft velvet grain. "These will last a lifetime."

The crowd had thinned considerably when the women left the mall, laden with several long curtain rods and two bags each, the packages stretched at the seams with the weight of the curtains. Ellie confiscated a rolling metal basket near the exit and placed her burden inside. Sarah followed suit. Ellie pushed, and then rode the basket like a carriage to her vehicle.

Tanner's first experience in a car earlier had been terrifying. The speed at which the conveyance propelled them along was astounding and nothing short of a miracle. He'd spent much of the trip holding on for dear life, eyes closed and praying. Sarah had indicated that Ellie's transport was called a mustang, of all things, but occasionally also referred to it as 'POS,' so he remained confused.

The name of the vehicle, however, was the least of his concerns. They'd covered a great distance in a very short time. More in control now, he managed to collect his faculties enough to recognize many landmarks on the return trip. Hidden among the phenomenal landscape of this new Fredericksburg, the buildings he'd once known were now renamed after former presidents. George Washington Masonic Museum, Thomas Jefferson Religious Freedom Monument, James Monroe Museum.

Tanner's senses crackled at the profusion of energy coursing through him from the evening's venture. He couldn't wait to get back and get hold of the books Sarah had borrowed, as well as peruse the other offerings downstairs. He hoped for a long night of reading by her side.

Ellie stopped the vehicle in front of Sarah's home. "You sure you don't want to go out for a while?"

"I'm positive. I can't believe I lasted this long. I'm tired. Thanks for going. I'm sorry if I ruined your master plan."

"Fear not. There will more scheming."

"That's what I'm afraid of."

Ellie got out and helped Sarah carry the purchases up the stairs.

Sarah frowned as she pushed her key into her door lock.

"What's wrong?" Ellie asked.

"I thought there might be a letter."

"Girl, you've got it bad."

Ellie carried in her haul and laid them across the couch. "How about I come over tomorrow and we can put them up? I still can't believe they were on sale for half-price. You are seriously, ridiculously lucky these days. I wish I'd have found that damned ring."

Sarah smiled. "Sure, tomorrow would be great. But not early."

"No problem there. All right. I'm going to see if Adam's home and if not, head over to the Ale House for a while."

Sarah hugged Ellie. "Thanks again."

"You're welcome. Good night."

Sarah closed the door behind her.

Not a half hour later, Sarah was dressed in her night clothes and under her covers. Much to Tanner's gratification, she reread his letters. He'd carefully hidden her replies to him. As of now, he'd shared only the vaguest details of his life, minus the last bit, of course. That explanation would require a delicacy he wasn't sure he was capable of.

When she finally dozed off, his letters by her side, Tanner was pleased beyond measure that he managed to extinguish her bedside light.

Emboldened, he moved the letters—one by one—to the nightstand as well, stacking them in a neat pile. Bitly watched with the calculating eyes of a predator, but didn't hiss at him this time. Yet another small victory. He'd take them as he found them.

As Sarah's breathing evened and deepened, he assumed his nightly ritual and penned another letter to her.

Dearest Sarah,

Your letters are the highlight of my every day and have sustained me through these difficult times of late. Adjusting to this new environment has been more trying than I could ever have imagined. There is so much wonder here.

I count you among the new things I am in wonder of. I know you're anxious for us to meet, and we will very soon. I feel I know you already and cannot wait to walk down Princess Anne Street with your hand in mine. My dearest wish is to court you as is deserving of a fine lady as yourself.

A few details must first fall into place before I can make my appearance. I hope your patience will hold. I've been caught in a sort of Purgatory since the war and am only now finding my way back to all that is good and light and beautiful. Much of that is thanks to you.

You awakened me, dear one. You who gave me the first spark of hope in...many years. Hope for a second chance at life. Hope that my true love might actually exist, even after I'd given up all notion of it and resigned myself to the darkness for all eternity.

But now? Now there is you.

Do not despair. Do not lose hope. Give me a bit more time and all will be revealed.

I will not disappoint you.

Ever.

Tanner

He folded the letter and slipped it under her door. Every few minutes, rounds of applause rose from Greysmith's. The sign had advertised an author reading tonight. Tanner had thought to look in but found himself entranced, memorizing Sarah's features instead.

It was a miracle she hadn't yet terminated their correspondence. Her overwhelming trust and faith in him—a stranger in every way—revealed the true character of her soul. She searched for and found the best in people, then worked to hang on to it, as was evident in her long relationship with that scoundrel.

The man was a beast. He hoped she held to her decision and didn't relent the first time he tested her resolve. A man in the flesh was much more difficult to deny than a man existing only on paper. Even now, filled to what he was sure was his full capacity of life energy, Tanner's body was no more real than a shadow. Invisible in every sense except to perform parlor tricks, which were sure to frighten Sarah to death without knowing the context.

The questions were how and when to breech the subject of his supernatural state. And then...the metaphysical plane.

He didn't think he could wait much longer.

CHAPTER THIRTEEN

Tanner turned page after page of *The Fredericksburg Campaign: Winter War on the Rappahannock* in rapt incredulity. It seemed the battle that took his life ended in a disastrous Union defeat. They'd lost dozens of men in the initial assault, and then nearly ten-thousand over the course of the next few days. Chatham Manor was transformed into a hospital for mostly Union, but also many Confederate soldiers. Somehow, much later, the Union had managed to win the war. His battle was one of many battles in and around Fredericksburg, and it would take more than a hundred nights of reading to learn the entire story. A task Tanner hoped to achieve.

Most disturbing of all was the fate of President Lincoln, his most respected and highest regarded leader. Shot down at a theatre.

Dear Lord.

Tanner was sure there was much more to *that* story than existed in any of the texts of the coffee shop.

The cacophony downstairs came to an abrupt stop and Tanner glanced at the wall clock. Midnight. Finally, Greysmith's was closing, which meant he'd be free to wander the stacks unhindered. He had questions begging for answers. As he rearranged the pile of books on Sarah's desk, movement by the door caught his eye. His letter was pulled from the hallway side of the door and the note vanished from his sight. Tanner was up and into the hallway in seconds.

Jason read the letter outside Sarah's door, his face reddening with anger.

Closing his eyes, Jason hesitated, his jaw clenched. He rapped on the door three quick knocks and waited. Tanner did not want Sarah to open the door. Surely, she wouldn't open it for him. She hadn't wanted to be alone with him in her apartment before they'd parted ways.

Tanner slipped back inside, and Sarah sat up in bed. "Who's there?"

Jason didn't answer, only knocked again, three short raps.

Sarah's forehead crinkled in concern, then Tanner's letter slid under the doorway with force and skittered across the wood floor. Sarah was up and to the door, slipping back the deadbolt in seconds.

"Wait, Tanner!" She pulled open the door, and Jason was upon her.

* * *

Sarah's air huffed out of her lungs as Jason shoved her across the room. Her knees caught the edge of the bed, and she fell back onto to it. Jason kicked the door shut behind him and flipped on the overhead light. He bent to pick up the letter he'd shoved under her door.

"Is this why you broke up with me? You've been cheating on me? How. Long?" He jutted the letter forward at her, punctuating each word.

She'd never seen him so angry. And the truly frightening thing was he wasn't even drunk. His eyes were clear and his speech unslurred. This was pure Jason.

"No. Of course not. I only met him after we broke up."

"*We* broke up? I didn't break up. You sent me a chicken-shit email, but that doesn't mean we're broken up. I say when we're broken up."

Sarah looked over at her nightstand. Could she use the lamp as a weapon if she needed one?

Following her gaze, Jason noticed the stack of letters sitting there.

Had she stacked them there? She didn't remember arranging them.

He snatched them up. Bitly peeked out from the corner of the bathroom, then quickly retreated. Sarah's heart pounded as he read the top letter, then glanced back at the other seven.

"What a bunch of bullshit. This what gets you off now? All this fancy bullshit talk? You want me to read it to you aloud? Would that make you hot?"

Tears welled in her eyes, making them burn as she tried to hold back her own anger. "Get out."

"No. I'm not getting out. I'm taking what's mine."

Jason threw the letters at her, and they scattered across the floor. He fell upon her, grabbing her flailing arms and pinned her to the bed.

"Stop it!" Sarah tried to bring her knees up between them to push his weight off her as she scrambled beneath him.

"It's been a really shitty week. Don't make it worse." Jason pushed his knee between her legs and forced them apart.

She gasped in a breath to scream, and he covered her mouth with his as she exhaled, swallowing her cry. He bit her lip hard, and she began choking on her own blood.

"You try to scream again, and I'll stuff that mouth full of something else."

Sarah's mind raced. This was not going to happen. He was strong, but she wouldn't stop fighting until he was gone. When he eased his grip on her arms, reduced to one hand as he worked his belt and zipper free, Sarah twisted beneath him and scrambled up and across the bed. He grabbed her by the ankles and ripped her back to him. Straddling the back of her neck, he pinned her shoulders with his knees.

She twisted her head sideways, craning to look behind her and opened her mouth to scream again. He stuffed her sleep mask between her lips, making it difficult to breathe. Tears leaked from the corner of her eyes, and she continued to kick, trying to buck him off her but his weight was too much. Jason stripped his belt from his pants, then stretched her arms up and above her head and knotted the belt around them. He yanked her fleece sleep-pants down and off her. Mercifully her panties held in place.

In the second it took for him to return to her, she twisted again, brought her knees up and kicked him square in the chest, causing him to stagger and knock the lamp from the nightstand. It crashed to the floor and broke. Undazed, Jason caught her legs and spread them apart for a good look.

"It didn't have to be like this. This is your fault."

His dress pants hung loose on his hips, but she could see his erection outlined against the fabric.

"You like that. Don't you," he said, following her line of vision.

Raising her gaze, she saw his black pupils expanding in his eyes, filling them with a determined hatred she'd never have believed.

A second later, his head snapped hard to the left. Then left again.

His face contorted in surprise and then a new emotion displayed. Terror.

An invisible blow to the stomach bent him in half at the waist, causing him to lose his hold on her legs. Sarah flipped over and rolled herself off the bed and to the floor on the other side. Spitting out the sleep mask, she scrambled to her knees, and then to her feet. Desperately trying to untangle the belt, she backed away a few feet, hitting the wall behind her.

Jason lunged toward her, and this time she managed a scream. Jason's forward motion was momentary as he met with unseen resistance. He flew backward across the room and into the wall as if shoved. Photos dislodged from their hooks and smashed to the floor, shattering. Trying to recover himself, Jason gasped in a breath and reached for the doorknob to flee, but was assaulted once again. Her wooden umbrella stand lifted from the floor and struck Jason across the side of the head. Blood gushed from his temple, and he slumped to the floor, losing consciousness.

Sarah gasped as a shadowy figure assembled before her. A man, holding the now splintered umbrella stand. The apparition turned to face her just long enough for her to recognize him, then dissipated to vapor, vanishing as the door crashed open.

Adam stepped through the door first, quickly followed by Ellie and Samuel from Greysmith's. Ellie ran across the room and wrapped her arms around Sarah.

Adam went for the belt, keeping an eye on Jason. Samuel kneeled, ready to subdue her groggy assailant. Blood poured from Jason's head wound.

Samuel rolled Jason to his stomach and pressed his knees into Jason's back, pinning him there. Adam bent Jason's arms behind his back and secured the belt around Jason's wrists at his waist.

Ellie covered Sarah with a blanket, then pulled her cell phone from her pocket and dialed 911. "We need police and an ambulance. No fire trucks, please. My friend has been attacked, and we have the intruder."

Sarah watched in detached awe as the next hour played out before her. The paramedics said shock was to blame. That seemed about right. The only problem was she didn't know if it was shock due to Jason's behavior or the fact she'd just witnessed the ghostly Civil War soldier from her dream beat him to a pulp.

She'd managed to leave out any details of Jason's invisible attacker. So far, everyone assumed she'd done the damage herself. It was also the only explanation that would keep her from being held for observation.

Her scream and the noise of the fight had brought Samuel and Adam running. Ellie's visit with Adam had apparently been going well. Adam stood shirtless, and Ellie's hair ratted in a nest around her head.

Jason came to right before the police arrived but hadn't uttered a word, except to lawyer-up. She doubted he'd be blaming an invisible assailant for his injuries either.

"That's all for now. He'll be in custody for a good long time. Thirty days most likely. Depends on the judge, his lawyer and whether or not you make it down to the station to press charges."

The officer gave Sarah a hard glare.

"I will. I'll come down Monday. I promise."

"Good. We can do a restraining order then too. Not that he's going to be around for a while, but he has money. Money can unfortunately sometimes get guys out of some bad situations. We lock 'em up, and the lawyers get 'em out." The officer flipped closed his notebook.

"Nice," Ellie said with derision.

"It's just as frustrating for us," he countered.

"You weren't the one who was almost raped in your own home," Ellie said.

"Enough, Ellie, it's over," Sarah said.

"This time," Ellie muttered.

The last officer left at three in the morning. Samuel and Adam waited by the door. Sarah walked to them.

"Thank you both. I—"

"You're welcome. Just make sure you follow through. None of us want anything to happen to you," Adam said.

"Come by tomorrow morning for a free drink." Samuel gave her a wink and squeezed her shoulder.

"I think it already is tomorrow morning. I'm sorry you've all been up so late."

"I'll go by The Home Depot as soon as they open and get some stuff to fix your wall. Unless you have a different plan?" Adam said.

"I can't ask you to do that," Sarah said.

"You didn't ask. I offered. Don't worry, it won't be early." Adam smiled and pulled Ellie to him. "You staying with me or what?"

Ellie blushed. "I should stay here with Sarah."

"No. Go. Please, go. Jason's locked up, and I'm not going to be any kind of company. I'm going to bed and sleeping until tonight is only a bad dream."

"Are you sure? You aren't afraid to be alone?" Ellie asked.

"Not with you two next door. Seriously. I can do this. I *need* to do this."

Sarah could tell Ellie was torn, but she was not ready to dissect what had happened any further tonight. And she certainly wasn't ready to admit to what she may or may not have actually witnessed, which she was already second guessing now that the adrenaline had fled.

"Right down the hall," Ellie said, squeezing her in a long, hard hug.

"I know," Sarah whispered in Ellie's ear.

CHAPTER FOURTEEN

A few minutes later, Sarah was alone in her apartment, her forehead pressed against the cool steel door. The crackle of her fireplace and the utter absence of people was small comfort after her long night. She slid the deadbolt closed.

Bitly peered from beneath her disarrayed bed. Sarah sat on the edge, running her hands across the rumpled sheets, trying to smooth away the replay of bad memories.

So close.

Tanner's unread letter lay to her left. She picked it up, then saw the rest of them scattered, some torn, lying across the bed and floor. She sat and gathered up the notes, working to smooth the papers, and reorder them by date. Her latest letter, the one Jason had discovered, shook in her trembling hand as she read it. She was thankful the two men hadn't run into one another in the hallway.

She'd been so excited when she'd opened the door, expecting to catch Tanner leaving his letter. No way would she have chanced it if she'd have known Jason waited for her instead. Jason was beyond redemption.

Monday she'd press charges, file for the restraining order, buy a can of mace and terminate communication with him for good. She also planned to call the landlord to insist a peephole be installed. The last thing she wanted was another surprise visit.

Her heart still hammered in her chest. It would be a long while before she could fall back to sleep. Even then, she feared she couldn't escape from her other troubles. The dreams. Had she imagined the faint image of her dream soldier holding her umbrella stand?

She hadn't imagined Jason being attacked. Of that she was certain. Something had struck Jason repeatedly and prevented him from raping her. A guardian angel, maybe? She'd never given much thought to such things, but then again, she'd never needed one.

The ring grew warm against her skin, and she pulled it from beneath her shirt. She slipped it from her neck to examine it. Every time something good had happened in the past two weeks, she'd been wearing the ring. The few bad things that had happened had also worked out in her favor. She really was beginning to believe the ring was a lucky talisman. Maybe she should have it turned into a proper piece of jewelry.

She still had just enough money left over after her purchases, thanks to the unexpected discount on the curtains, to have the stone set into a custom piece. Next week, she'd take it back to Caroline Creations and have the stone reset. Maybe she could even trade her platinum chain toward the piece. She didn't want any more reminders of Jason in her life than necessary.

At nearly five o'clock, she straightened her bed and crawled beneath the covers, already wishing her new drapes were installed and closed against the coming day. Greysmith's would reopen in an hour and the sun would be up soon after. Life would continue whether she was ready to join in or not. She prayed for a few hours of rest before it happened.

* * *

Tanner couldn't tear his eyes from Sarah and was in awe of her resilience and strength. She'd fought valiantly against the wretch, but he'd outweighed her by a hundred pounds. A few more moments, and he would have violated her before Tanner's eyes. An act Tanner refused to allow.

At first, Tanner had hoped to merely drain the wretch of his energy when he punched him in the face. But when the beast's head snapped with the effort, Tanner had repeated the action with equally satisfying results. Infused with an overabundance of energy from partaking of the coffee shop patrons earlier and the profusion of emotion coursing through him, Tanner had focused his very essence on the sole task of putting a stop to Jason.

And he'd succeeded.

Still, he was amazed with his success. Nothing had pleased him more than to finally see the authorities arrive and take the louse away. Had he been at his full force, Tanner had no doubt he'd have killed Jason with his bare hands. A thought made more appealing with each passing moment.

How must his actions have looked to Sarah? He'd assumed she'd be frightened beyond measure, yet she hadn't mentioned any of it to the police. Truly, it was unexplainable in every sense. For the briefest moment, he'd been sure she'd seen him—really seen him. But then in the chaos of his battle, the moment passed, and he'd faded back to the ethereal.

If he couldn't maintain his form for more than a moment, he was doomed. Letters wouldn't sustain her interest much longer now that she knew something was afoot. He had no choice but to reveal himself completely and hope Sarah would— *could*—accept his explanation and help him break the hex.

He couldn't bear the thought of failure. If she was too frightened of him, he was lost. Pondering his options, he watched as she tossed and turned in fitful sleep, the first vestiges of the new day crept in through the still unadorned windows.

She needed the rest and after the night's efforts, Tanner found he had greatly depleted his energy as well. He refused to draw from Sarah, and further refused to leave her side, even as the sounds of the coffee shop opening below and the energy of their many morning patrons beckoned him. He'd stay as long as it took for Sarah to rise, and he could know she was safe before tending to his own selfish needs.

Too weak to manipulate more than his thoughts, he sat in her chair in front of the fire and waited. To his great shock, Bitly pounced onto the back of the couch behind him, then eased his way onto Tanner's incorporeal lap, curling and pawing until his nest was made, before finally settling down. Tanner reached a tentative hand to the cat's head and stroked his fur, eliciting rumbling purrs of satisfaction from the beast, indicating his efforts were not without effect after all.

Well, at least the cat was warming to him.

"Good kitty," he whispered.

* * *

Sarah's solider returned to her in a dream.

Blood bloomed across the soldier's chest, staining his Union blues an even darker shade before he fell to his knees on the battlefield. He stared ahead, over the edge of the terraced lawn and into the ravine and river below. The soldier's dark black, unkempt hair tumbled free as his cap dislodged and dropped in his fall. Curls plastered to his forehead as sweat broke across his pale but handsome face. Shots rang out around him. His eyes blinked with each labored beat of his slowing heart as he tried to focus and hold on to the here and now.

"Lieutenant Dawson! Hold on, Lieutenant! James!"

He heard the words. Felt the press of hands to his chest to staunch the bleeding, but couldn't seem to formulate a response. His eyes closed and the only sounds that remained were the slow thump of his failing heart. Thump. Thump. Thump... Thump...Thump.

Then nothing.

Sarah awoke covered in a sweat of her own. Her heart pounded a precarious staccato that filled her ears like a bass drum. She replayed the dream, the most vivid yet, calling each detail to the surface as she leaped from her bed and sat at her table. After searching the disheveled desk for a piece of paper and pen, she quickly scribbled out the details she remembered.

A blue uniform.

A Union soldier

Lieutenant Dawson.

James Dawson.

She had a name. The pounding of her heart now had more to do with the lead she'd discovered than the horrific details of his death. She was no artist and while she couldn't sketch out a likeness of the soldier in her dream, she was certain she could recognize him if she saw a portrait or photograph. A lieutenant would surely have sat for a portrait at some point, if there ever even existed such a man.

Someone or something very similar to her dream soldier had existed, however briefly, in her apartment only a few short hours before.

And had saved her life.

Sarah didn't know how any of this was possible, but she planned to find out. Leaning back in her chair, she closed her eyes and tried to relax. Her head pounded. Her blood pressure was likely sky-high after her abrupt awakening, but she had to capture the bits of her dream before they escaped into the ether, as dreams were wont to do. Too bad real life didn't evaporate as easily.

Memories of last night crept into the light of her apartment and threw dark shadows across her mind. She would get that restraining order Monday. She thought about calling her folks, but didn't want to upset them. Between Ellie, Adam and the coffee shop guys downstairs, she felt safe enough for now. The physical threat was gone, behind bars for thirty days...she hoped. The emotional replay became her biggest threat now. She stuffed it down and gave herself a physical shake, willing the bad energy away.

Sarah flipped open her laptop and typed "Lieutenant James Dawson" into the search engine. Four hours, 151,000 results and at least a thousand photos down the rabbit hole later, she still hadn't stumbled across anyone resembling the man in her dream...or her bedroom.

She rubbed her eyes with the pads of her hands and rested her face in her palms. What was she doing? Snapping out of her internet induced fog, she rose and crossed to the windows. The day had started without her. Another Saturday.

She startled at the knock on her door, her heart ratcheting up its dangerous tempo again. At this rate, she was going to die of a heart attack, if nothing else. She wasn't sure how much more she could take.

She crossed to the door, then hesitated before sliding the deadbolt free. "Who is it?"

"It's okay, Sarah. It's me and Adam."

Relieved, she slid the bolt and opened the door.

Ellie eyed her knowingly and pushed past her carrying an armful of tools as well as a bag of food. Adam followed equally laden with materials and tools.

"I assume you haven't eaten?" Ellie asked.

"Not yet."

"Did we wake you?"

"No. I was just...I haven't been up long."

"I don't blame you. Someone in your building is an eager beaver though, up at the butt crack of dawn." Ellie gave Adam an endearing smile. "I'm not going to hold it against him though, since it was for your benefit."

"I went to The Home Depot to get the stuff to fix your wall. I figured the sooner the better," Adam said.

"And I brought us sustenance. If Handy Dan over here is going to fix your wall, I figured we could bribe him into helping us hang those drapes as well. I made a down payment on your behalf early this morning, but I figured a late breakfast bribe wouldn't hurt either." Ellie waggled her eyebrows at Adam and a blush crept across his face before he turned to inspect the wall damage.

"Ellie," Sarah said.

"What? Just doing my part." Ellie pulled breakfast sandwiches from the bag and eyed Sarah's coffee pot. "Do you mind if I get a pot started?"

"Go for it. I need to change clothes. I'll be right back out. Thank you, both."

Sarah grabbed a change of clothes and shut the bathroom door behind her. She'd wait to shower tonight, but should at least get dressed and brush her teeth if she was going to have company for a few hours. There was little chance she and Ellie would have been all that successful alone with the curtain installation. While she wasn't exactly inept, measuring and leveling were not her strong suit. That, and the fact she had no actual tools. She appreciated Adam's help more than he could possibly know, and from the blush on his face, Ellie had indeed already settled any debt.

A friend in need…

Sarah was happy that Ellie had finally found a quality guy. She brushed her teeth, feeling refreshed and ready to face the rest of the day. In fact, if she got Ellie and Adam out of her apartment soon, she could even make it over to Chatham for a few hours of research.

She couldn't shake the thought that James Dawson was a real—if not live—person, nor the nagging sensation that her dreams and Jason's assailant were more than mere coincidence. Something strange was happening, and while she wasn't exactly afraid of it, it made her curious enough to pursue the leads she had. In the meantime, she'd keep her crazy on the inside until she had something more substantial to share.

Any hint of what she was thinking and Ellie would make it her mission to untangle the mystery. Not a bad thing, but something told Sarah the situation required more finesse than Ellie could handle. Taking a deep breath, she opened the door and joined Ellie and Adam in the living area to work on her home improvement projects. Somehow she needed to convince them both that she was okay.

Now if she could only convince herself of the same.

CHAPTER FIFTEEN

A little after two that afternoon, Ellie and Adam finally gathered their things to leave.

"Thanks again, you two. The wall and the curtains are beautiful." Sarah hugged Ellie hard and put a chaste kiss on Adam's cheek.

"Are you sure you don't want me to stay? I could sleep over. Really, it would be fun," Ellie said, standing in the doorway.

"No. I have errands to run, and you have things to do too, I'm sure. You don't have to babysit me. I'm fine. Really."

"I could go on your errands with you. I don't mind. I like errands."

"Ellie, no. For real. You've done enough. I'm not going to keep being a burden to you." Sarah nodded to Adam. "Either of you."

"I called the landlord this morning, and he'll come next week to install that peephole in your door," Adam said. "I offered, but he wants to hire someone to do it. I didn't see any reason he needed to know about your wall, though. No need for you to lose your deposit someday over something that wasn't even your fault."

"You two are the best. Now go. I'll see you Monday, Ellie."

She watched as they walked the short distance to Adam's apartment. They leaned against Adam's door and said their goodbyes to one another. Sarah closed her own door and slid the bolt. If she hurried, she could spend a couple of hours at Chatham Manor. Even though she knew her search was of the needle-in-a-haystack variety, her heart was light with the possibilities. Maybe the distraction was what she needed after everything that had happened. She was sure she would find some evidence of her dream angel, although what she would or could do with the information, she had no idea. Only the all-consuming need to chase down her dream and unearth whatever was buried within it.

After slipping on her running shoes and coat, she hurried out the door and down the stairs. She spared a glance through the glass doors of Greysmith's, and then along the entire front, street-side windows on the off chance her secret admirer was inside. She'd left her latest letter under her doorway, just in case.

* * *

Tanner's curiosity rose as he followed Sarah down the street in a different direction than she'd traveled before. He'd watched as Sarah scribbled the note after she'd awakened, and anxiety had filled him. What were the chances that she had randomly deciphered details of his life? The facts she'd written were the exact details of the dream replaying most often in his *own* mind as of late. Had he somehow shared unconscious thoughts?

Memories? Dreams with her? And if so, what else might transpose to her? The hex?

The thought of bringing his darkness upon her terrified him.

As they entered a large structure, he was further unhinged to discover she apparently had a conveyance of her own. Sarah opened the door to a car and climbed inside. It wasn't long before he knew exactly where they were headed. His heart picked up its cadence as he rode along what was now named Kings Highway and crossed over the Rappahannock River. The bridge, a much more elaborate piece of construction than he'd entered the city upon more than one hundred fifty years ago, was truly a marvel of engineering. The landscape had changed drastically, farmland having given way to a sprawl of urbanity. Tears of nostalgia sprang to his eyes as they turned down the long lane and Chatham Manor came into view.

The estate was as he'd remembered it. The stately grounds were protected by surrounding forest and farmland. Sarah parked her car well away from the buildings and exited. They walked along a soft path toward the manor. As they approached, Tanner saw the first visible battle scars on the home. One of the books had mentioned the manor had been used as a hospital. How the structure had survived at all was a miracle in itself, and a testament to the era's carpenters and masons. None of the more recently raised buildings he'd viewed thus far in his travels had been nearly as beautiful nor as outwardly well-constructed. Brick, a sturdy substance, defied the elements and man as well.

Memories flooded him as his feet traveled the familiar pathways. While he could have lodged inside the manor, he'd chosen to remain outside in his tent as did his men. The Major General, high-ranking officers, and many others of his regiment often took full advantage of the accommodations of the manor, relaxing before the fire on the cold December nights. The Major General himself occupied the entire second floor of the home. The adjacent building attached to the manor's left side housed the War Room. As Tanner followed Sarah into the building, nostalgia beat against his chest. Dread and longing for fulfillment of the second chance he held so close consumed him.

A group of school children, led by their teacher and a uniformed gentleman in the dress of Tanner's day—the first he'd seen thus far in his new surroundings—drew near. Tanner shuddered as several of the children passed completely through him. Their white hot energy sparked and crackled within him, and for a moment he feared he'd manifest before them, engorged with the charge. This was the wrong place to make himself known, and he struggled to consume and compress the vital energy within him and store it for later. Sarah would not be put off much longer, and if she discovered anything of him here in this place, he'd have no choice but to make a more tangible contact with her.

Soon.

His energy emergency temporarily at bay, he passed unnoticed behind Sarah as she approached another uniformed but very elderly man seated behind a desk. His badge read, "Vernon, Volunteer Park Ranger."

* * *

"Excuse me," Sarah said. "I was wondering where I could find archives of soldiers who might have served in battle on the Chatham grounds."

The elderly gentleman looked up from his newspaper. "You'd want the microfiche archives for that. We have some exhibits here, but most of that stuff is over at the Fredericksburg Battlefield Visitor Center.

Ruby might have some archives of interest for you, though. She's leading another tour right now. You can look around the library exhibits if you want until she gets back."

"Great. Point me in the right direction. I'd love to take a look."

"Follow me."

Vernon proceeded at the speed of silence, his rickety, skeletal form shuffling across the hardwoods, and his feet never actually seeming to lift. When they finally reached the room marked "Library," Sarah released the breath she'd been holding, relieved the man hadn't actually died of old age on the trip.

He crossed to the card catalog against the back wall. "Here are a few things you might be interested in. While there's not a list of every soldier who passed through Chatham, there are some names in here. If you can't find what you're looking for here, Ruby can point you in the right direction. She should be back in a couple of hours, but we'll be closing by then. Have a look but don't touch anything under the glass. I'm supposed to stay in here with you, but I'm the only one left today. You can make an appointment with her and come back if you don't find what you need in the card catalog."

"Thanks so much," Sarah said.

"Yep." Vernon turned and began the long traverse back to the information desk, leaving Sarah alone.

She started with the Ds, removing the narrow drawer from the cabinet and carrying it to a long table. Flipping through the tabs, she searched for any mention of a Dawson. She found several, but none for James Dawson. Next she tried a new strategy and pulled another drawer from the archive. Searching through the Js, she still found nothing. She repeated the strategy with O for officers, L for lieutenants, G for generals. Nothing.

Growing exasperated, she returned the drawers to their homes.

Maybe this was a fool's errand after all. She was glad she'd not said anything to Ellie.

The wall clock chimed five p.m. The park was closing. Sarah sighed, pulled her hair into a ponytail, and slipped on a holder from her wrist to wrangle the annoying mess out of her face.

A book in an exhibit across from her caught her eye. Despite Vernon's warning, and against every rule-obeying bone she had, she lifted the case lid and pulled the small leather bound book from the display. The Masonic compass and square symbol emblazoned in gold on the cover increased her boldness. Turning the yellow pages carefully, she paused when a familiar symbol caught her eye. She stopped cold at the title page inside. A one inch by one inch etching of the dragon engraved on the ring, which hung from her neck, sat dead center on the page. Written in calligraphy directly below it were the words, "Brothers of Peril." The pages that followed were blank with only the slightest indentations etched across the paper. She turned the first page and traced her index finger across the back side of the parchment, following the pen indentations across like a river of Braille.

Strange a supposed secret society would have any sort of written record at all. Of course, as it was, no visible writing actually appeared.

Perhaps the ink had simply faded over time. A hundred and fifty odd years under the right or—more likely in this case—wrong conditions could certainly do such a thing.

So curious.

"Interesting, isn't it?"

Sarah startled and nearly dropped the book before turning to find a female park ranger standing in the library doorway. Her name tag read, "Ruby."

"Yes. Very. I'm so sorry. I just…" Sarah returned the book and lowered the glass display lid, embarrassed to be caught handling the relic.

"Did you find what you were looking for?"

"No. I'm looking for a soldier. Or at least I think I am. I…he may not even exist. I have a name and a rank. He may have been here, at Chatham, but I couldn't find anything on him."

"We're closed now, and we really don't keep those sorts of records here. The few we have are in the back card catalog. Are you a local?"

"Yes. Princess Anne Street."

Ruby laughed. "Can't get much more local than that. If you want to leave the information you have and your number, I'll take a look this week during my downtime. I'll call if I find anything."

Sarah looked again at the raised Masonic symbol across the cover of the book. She pulled at the collar of her shirt as the ring beneath grew warm against her skin.

"Can you tell me anything about this book?" Sarah asked.

"Not much. A few historians tried to take rubbings from it, but it's apparently written in some sort of code, which they haven't been able to break. Every few years someone gets fired up about it again and makes a run at it."

"It's very intriguing."

"It is. Lots of urban legend surrounding the Brothers of Peril. This book confirmed their existence, if nothing else. Everything else we do know is in a book by Edward Carnahan in the park bookstore. There's one copy…" Ruby reached for another book behind Sarah. "Here. Edward was a local guy but he died a few years ago." Ruby frowned and shook her head. "Good guy. A regular volunteer and guide here at Chatham. We miss him. He mined mentions of the Brothers of Peril from journals and letters through the years and collected them. Finally had them published by a vanity press. There are only about a hundred copies or so in circulation. He found that book…" Ruby pointed to the book in the case. "Only after he'd written his own. I heard he was working on a new edition when he passed. Of course, it's hard to get much actual proof of a secret society. They did a good job keeping it secret. Even to the grave. This book was discovered in an estate bequeathed to the park upon the owner's death. Edward swooned until he realized it was written in invisible code."

"I heard they used some sort of witchcraft or the occult to manipulate the war?"

"Well, they didn't practice themselves supposedly, but employed and consulted others who did, including some direct descendants of Salem witches, if the stories can be believed. The idea of it makes history a little more exciting, doesn't it?"

"Yes."

"There are copies of the engravings for sale on a flash drive if you are interested. For twenty dollars, they can be yours if you'd like to make a run at it yourself. This copy of Edward's book is for sale as well."

"That would be wonderful."

"Come on. I'll ring you up on the way out."

Sarah followed Ruby back to the lobby. Vernon sat behind the desk with his head canted at an odd angle, a little line of drool stringing from his mouth.

"Oh, no. Is he…"

"Vernon!" Ruby shouted, giving the man a little pat on his shoulder.

Vernon's eyes sprang open, and he blinked rapidly, taking in his surroundings, clearly trying to regain his bearings.

"You nodded off again. Time to go home, buddy. I'll bet Gertrude is waiting in the parking lot for you."

"Oh yeah. She'll be hot that I'm late. I better get a move on."

Vernon's moves were no faster than Sarah had witnessed earlier. In fact, she was fairly certain he'd still be walking to the lot long after she wrapped up her purchase. She watched him disappear inch by inch into the early winter's evening until Ruby snapped her attention back.

"$41.15 with tax. So your soldier... Do you have that name and rank?"

Sarah reached for a scrap of paper and pen and wrote the information along with her phone number, name and address, then handed it to Ruby. "Thank you."

"No problem. But you have to promise if you figure anything out, you'll come back and share it with me first. I've been dying for someone to crack that code."

"You bet."

"Good night."

Sarah walked the soft path back to the parking lot and couldn't help but watch the ground on the way. No telling what treasures still remained buried here. So much history.

But there was only one piece of it she wanted to track down.

Lieutenant James Dawson.

CHAPTER SIXTEEN

Tanner couldn't believe they'd found the Brothers of Peril grimoiré. The Major General was charged with its protection. He could only assume Sylvia had turned her attentions to the Major General after she had successfully dispatched him. What he couldn't imagine was what horrors she might have visited upon the Major General to make him relinquish the relic.

The Brothers of Peril had been recommissioned by Lincoln himself. The group had gone dormant after Washington's term in office ended in 1797. The original members were long dead sixty-three years later. Tanner had been recruited into the new incarnation for his communication skills, not his supernatural abilities. His current state of existence was his only personal experience with the true supernatural. He'd been sent to the war as a correspondent after a stint at startup newspaper, *The New York Daily Times,* then later as a liaison. At first, the Major General had considered Tanner's journalistic skepticism an asset. A check and balance to the other members' tendencies to look to supernatural answers for every battle impediment along the way, sometimes at the expense of employing actual battle strategy. What had begun as an advantage had become a crutch.

As time went on and tensions ramped up, more and more members were recruited. Their active grimoire was penned from a collaboration of texts through the years, including *The Sixth and Seventh Books of Moses* and *The Philosophical Merlin*. It had remained a handwritten guidebook, finally transcribed and encoded by Tanner's own hand and the key trusted only to the Major General...and Tanner's memory. All remaining copies of the book had been destroyed under Lincoln's orders, once the transcription was complete, to retain the secrets of the Brothers of Peril and their influence. It both pleased and terrified him the book remained intact and was available for public consumption—a fact that would have to be remedied at his first opportunity. The tome's value and power was staggering to consider, even though he currently saw no evidence of war here in Fredericksburg. The book and its influences, however, had been and were still capable of not only winning a war, but of starting one.

And now with everything else he faced, he knew one thing for certain—he needed to protect that book.

* * *

Sarah stopped for dinner at her favorite Italian place on the way home. She needed a good meal and a pick-me-up. Her trip to Chatham had been disappointing, but she hadn't come home empty-handed. She flipped through the pages of Mr. Carnahan's book as she waited for her pasta to arrive. Thankful her stomach had settled enough to eat, she had half of her loaf of bread gone by the time she'd read only a few pages into the first chapter. The book was fascinating. If even half of what it promised was true, the possibilities were amazing.

She'd never believed in the paranormal—not really—and until last night, nothing unexplainable had ever happened to her. In fact, her mind still played tricks with her even now as she recounted the actual events of Jason's attack, alternating between calm assurance and incredulous uncertainty as to what she'd actually seen. And to think there had been an entire society dedicated to using such supposed supernatural forces against their enemies. People were crazy sometimes. While Ellie was much more attuned to supernatural possibilities, Sarah couldn't deny what was happening to her.

Clearly the ring she'd found was tied to her current predicament, and much more than a lucky talisman. On the one hand, she'd love to turn it into a piece of jewelry, but her trip to Chatham had proven the ring was, indeed, a precious artifact. Yet she couldn't bring herself to give up the object.

Looking back down at her plate, she noticed half of her pasta had already been consumed. When had she eaten it? She'd been so absorbed with her thoughts, then the book, she hadn't even realized what she'd done. She motioned for a to-go box from the waitress, then quickly gathered her things. She scraped her leftovers into the box before heading to the counter to pay.

All she wanted to do was get home and pour through the rest of the book while sitting in front of her fire. Tomorrow, she'd tackle the flash drive. Coded language was her thing. Sure, she spent all day, every day, working with computer languages, but she also had some specialized training in encryptions and cryptography. Who didn't love a good puzzle? While greater minds than hers had more than likely already taken a crack at breaking the coded message, what did it hurt to try?

Sarah eased into her parking space in the garage and made the short walk back in record time, motivated to continue her search. When she reached the top of her apartment stairs, her heart sank. Her letter to Tanner remained exactly where she'd left it.

It was getting silly that he lived so close, patronized the coffee shop directly beneath her, and they still hadn't met. She was growing more suspicious. She had enough mysteries going on right now. It was time to press him into action. Snatching up her letter, she resigned herself to writing a new letter in its place, demanding a face-to-face meeting. Clearly, they both had problems that needed to be dealt with. Sarah was at least somewhat in control of her own side of that equation, but growing tired of waiting for someone else to make the next move.

Slipping into her apartment, she smiled as she noticed her gorgeous new drapes against the street-side windows. She crossed to the windows, then pulled each panel loose from its ties and slid them closed. The heavy, rich velvet blocked out all but a dim glow seeping through the cracks between the drapes. Tonight, she'd sleep in a cave instead of a showroom. And it would be wonderful.

* * *

Tanner paced as Sarah showered. Why had she retrieved her letter? Had she already lost interest? How much longer could he play at this game with her before she grew tired and cast him aside? Perhaps some contact, even if it was less than ideal, would be better than no contact at all. He was certain now that she was beginning to piece together their connection, even though she didn't yet know where it would lead. She was a smart girl. He was equally as certain, however, she would not be able to break the code.

Only two people had the key and the Major General was dead. Truly dead. Of that Tanner was sure, or the book would never have survived. How the current government hadn't tracked down the book before now, he had no idea. Lincoln had, of course, known of its existence, and, Tanner assumed, even more of his many aides and trusted confidants knew as well. Yet it had been placed upon a dusty shelf in plain sight? He shuddered. To think the key to all war and peace could possibly lie in his bewitched brain was even more overwhelming than his condition.

Enough residual energy remained, likely from the group of children, that Tanner managed to peel open the drape and he peered below. When his hand materialized into view before him, he startled and jerked it back. He patted it along his chest and shoulder, feeling his form begin to solidify beneath his touch. Finally *seeing* his own physical body once again made flesh was miraculous.

His heart raced as he heard the water turn off in the small bathroom. Half materialized in her bedroom in the dark was not how he wanted to meet Sarah for the first time. Tanner fled to the door and came to an abrupt stop against it as his formerly ethereal form refused to pass through the wood. The resulting *thunk* caused him alarm. He spun around to see if Sarah heard it as well. Panic filled him and he fumbled for the door handle, desperate for escape before it was too late. The door refused to open, but then he remembered the bolt. He slid the lock open and turned the knob. He stepped into the hallway just in time. The door snicked closed quietly behind him.

The hallway presented the next challenge. He was relieved to find it mercifully empty, but he didn't know how long his good fortune would hold. What to do next?

With more energy, he might be able to come to full corporeal form, but for how long? Seconds? Minutes? Longer? And as he was, half-spirit half-man, he couldn't exactly walk into the coffee house downstairs and leech energy from its patrons. He also couldn't remain in the hallway. Eventually, one of Sarah's neighbors would wander by, and then what? Still tethered to the ring, he couldn't go far. He walked down the stairs and stopped at the door marked Service Entry. Trying the knob, he was intensely relieved when it turned without resistance. After slipping through, he stood in the darkened room until his sight adjusted. Sounds of the coffee house drifted through the closed storage room door from the shop and light seeped beneath revealing steel racks filled with supplies.

Tanner tried to calm his pounding heart. He had to make his move. With each passing moment, each energy boost, he was becoming more and more corporeal. He had to reach out to Sarah.

He'd do it tonight.

CHAPTER SEVENTEEN

Sarah sat curled by her fire, consumed by Mr. Carnahan's book. She'd already rewritten her letter to Tanner and slipped it beneath her door. Now she read, captivated by what she found. It was all so crazy. And although it was mostly urban legend, if an *nth* was true, what an amazing story it was. It made her wonder what other insanity the government had secretly been up to all these years. Conspiracy theories abounded on the internet. The longer she searched, the more she realized there was a website, group or both for every theory under the sun.

She googled "Brothers of Peril" and came up with tons of links, but none related to the book. It seemed very little pertinent information on this particular conspiracy panned out, which she found even more intriguing. Unless, of course, research into the group had already been quashed online? Hundreds of broken links and dead ends made her wonder. But if so, why did the book remain at Chatham? And Carnahan's book? And the easy access to the flash drive? Encouragement, even?

An icy shiver ran up her spine as she considered the possibility she was a spider caught in an invisible trap. Maybe *the government* waited for interested parties to come to *them*. If one was persistent enough to track the information to Chatham and find the book, then perhaps that same person might be helpful in solving their mystery?

And the park ranger, Ruby, had all of her pertinent information. Which Sarah had willingly provided.

Good grief.

How easily she had fallen down the rabbit hole.

No. This was no conspiracy theory. She hadn't been pulled into some governmental intrigue. Her imagination ran wild. What she needed was sleep. And a fresh start tomorrow when her mind was not jumbled with all of this nonsense. Clearly, her subconscious mind couldn't adequately process her experience with Jason last night.

Good God, was that last night?

She rubbed her eyes and gave Bitly a scratch behind the ears, which led to his full-throated worship in return.

"Time for bed, boy. God knows what I'll dream up tonight with all this strangeness floating around in my head."

She laid the book on her table, switched off the lamp, and then climbed into bed, her body sinking into the mattress. Staring at the ceiling as her eyes adjusted, she tried to remap her apartment in the new darkness provided by her drapes. The familiar shadows of the past few months were all different now and her home felt more like a cocoon. Sarah rolled over and pulled the covers tight around her. The bed rocked as Bitly pounced upon it, pawing at her through the covers as he made his nighttime nest beside her.

One uneventful night was all she needed.

* * *

Tanner waited for hours in Greysmith's storage closet until the last of the customers had left and the front door was finally locked. He needed energy. A lot of energy to succeed, however briefly, in his plan. Even then, there was no guarantee he'd be able to manifest long enough to make his case to Sarah. His heart lay like a lead ball in his chest. He had to try.

It was no surprise when Samuel entered through the storage closet to lock the back door. Tanner had heard Samuel greeting and serving customers all night as he waited for his opportunity. Stepping into Samuel's path from the shadows, Tanner let the young man pass through him and the boy stumbled. Falling to his knees, Samuel's eyes filled with fear. He blinked rapidly. Tanner felt his body begin to solidify after the infusion of Samuel's energy. His hands took form first, then his torso, as he returned to visibility and literally appeared before Samuel's eyes. Tanner could only imagine how unsettling that must be.

For the first time in more than a hundred fifty years, Tanner heard his own voice say, "I'm sorry." And he was sorry. Draining the energy from someone was likely to have consequences. He worried a complete exhaustion of another's energy could be catastrophic. Bringing harm to one of Sarah's friends was unthinkable, yet his situation demanded action.

Tanner's voice was the last thing Samuel heard before he passed out cold on the floor.

With not a moment to spare, Tanner soaked himself in the aura surrounding Samuel. Samuel was a healthy young man and Tanner absorbed his energy. When Samuel's aura—his life energy—began to change to a dirty gray, Tanner tore himself away from his sphere of influence. Remorse filled him. Even knowing what he was doing was the only course, it didn't make his actions any less deplorable.

Samuel's pale face glowed like a moonflower in the dark storage room. Regret crept into Tanner's conscience, but what was done was done. Tanner was only glad he hadn't tried it first on Sarah. Infused with Samuel's energy, Tanner strode from the storage room and into the empty coffee shop. He made his way to the lavatory, where he'd seen a mirror earlier in his investigations while Sarah had scrutinized the shelves. He was curious how he appeared, now that he was corporeal. Would he be decomposed? Hideous?

Flipping on the light, he gasped when he caught sight of his reflection in the mirror across from him. He hadn't aged at all. He appeared exactly as he remembered himself the day he'd gone to battle. Only his clothing had changed. After burial, he had been dressed in his finest long Union blue coat and woolen trousers. Gone were the bloodied and torn clothes of his demise. Impulsively, he pressed his hand to his face and dragged his palm across his beard-roughened jaw and then his forehead, unable to believe he was whole again. It was a miracle.

Fumbling at the buttons of his coat, he finally forced one through a buttonhole, then another. He lifted the shirt beneath to inspect his not-quite-so-mortal wound. Pocked scars across his upper chest marked the points of impact for the gunfire that had taken his life—otherwise he was living flesh.

For how long was the question.

Tanner hurried back to the storage room and checked on Samuel. He briefly considered undressing the boy and stealing his clothes as well. While his current attire might be more convincing, he didn't want to overwhelm her. His odd midnight calling would be unusual enough.

He laughed at the absurdity of that understatement. Honestly he had no idea how he would even begin the conversation with her. But it had to be done.

Deciding against changing his clothing, he bent to feel for a pulse in poor Samuel and was relieved to find one. Sarah liked the young man and Tanner certainly didn't want to be responsible for bringing any more unnecessary grief upon her than he was about to. He made his way out of Greysmith's and up the ever-stretching staircase to Sarah's home.

He stood for many long minutes outside her door, praying for the courage to knock upon it.

CHAPTER EIGHTEEN

The soft knocking at her door had Sarah sitting straight up, her heart careening inside her chest. Off kilter in the still-new darkness, she tried to place exactly where she was. After several long seconds, she threw back the covers and went to the door. This time, she didn't slide the bolt and throw it open as she had the night before. The bolt was already open. Had she forgotten—after all that had happened—to slide the deadbolt?

Oh, how she wished the peephole had been installed already.

In her mind, she knew it couldn't be Jason again. She still needed that restraining order, however, regardless of how long he did or did not stay in jail. Although she wasn't all that confident a piece of paper would keep him away. The fear of ruining his reputation was the best card she could play. And she would.

Another quick series of soft knocks revved up her heart and the words stuck in her throat before finally coming out.

"Who is it?"

A long pause stretched between her and the visitor as a shadow shuffled intermittently under the door.

"Sarah…it's…Tanner."

Sarah looked to the floor again and saw her letter to Tanner was missing. Had he read it in the hallway and responded so quickly? She glanced back at her illuminated clock. It was after midnight. Way too late for this and dangerously inappropriate, especially considering her experience the night before…with someone she knew and had once trusted.

Still, curiosity got the best of her.

It killed the cat, the voice of reason in her head reminded her.

Satisfaction brought it back, Sarah countered.

"Just a minute." Sarah sped to the bathroom and retrieved her robe. She stuffed her phone and, on second thought, her scissors into the robe's oversized pocket. Just in case he turned out to be a homicidal maniac. Which totally would not be the case. Most likely.

She clicked the handle lock open, then gripped the knob with a damp hand.

This is stupid. This is stupid. This is stupid.

At the very least, she should call Ellie and tell her what was going on—or Adam, even. How many times could she expect them to come to her rescue?

She pulled open the door and stared into the face of the Civil War soldier from her dream.

Lieutenant James Dawson.

Tanner.

Dear God, what is going on?

Sarah had meant to step into the hallway and not let Tanner into her apartment until she had a strong vibe of safety about him. Instead, her legs grew wobbly as she tried to reckon with the improbability that her dream soldier and Tanner were the same person.

She forgot how to stand. Her resolve crumbled along with her upright position and when she came back to her senses, the man hovered above her.

Gah! I'm a hazard to myself.

Shaking the fogginess from her head, she scrambled back, away from him. Distance was what she needed. *And the scissors maybe?* Just-in-case seemed suddenly rather imminent. Her door was closed, and Tanner—the soldier—stood in front of the fire, covered in shadow. The flames made him appear to flicker so she couldn't make him out clearly. The brief glimpse she'd had in the hallway before her brains went south wasn't nearly enough. Her curiosity wanted to see him up close, but her good sense warned her otherwise.

She reached back for the lamp on her nightstand.

"Please don't turn it on," Tanner said. "Not yet."

Her heart did a stutter that had everything to do with fear. She gripped the scissors. She could scream and Adam would come running. Probably. *Damn those new drapes.* If they were open, she could see him plain as day.

She eased against the bed and drew her knees up to her chest. "Why are you here, Tanner? So late? Why are you…dressed that way? You're scaring me."

Tanner fussed at the tails of his long coat and light flickered off the large gold buttons lining the center of his chest. He lowered his head, drew in a long breath and held it, eyes closed.

"I am truly sorry to have inconvenienced you with such a late night intrusion but I felt…I felt it imperative that we meet."

"Because of my letter?" Sarah asked. "I'm very confused."

Tanner hesitated. "Your letter, among other things, prompted me to action. Yes. Please don't be frightened."

"Then let me turn on the light so I can see you clearly."

"I don't think that's a good idea just yet."

"And why would that be? What are you hiding?" Sarah pulled her phone from her pocket. She couldn't make a call without him noticing the glow in the darkness, but if he turned away—even for a second—she would certainly try.

"Sarah." He hesitated. "There's no easy way to explain this."

"Start at the beginning then."

"The beginning. That's the very problem. The beginning was 1862. The day I died."

Tanner turned toward the fire, and Sarah noted his strong profile illuminated by the glow of the firelight. His eyes glistened as he composed himself, and she tried to make sense of his last statement.

"I'm sorry. The day you died? What are you? A reenactment soldier? Cosplay nerd? Funny you didn't mention any of that in your letters. Were they all a lie too? Are you another crazy stalker...or...something worse?"

"Worse."

Sarah pulled the scissors from her robe pocket and slid her hand behind her back, her fingers laced in a death grip around the handles. She pushed herself up from the floor and backed against the wall, measuring the distance to the door, and then to Tanner. If she attacked him first, would it still be self-defense? She'd let him in her home, after all. Sort of. Finally, she couldn't bear the silence any longer. If he was going to make a move on her, let him get on with it. The suspense of waiting was killing her already.

"What are you?" she asked.

"A ghost."

So not how she expected him to answer.

She stared at a crazy person. A crazy person who would, in all likelihood, kill her and chop her into tiny pieces. Hopefully in that order. Her only chance was to convince him otherwise or start screaming. Just as she was about to make her choice, Tanner reached for the light switch by her door and her heart stopped in the split second between darkness and light.

The man standing before her looked every bit a soldier. Or more the *idea* of a soldier. What had seemed solid, substantial, and foreboding in the darkness, diminished in the light. Not exactly transparent, he flickered like a poor satellite transmission, twitching in and out with the strength of the signal.

"You're..." Sarah felt her mouth gape, and she blinked to clear her vision. It didn't help.

"A ghost. Yes."

"How? Why? What are you doing...here?"

"You brought me here, Sarah. With the ring."

"What? No... it's only a piece of jewelry."

"One that I am bound to by a hex. A hex that has kept me in limbo for more than a hundred and fifty years. I've been alone in a living hell all that time. Until...you. You sparked life back into me. You gave me something to live for. You gave me...hope."

"This is crazy."

This is crazy. This is crazy. This is crazy.

"I agree with you, yet it's the absolute truth. I am tethered to the ring by magic. I can't seem to be more than a hundred feet or so away from it. Trust me, I've tried everything not to involve you, but you—"

"What is your real name?"

"Lieutenant James 'Tanner' Dawson. I fought at Chatham. I died at Chatham. And with your help, I may live again."

Sarah heard the blood rush into her ears like ocean surf, and the pounding of her heart drummed in her head.

HAUNT MY HEART

Don't pass out. Don't pass out. Don't pass out.

* * *

Tanner strode to Sarah in two long steps, catching her before she could hit her head on the edge of her night table as she lost consciousness. He eased her onto her bed, and saw himself weakened with the task. Every physical effort cost him energy he couldn't regenerate on his own. Hell, he couldn't even store it for longer than a few hours. This foray was proof of that. His only comfort was that she hadn't run screaming from the room. Most likely she had no inclination to believe him and was now in shock.

The absolute worst thing that could happen to him at this point was that she would dispose of the ring, and she'd be lost to him forever. Even though this was their first true meeting in the flesh—or as close to flesh as he could get at this point—he'd grown quite fond of her. And not just because she seemed his one shot at redemption. Sarah was kind-hearted, generous and lovely in every way. And stronger than she knew.

Tanner worked to unwind her fingers from the scissors gripped tightly in her hand. He didn't blame her for preparing to do him harm. Considering the circumstances and the timing after her encounters with Jason, another man in her home with unclear intentions was the last thing she needed.

He brushed the hair from her face and inadvertently drew energy from her, like flame to oxygen. Her light flared and engulfed him. Closing his eyes, he let himself be overcome by her energy. A soft moan from Sarah snapped him to attention, and he hopped back from her aura. The small encounter was enough to solidify him again.

In every way... he realized, much to his horror.

Good God.

Biology would not be denied. Even in his immortal damnation. Clearly a cruel joke of some sort. A parting gift on Sylvia's behalf? He honestly didn't know how much more he could take. It wasn't like he could leave Sarah to return to her life. Not when his own depended on her so thoroughly.

He returned to the couch and sat heavily upon it, staring at the hypnotic flames in the fireplace. Luxuriating in the heat warming his skin, his mind cycled through the many possible reactions he could expect from Sarah when she awoke. Bitly skulked out from under the couch, eyeing him discerningly, then leaped onto his lap. The cat extended himself up the length of Tanner's vertical torso, planted his front paws just beneath Tanner's chin and stretched up to sniff at his breath. Satisfied, Bitly closed his eyes and began to purr. The rumble filled Tanner's body and before he knew it, his own eyes drifted closed. The three of them slept the remainder of the night in Sarah's apartment, not knowing what the morning might bring.

CHAPTER NINETEEN

Sarah awoke and blinked into the thin laser of sunlight piercing between her new drapes. Morning? Her brain struggled to catch up and she quickly worked backwards, sifting through her last memories. As the pieces fell into place, she sat up with a start. A quick examination revealed she seemed to be intact. Shaking her head, she tried to clear the last vestiges of her bizarre dream. Maybe she was ill. Maybe she had a fever. Maybe…

She snatched up her phone from the nightstand and punched it on with her thumb. Ten thirty a.m.? On *Monday* morning? She'd slept through an entire day?

Not only that, but now she was late. Really late. Noticeably late. Somehow she hadn't set her alarm. Nothing made sense to her as she fled to the bathroom. Desperately, she reached to rearrange her scattered puzzle pieces as she changed clothes, brushed her teeth and scrambled out the door to work.

No way would she skate by this time. Candace's Monday morning meetings were mandatory. Even for the salaried. And it had already begun a half hour ago. She was screwed. She tore open the door to leave. Grabbing her rain jacket and purse from the hooks, Bitly's admonishment brought her around again.

"Sorry." Sarah stepped back inside and poured Bitly's kibble into his bowl and gave him a quick stroke across the back. The cat arched against her attentions and purred. "You may be seeing a lot of me after today. I'll be fired for sure now."

Out the door and down the stairs, she broke into a quick trot as soon as she hit the bricked sidewalk, her hood refusing to stay on against the howling wind. She raced down the deserted sidewalk. Everyone who should be at work was already at work. Even the tourists had found a coffee shop or boutique to take refuge in against the cold sleet. The sidewalk, already slippery from the frozen precipitation, slowed her pace. She took more care after nearly losing her balance. Her phone buzzed two short vibrations indicating she had a text. She fished the phone from her pocket as she forged ahead.

WHERE ARE YOU?

Ellie had texted at 9:55.

The current text read:

DON'T COME IN NOW. CALL IN SICK. I TOLD CANDACE YOU HAD THE FLU.

Sarah skidded to a stop three doors down from her office and scooted against the building under an awning, just in case anyone upstairs saw her on the sidewalk. A sick day? Ellie was a genius. It hadn't even occurred to Sarah to call in for a sick day. Her heart hammered in her chest from the stress of running and trying to make it to the office in the sleet. Her soaking wet hair plastered to the sides of her face, and the cold chilled her to the bone. Call her paranoid, but now she actually did feel sick. She hit her office speed dial number and practiced her call in her head as she waited 'for someone to pick up the line.

After a dozen rings, the receptionist desk voicemail picked up instead. Everyone was at Candace's Monday morning meeting. Sarah's guilty conscience almost got the best of her, and she struggled not to chicken out and hang up. When the beep demanded she leave a message, she managed to squeak out a quick apology for being ill and a promise to be back in as soon as she could. She hated lying, but even if she had gone into the office, she was sure Candace would have taken the opportunity to fire her. In front of everyone. And with gusto. Ellie had saved her bacon for sure. It paid to have a devious friend.

Thinking of devious friends reminded her of her promise to file that restraining order against Jason. Now that she had a free day, she had no excuse not to do it. She searched inside her purse for the paper the officer had given her and found the ring instead. Pulling the ring from the depths of her purse, the object made her hand tingle as it sat on her palm and warmed against her skin. What the hell was going on with this trinket?

In her heart, she knew she hadn't dreamed her encounter and now in the bright, although slightly foggy light of day, she let it come back to her, replaying the conversation in her head. Of' course, Tanner had vanished by the time she'd awakened. He must have let himself out. But how and why had she slept through and entire day and night? The entire situation was so surreal. It had happened. All of it. Tanner had visited her and then she'd checked out for a day. But he *had* been there…and nothing like she'd expected.

Certainly nothing she could explain.

Only one person would believe her story. Ellie.

She'd tell her tonight, after work. She'd tell her everything. And then they would decide what to do. In the meantime, Sarah pulled her rain jacket hood over her head, shivering when the icy water skittered down her spine.

First things first.

* * *

Tanner followed Sarah through the dreary day and wished more than anything he could speak with her and understand what she might be feeling. His energy had faded considerably. When he realized he'd inadvertently drawn too much energy from Sarah, he'd retreated. She'd slept through the entire next day as a result, and he'd watched her from the chair by the window, keeping his distance so she could regenerate her reserves. It was a mistake he wouldn't make again. Too worried about her condition, he'd not left the room until she woke and raced from the apartment. Now his strength had abated completely, his temporary corporeality and his meeting with Sarah seemed like a dream. Mercifully, his current state lessened the possibility of manifesting unintentionally, but now that he knew he could manifest at all, his impatience only increased.

He existed in the constant fear that at any moment all could be lost.

He'd watched as Sarah filed paperwork at the police station, pleased she'd followed through on her promise. If Jason chose to visit her again, it would be at his own peril. Not only would she have the law on her side now, she'd have the full and complete wrath of a recently revived Union soldier.

Sarah bought lunch from a pub and carried it with her as she walked along the Rappahannock River. His eyes drifted by habit up the bluff on the opposite side of the river to Chatham. How different it looked now, yet his nostalgia spurred inside him and quickly turned sour as he remembered anew his predicament.

All that had happened to him so far was a result of Sylvia and his mission with the Brothers of Peril. But those actions had led him to Sarah. Without the hex, he would never have met her at all. Still this Purgatory in which he lingered was worse than any other damnation he could imagine.

There was no resolution here.

One thing he knew for certain. He wouldn't return to the darkness. Whatever it took, he'd be freed whether by life or death. Either would be a blessing.

Finally home again, Sarah hustled inside the shared entrance and spared a glance into the coffee shop, looking for him no doubt. Regret clutched at his heart. He'd had to render her friend Samuel unconscious to see her in the flesh. A similar plan would be needed to resume their conversation. He was willing to do whatever it took to make that happen again. This nightmare needed a resolution more substantial than mere letters could provide. One way or another, this needed to end.

* * *

Sarah set her sandwich on the table and stripped off her wet clothes before even opening the bag. She was thankful her drapes were still closed, and she could walk around her apartment without fear of flashing the block. Her skin warmed as she stood before the fireplace. She turned the knob to crank it up even more. She pulled her hair back into a ponytail and twisted water from her hair into a small puddle on the floor, which Bitly pounced at and quickly began to lap up. Sarah walked to the shower and closed the door. After dialing up the hot water, she watched as steam began to fill the room.

She was especially glad she'd gotten the restraining order after learning Jason had been released first thing Monday morning. It was a miracle they hadn't crossed paths at the station. She wondered what he was doing now. Probably consulting with his lawyer as to his next move. It was only a matter of time before she would get the calls asking her to drop her charges. To be reasonable. To consider his future...and hers.

Honestly, she didn't know what she wanted. Except that she did not want him in her life in any way. Ever again. That was crystal clear. Despite his actions and despicable cruelty, she didn't want to ruin him. Even now, she held hope he was somehow still redeemable. But she wouldn't be the one redeeming him this time.

Besides, she had much weirder and more pressing problems. Like Tanner...and the ring. She'd texted Ellie on the way home and asked her to stop by to talk after work. She wasn't even sure where to start, but she had to tell someone what was going on, or at least what she thought was going on.

Stepping out of the bathroom and into her empty living room, she considered her last few hours. Her life seemed sort of ridiculous to even try to explain now. Maybe she was cracking up. Maybe too much time alone had finally gotten to her. Maybe this is how every crazy cat lady began.

On cue, Bitly wound between her feet, pressing against her and licking the water from her leg with his sandpaper tongue.

"Thanks."

She shooed him away and dried her hair with the towel. Pulling on her fleecy jammies, she eyed her lunch bag. She snatched it up and carried it to the chair by the windows, then pulled open the blinds. Yep, still dreary.

She ate snuggled in her chair watching the afternoon pass by.

Her mind filled with questions and the computer finally pulled her in. She plugged in the flash drive.

With three hours still to kill before Ellie got off work, she might as well give the mystery a go. Not that she expected to find any of the answers she searched for, but it beat trying to decipher the events of the past few days.

The first page of the Brothers of Peril handbook appeared on her screen—the same page she'd seen in the physical book at Chatham. The identical insignia as was engraved on the ring filled her screen. She traced the lines with her finger across the smooth surface, then got up to rummage through her purse for the ring.

Holding the ring up to the screen, she studied both for comparison. They were exactly the same. The growing evidence before her eyes was too much to cast off as mere coincidence. Still, she couldn't piece them together into a logical tapestry.

And where was Tanner now? This very moment? She couldn't bring herself to accept the word that kept popping up, because it was too much to fathom.

Ghost.

No. A ghost hadn't written the nearly two dozen letters to her, or spoken to her Saturday night in her apartment or—she shuddered—put her to bed and locked the door behind him when he left. Everything she'd heard or watched or read of ghosts touted them as lost souls, condemned to haunt the ether until their release. Many of them were vengeful and dangerous. Was that the story of the ghost haunting her? Was he somehow trapped by the very object she held in her hand, just as he'd said? And if so, could he be summoned at will? Dare she try?

Ellie would want to take her to Alex, her psychic. At this point, visiting with Alex was beginning to seem like a reasonable option…either to prove her sanity, or lack thereof. She wasn't sure which answer she wanted.

If Tanner were indeed real, then how and what was she expected to do with that knowledge? What were her obligations? She'd merely found a ring, for God's sake.

If he wasn't real and the psychic confirmed that the ring was nothing more than the piece of history it appeared, then what?

Clearly, she was cracking up.

Sarah straightened in her chair and flipped the page on her screen. The rubbings popped out at her like a 3D puzzle photo. She concentrated hard, shutting all her worries out of her troubled mind. There was a code here. And every code could be cracked. She couldn't imagine it was all that complicated. Not really. Surely if the CIA or NSA had any real interest in it, they'd have assigned resources to it and not left it up to crowdsourcing to ferret out.

After several long minutes, a pattern began to emerge. The pattern repeated so scarcely it would have been easy to miss for someone without her background, but it was there. Sarah grabbed a notepad and pencil and began to tease out the letters she could assign to it, filling the page and flipping excitedly to the next. While the message made no sense, it was clearly in English, which meant eventually she could figure it out.

Four hours and seventy filled pages of gibberish later, Sara startled when her phone sounded, nearly giving her a panic attack. Torn from the black hole she'd been ensconced in, she searched her desk, shuffling through piles of papers for the buzzing phone. She hadn't even called her parents to give them her new number yet. In fact, only one person had it.

"Hi, Ellie."

"You are not going to believe where I am."

Sarah walked to the window and eased into her favorite chair to watch the coffee shop arrivals and departures, unable to help but wonder if Tanner had ever been downstairs in the shop at all.

"Where are you? Are you still coming by?"

"That's what I called to tell you. Candace got fired today, and I'm on a plane to New York."

CHAPTER TWENTY

"How did that happen? I miss one day and the world goes crazy?"

"It was that flash drive! You know how she was so crazy to find it, right? The FBI actually showed up today with a warrant and searched her office for it. Right there as she watched. As we all watched. And then they led her away in cuffs. She'd been stealing customer transaction records from some of our biggest clients for some big hacking ring. She had access to all of our client passwords. That flash was filled with them. Candace is in jail!"

"No." Sarah stood and pressed her forehead against the window pane.

"Yes! And I'm on a plane to New York to meet with the web developer franchise office. They want me to temporarily fill her spot. *Me.* I think your luck is rubbing off."

"I don't know what to say. I mean, I knew Candace was bitchy, but this? I'm shocked. Shocked. Congratulations. How long are you going to be gone?"

"Until next week for sure. That's also what I called to tell you. The office is closed for the rest of the week, pending an investigation and the collection of more evidence. You'll need to drop by your laptop too. Sorry. It's evidence now as well. Don't delete anything. Just shut it down and bring it by tomorrow. There are scads of FBI guys all over the building."

Sarah ran a hand through her hair. "I can't get over it. How long do you think the office will be closed? Will we get paid? I can't afford to go without a paycheck."

"That's one of the reasons I'm headed to New York. To sort all of that out. They did say everyone, who's not implicated of course, will be compensated as usual. You just got a week, maybe two, of paid vacation, baby. You can thank Candace for that."

"Seems like everyone I know is going to jail. You be careful in New York. I can't afford bail money for you. I'll miss you."

"Don't worry about me. I'm sorry I won't be there tonight. Speaking of jailbirds, no word from Jason, I hope."

"No, but I filed for the restraining order, and I know he's out on bail."

"So much for the thirty days. I'm calling Adam next. I'm sure he'll be willing to help you if that asshole decides to visit again. Promise me you won't let him in."

Sarah was silent a beat too long.

"I mean it, Sarah."

"Oh don't worry. I won't. Nothing could make me open the door to him again. But that's what I was going to talk to you about. I did have a visitor the other night."

"Who? What happened?"

Sarah hesitated, already regretting telling her over the phone, but closed her eyes and forged ahead. "Tanner."

"Your secret admirer? Seriously? What does he look like? Tell me everything."

Sarah walked to the couch and sat, pulling the ring from beneath her sweater. The words she wanted to say seemed ridiculous. *Were* ridiculous. But she felt safe with Ellie, and if anyone was open-minded enough to hear her story, it was her.

"I think…he…"

"What? Did he hurt you?"

The ring began to heat in her palm, and she peered down at it. A faint glow emanated from it and it grew warm, but not to an uncomfortable level.

"No. But he did frighten me. He appeared very late and he was…"

"What?"

"I'm sorry. I don't know. It was a strange meeting is all. It's probably nothing."

"Sarah Elizabeth Knight, if you have a not-right feeling about this guy…*at all*, you do not see him again. You lock yourself in that apartment and stay there until I get back. I mean it."

"I can't do that. I don't think he's dangerous. If he were, he could have had his way after I passed out."

"Passed out? Jesus, I'm coming home. You can't be alone."

"No! I shouldn't have even told you. I'm fine. It's fine. I probably won't even see him again after last night. I'm pretty sure he's gone."

Silence stretched across the connection, and she could feel the weight of Ellie's worry, and now guilt.

"A few days ago you didn't think Jason was dangerous. How do you feel about him now?"

Sarah went cold. It was true that her perception of men was perhaps flawed. She'd always been too trusting. There was no way she could tell Ellie the rest of what was going on over the phone.

"Don't worry. Go. Save the company. Save my job. Be awesome. I'll see you when you get back."

Ellie sighed. "I'm assigning Adam as your bodyguard while I'm gone. If anything happened to you…"

"Nothing is going to happen."

"Shit."

"Quit worrying. And I don't need a bodyguard. A helpful neighbor is plenty. Thank you. I'll try not to break him while you're gone."

"I'll call you every day."

"Perfect."

* * *

Tanner's relief was great when Sarah's conversation finally drew to an end. Ellie was clearly delayed for a few days, Sarah was without employment and now, hopefully, he would have another chance to reach out to her. She reached for her phone again and called for the delivery of something called pizza.

Drawn back to her computer, she sat and continued to study the images on the display. He'd read what she'd transposed into the notebook over her shoulder as she wrote, and again as she'd entered her conclusions into the computer. Her notes appeared in a neat font disappearing down the screen into oblivion. Miraculously, she had in fact broken the code, but the resulting message was also coded as a fail-secure. There was no way she'd break the second code. That key resided within him alone.

As the evening passed, Sarah devoted herself to her task, filling the notebook and screen with more and more still-unbreakable pages of the Brothers of Peril grimoire. It would take weeks to transpose the entire book, but she had the first chapter nearly completed. The sustenance she'd called pizza, which had been delivered hours earlier, had smelled so wonderful he was amazed she hadn't heard the growling of his reawakened stomach. Food had suddenly and unexpectedly begun to seem like a good idea again. Hours later, half of the meal sat untouched and cold on her desk.

At last, she rubbed at her eyes and stretched, her spine crackling with the realignment after spending the bulk of the day hunched over her work. Bitly had long ago abandoned his efforts at gaining her attention or affection and lay curled in the chair by the window. She crossed and stared down into the street.

"Where are you, Tanner?" she asked the night.

Tanner had already accosted one of her friends in his efforts to achieve corporeality. And as his own energy faded, he was sure he'd need to do it many times over this night for his next attempt with Sarah. Time was running out.

While Sarah performed her nightly rituals in the bathroom and prepared for bed, Tanner once again slipped out and into the hallway. His lack of energy feeding had left him weaker than he liked, and he easily passed through the first two apartment doors along her hallway to feed like some sort of parasitic incubus from her neighbors' energy while they slept.

This was what Sylvia had reduced him to. Small consolation that, so far, none of his victims had been seriously damaged...or killed. Yet.

When he'd achieved a full and corporeal form once again, he reveled in the miracle for only a few seconds before slipping down to the coffee shop. He'd worried about his clothing, but it seemed the shop's many patrons found his appearance mildly amusing and nothing more. Fredericksburg was clearly a historically-minded city, and he assumed they took him for a 'volunteer' from Chatham Manor or the like, if they questioned his attire at all. No one asked and he didn't offer any explanation. In fact, he made it a point to be standoffish, lost in the perusal of the vast volumes the shop boasted in the hopes of avoiding conversation all together.

His mere proximity to the remaining patrons would hopefully be enough to sustain his form for his next encounter with Sarah. It had to work. Now, if only his powers of persuasion were half as effective. He browsed the shop for more than an hour before he noticed the staff winding down for closing. Soaking in the warm flow of energy from each person he came near, he let their auras feed him, making him feel stronger than he had since that fateful day at Chatham, before he'd lost his life.

Filled to overflowing, he marveled at his reflection in the bookstore window. For the first time since he'd been reawakened, he realized he manufactured an aura of his own.

A few minutes before the coffee shop closed, Tanner climbed the staircase to Sarah's apartment once more and stood outside her door. What if she didn't open for him this time?

What if she did?

He couldn't shake the certainty that the moments that were about to follow would determine his fate once and for all. Once again, he was at the mercy of a woman.

This time, however, it was a woman he was certain he could love.

CHAPTER TWENTY-ONE

Sarah groaned. *Again with the knocking? What was this? Grand Central Station?* One night of peace was all she asked. One. Night.

A quick glance at her phone revealed the time as 12:02 a.m.

She flipped back the covers and padded to the door, pressing her ear to it for any clue as to the identity of her visitor. Drawing in a deep breath, she resigned herself to whatever lay ahead.

"Who is it?" she asked.

"It's Tanner, Sarah. May I come in?"

Indecision beat at her as her heart rate kicked up. She considered calling Adam. "I don't know, Tanner. I don't think this is going to work out between us."

A long silence followed, and she thought perhaps he'd slipped away, when a thin book slid beneath her door. She bent to retrieve it.

The Supernatural Civil War: Ghosts, Legends and More

"Have you read this one?" he asked.

"No."

"Turn to page 167, if you would, please."

She did and slumped against the doorway, its support the only thing stopping her from sliding to the floor. The title of the chapter beginning on page 167 was "The Brothers of Peril." Her mind raced. Everything and nothing made sense at the same time. She had all of the pieces but still couldn't see the big picture. Answers skirted the edges of her consciousness, like a name or a word you can't quite retrieve but know you *know*.

"What does this mean, Tanner?" she asked through the door, wanting and not wanting to hear his answer.

"I am the key to your book, Sarah. Let me in, and I'll tell you everything."

After several long moments, Sarah opened the door. She'd backed as far away from Tanner as she could in the small apartment, clutching her scissors in her hand once again as he sat soldier straight on her small couch. The air around him radiated like a heat mirage, making him seem otherworldly. Only Bitly's open acceptance of him as he rubbed his large feline head against Tanner's hand relieved her anxiety, turning it down from an eleven to a ten.

She studied him as he sat, clearly gathering his thoughts and stroking Bitly's back and ears. The silence finally overcame her, and she broke it.

"Are you an angel?" she asked, her heart skipping ahead several beats.

"Hardly." He laughed and the tension cracked a bit. The sound of his laughter warmed her in places it shouldn't have, catching her off guard. His dark black hair shone in the firelight, curling at the over-long ends along his uniform collar.

"Then who? What?"

"As I told you earlier, at this moment, I'm a ghost, although a bit more corporeal than I was when we last met." He smiled. "The book you are trying to translate is a grimoire, which belonged to the Brothers of Peril. I was a member of the Brothers of Peril. Not a practitioner of magic, but a liaison. My name is James 'Tanner' Dawson. I was a journalist before I joined the war. My family had money and connections. That wasn't why I was quickly promoted to Lieutenant, however. I had…some skills. I encoded the pages you are trying to interpret. While you've done well so far, the key lies in me alone, and I can't allow the book or its translation to fall into the wrong hands. The book is dangerous."

"So that's why you're here? To retrieve the book? And whose hands exactly would it be you are trying to keep it out of? Our government? Because I don't have the actual book. It's across the river at Chatham. A national park, by the way, and on display for anyone to see, which is pretty surprising if it's that dangerous."

Tanner bowed his head in acquiescence. "I don't even know anymore which side to entrust it to…if any. I've been hexed to Purgatory for more than a hundred and fifty years. When you found the ring…somehow, your energy awakened me." Tanner twisted his hands together in his lap and rocked forward, eager to continue. "Sarah, I don't understand the sorcery behind what has happened to me, and now to you as well. What I do understand is that I have grown to care for you in the short time I've known you…gotten to know you. I don't want anything to happen to you. But I need your help."

"You saved me from Jason?"

"Yes. I wish I could have done more. I wanted to."

"You did enough. You stopped him before he could…"

Tanner rose and turned to her. Tall and striking in his uniform, rumpled though it was, he appeared a handsome man. Very handsome, if she wanted to admit it. Certainly he wasn't the troll she'd feared him to be. But a ghost? He seemed real enough standing before her now. But she couldn't shake the tremors of uncertainty running through her, leaving her skittish and on edge. Everything about Tanner, from his letters to his actions earlier with Jason to his demeanor now, told her she had nothing to fear from him. Supernatural entity or not, he was here to help, not harm her. The sincerity in his eyes—his bright blue eyes—weakened her resolve and tears began to stream down her face before she could hide them.

He'd been kinder to her in the two weeks she'd corresponded with him than Jason had in five years. Tanner was the sort of man she wanted to love. If he were a man at all.

She felt him close the distance behind her as a war of indecision battled inside her. The practical side of her warned her to be afraid, to run from him, but the other part of her begged her to give him a chance and be open to the possibilities, impossible as they seemed.

His very real hands closed against her shoulders and a static electricity sparked between them, then spread down her arms and through her chest, erasing her fears and good sense. After her encounter with Jason, enduring a man's touch was the last thing she could have imagined herself doing. Yet, here she was.

She turned toward him and searched his eyes, studied his face and wondered at him. "How can this be so? How can *you* be so? It's all too much. Were the letters real? Or a ploy to get to the book?"

"I meant every word of my letters. You are a bright light and have pulled me from a living Hell."

"I don't know what to believe. It's all so…crazy."

"I know. It's like a dream." Tanner reached a tentative hand to her face and slid it along her jaw and into her hair. Her eyes closed, and she leaned toward him, drawn to his light and his touch.

His lips pressed to her forehead and when she pulled away to look up at him, a passion ignited within her she hadn't known existed. Pulling his head down to meet her, she pressed her lips to his and his arms engulfed her. Lost in his kiss, the room, her troubles, her questions all faded away. She was consumed by the press of his firm body against hers as he gripped her tightly to him, like he was hanging on for dear life.

Only the need for air brought her back to reality. Embarrassed at her reaction, she pulled away first and backed to the window to distance herself from him.

"I don't know why I did that. I don't even know you," she offered in defense.

"I feel like I've always known you."

The sudden closeness of the room overwhelmed her. "None of this is real. You aren't real."

"That kiss. Your touch. That was real. You make me real again. You can give me back the life I lost."

"How?" she whispered.

"By believing me. You know what I've told you is true."

"It's what you *haven't* told me that I worry about."

His brow crinkled in concern. "It's too much for one night. I should go."

Tanner turned and walked to the door. Bitly leaped from the couch and wound between Tanner's legs as he made his way across the room, a feline obstacle course slowing his departure.

"Don't go," Sarah said, her request surprising her.

Tanner hesitated, hand on the door knob. "I don't want to go. But I don't know how long I can stay. I may fade away again."

"Then stay until you do."

CHAPTER TWENTY-TWO

Tanner's greatest dream stood behind him and every bit of his essence demanded he seize what was his for the taking. The kiss had catalyzed him in a way no other energy exchange had thus far. His body was alive—truly alive—in every way, and walking away from Sarah was the last thing he wanted. But it was too soon. Too much to ask of her. Too much to expect from her. Too much to wish for...until she said the word.

Stay.

His good intentions crumbled and desire quickly filled the space they'd occupied since the moment his lips touched hers. He couldn't imagine leaving her side again. Ever. As real as he felt now, his essence filling his body as sure as it had before he'd passed, the fear remained. How long would his corporeal state last? What if he faded away before her eyes? After all Sarah had endured thus far, would that be the final thing that pushed her over the edge?

He wondered if he could survive it himself.

Tanner wanted his body back. His life back. But in this moment, he wanted Sarah more. He found himself in her arms before he could even think on all of the reasons he shouldn't. Her eager gaze spurred him onward despite his reservations as his emotions, and then his biology, got the better of him.

His member hardened like the attentive stance of every good soldier.

He kissed her hard and with a hunger he wasn't sure could ever be satiated. Sarah's hands tangled in his hair, and she radiated with light before him. The taunt muscles of her lean back strained beneath the cotton of her thin shirt as she clutched at him and returned his kiss, demanding more and everything from him. A sweet vanilla scent drifted from her hair, and her hands worked at his Union jacket, struggling to undo the buttons between them. His long neglected heart rent in half when her warm hands slid beneath his own shirt and up his ribs, nearly bringing him to his knees. The contact sparked electric and light energy surged through him.

"Are you okay?" Sarah's terrified eyes asked the real question.

"I'm better than I've ever been." It was the truth. And a miracle.

"Do you think…?" she asked, but Tanner kissed her hard, shutting off her words.

"Let's not think any more tonight. Let's make the most of this opportunity."

Sarah grasped his hand and pulled him toward the bed. Tanner followed.

* * *

Sarah was clearly out of her ever-loving mind. Bad enough she'd allowed a strange man into her apartment, but now she was unabashedly seducing a stalker at best, a potentially supernatural entity at worst. The problem was there was nothing unnatural about the man before her now. Something about Tanner made her more than willing to forget her caution. Suddenly, the world seemed brighter and full of possibilities. So many things had gone wrong and right since she'd found the ring. But this—with Tanner—felt very, very right.

He shed his coat and shirt and stood before her as she sat on the edge of her bed. She couldn't resist the urge to skim her hands up and across his strong chest. Tanner's eyes closed as his skin warmed beneath her touch, and he sucked in a sharp breath. His erection pushed against the front of his trousers, and she reached for him, wrapping a hand around him and eliciting a groan.

His blue eyes opened and brightened briefly before he reached for the hem of her shirt. Pulling the blouse up over her head, he bared her breasts. For the longest moment, he didn't move and seemed transfixed, staring down at her like he was seeing a woman for the first time. His member throbbed beneath her hold. He lowered himself to her, his bare chest gliding against hers, pressing her back against her bed and sending a flood of warmth through her entire body to pool hot and low.

Sarah urged his trousers lower on his hips and tried to push them off, but felt him pull back.

"Sarah, are you sure you want this?"

"Yes."

A nip on her neck was his response and shivers shimmered through her, bringing her flesh to goose bumps. She scanned her eyes up his torso as he rose to unlace his boots. After removing them, he lined them up neatly beside the bed. His trousers were next, and he unfastened them, then let them drop to the floor. As he stepped out of his pants, her eyes followed the transaction with acute awareness. He was taller than Jason; where Jason was soft, Tanner was hard and lean. Only his words were softer and his touch.

When he ran his hands alongside her ribs, then down to pull her fleece pants free, her heartbeat picked up and hammered in her chest. This was happening. She was having sex with a stranger.

Not a stranger.

Not really. They'd corresponded, at least. Dozens of letters. Lots of girls her age brought real strangers home from bars and had sex. Ellie had been encouraging her for years to meet someone else. She would have been thrilled with the prospects of a one-night stand. Regardless, Sarah knew Tanner much more than any of those girls would have known their bar dates. Yet, she'd never had a one-night stand. And Jason was the only man she'd been with. Ever.

His hands stopped their roaming, perhaps sensing the tension building in her.

"Don't stop," she said.

"You're having second thoughts."

"I'm not. Please."

Tanner began to pull away, but she clasped her hands around the back of his neck and pulled him back down to her, kissing him until his body loosened, pressing back against hers like a missing puzzle piece.

"You're so lovely, dear one."

Sarah felt a blush sweep across her face. It wasn't true, of course. She was average at best. How many times had Jason told her how lucky she was to have someone like him taking care of her, looking out for her? Otherwise, she'd be alone.

Tanner was the lovely one. No, *remarkable*. Jason had stayed with her as a matter of comfort and necessity. His. Not hers. It occurred to her that perhaps Tanner *was* somehow bewitched, or he'd never have likely found her interesting at all. And after tonight, he'd probably be gone for good. Her confidence failed, and she pulled away.

"What's wrong?"

"I…this may be a mistake." Her eyes burned and began to fill with tears. He'd hate her for sure now. Leading him on so far.

Tanner stroked her hair. "Why do you say that? Now? What has changed your heart?"

"It's just…I haven't been with anyone other than Jason."

Tanner laughed. "Dear one, I haven't been with a woman in a hundred and fifty years. We'll make do."

Sarah nodded and closed her eyes to avoid his concerned gaze.

Tanner kissed the tears from the corner of one eye, and then the other. "Yes?"

"Yes."

His erection pushed against her mound, and she gasped, pressing against him, rubbing her tender bits along his shaft and driving her doubt to the shadows once more. Tanner's fingers wandered below and brushed her slickened opening. She pushed downward onto his hand, willing him to slide his fingers inside her. When he did, her back arched, and she gasped again.

"Tanner."

Tanner trailed a row of kisses across her chest, then settled his cheek on her breast near her pearled nipple. His warm exhale nearly brought her to climax as he worked her below. Her stomach muscles tensed, and when he flicked his thumb across her nub, she cried out.

It was more than she could endure. The tension built inside her, winding tighter and tighter, and stars burst beneath her closed eyelids, preceding the most intense release she'd ever experienced. Riding the wave, she clawed her hands, raking them across his back, digging into his skin as she held on to him.

Her body shuddered and twitched beneath him until at last her muscles relaxed, leaving her a rag doll in his arms. Tanner administered soft kisses across her body as his sputtered breathing began to subside, his own release not yet relieved.

"Don't stop now." Sarah parted her legs and his body aligned with hers. "I take birth control pills. I won't get pregnant."

"There's a pill for that now?" Tanner asked, incredulous.

'Please, Tanner."

The head of his erection stroked her engorged nub as it slid past, eliciting another shudder from her over-sensitive body.

Tanner cradled her head in his hands, and she watched his face change from concern to ecstasy when the head of his erection pressed against her opening. The fullness there demanded action, and she pushed her body onto him, insisting he fill her, truly and completely. His first penetration brought renewed tears to her eyes as she let go of years of not being enough. This moment alone proved she could be happy without Jason. Someone had cared about her enough to see to her needs first, not his own. It was the first time she'd been brought to climax without a battery-operated aid.

Tanner rocked in and out of her, filling and retreating, until his rhythm became more frantic. The muscles in his neck tensed, and she felt his body stiffen beneath her hands. His face buried against her neck and into her hair, and she raised her hips, clenching her inner muscles around him.

And that was it. He stilled and exploded inside her, his warm release filling her.

Five years.

And this was the first time she'd ever enjoyed sex.

CHAPTER TWENTY-THREE

Tanner knew there were words he should say. More explanations he should give, but none of them were enough to convey the warmth in his heart or his unbridled fear. He was so close to having everything or nothing at all. If he were to be returned to the ring or lose Sarah after tonight, he couldn't bear one more day of his existence. She was everything he'd ever dreamed of and nothing he had ever encountered in his time.

It had taken a hex and a hundred and fifty years to find true love. Now he feared true love might not be enough. Or returned. What if her feelings weren't the same? What if feelings alone weren't enough? What if there was no breaking of the hex and this was just the next phase of Sylvia's everlasting Purgatory, a cruel reprieve to make the next chapter more agonizing? His emotions were based on circumstances he could never expect Sarah to believe, yet she seemed... receptive, despite her understandable reservations.

It was more than any reasonable person could or should be expected to accept. Yet, her warm, lush body filled his arms as she curled against him and the line between what was possible and what was not grew preciously thin. Within her hold, he found his own energy needs satiated for the moment and was at last able to relax. He reached down and pulled the blankets over them, basking in her afterglow, unsure now where her ecstasy ended and his began. The constant and intimate contact left him feeling like he could conquer any foe.

Sarah strengthened him in ways that were both real and supernatural.

She stirred in his arms, and then stilled. His heart stopped beating as he waited for her response. He prayed it would be positive and not filled with regret.

"Hey," she said, her face lit by the soft glow of the fire.

The corner of his mouth hitched up in a slow smile. "Hello."

"I guess I dozed off."

"For a while."

Sarah smiled and blushed, but didn't look away from him. She held his gaze for the longest moment, and he tried in vain to puzzle out the questions she wasn't asking. Instead, she sighed and pushed the hair back from his forehead.

Tanner savored every look and every touch, for he didn't know when either might be his last. His stomach growled loudly, shocking him.

"Hungry much?" Sarah teased.

"Indeed."

Tanner eyed the box of half-eaten pizza on her desk, and Sarah tracked his gaze there. She frowned. "It's been sitting out too long. We could drive to the all-night diner but—"

Sarah froze.

"What?"

"Why is the webcam light activated on my computer?"

Tanner looked at the contraption and did indeed see a white pinprick of light beaming from the top.

Sarah was out of their warm bed and across the room in a heartbeat. She grabbed her robe from the end of the bed and put it on as she investigated. "My camera is on. How did my camera get turned on?" She manipulated the device, clicking away at the keys until the light extinguished, then she pulled the cord from the wall.

"Dammit, that flash drive must have had a virus on it. No telling what's infected my computer now. At least I wrote down most of the translations in my notebook too. I guess the FBI can have fun with this disease-ridden thing now. I'm supposed to turn it in tomorrow anyway."

She closed the lid down and folded the machine in half. "So? All-night diner?"

Before Tanner could answer, three quick knocks rapped at the door and the inside of his chest grew cold. Sarah paused, looking at him. "I honestly don't know who else it could be," she said.

She crossed to the door and hesitated, hanging her head and pulling in a deep breath. "Who is it?"

"Agent Sykes and Agent Falkner of the NSA, ma'am. We need a word."

Sarah's eyes grew large and round, and she mouthed the letters "NSA" to Tanner. He shrugged in reply. He had no idea what the NSA was or why they had 'agents' knocking on Sarah's door at this hour.

"Let me see your badges. Slide them under the door."

"We can't relinquish control of our badges, ma'am, but if you'll open the door, we'll gladly let you inspect them."

Sarah pointed Tanner toward the bathroom and indicated he should hide. Perhaps wise, considering his unstable condition, but he didn't like it. Not one bit. Something felt very wrong about this situation. For a wild moment, he wished he was invisible and intangible again and could pass through the door to scrutinize the visitors himself.

Against his better judgment, he gathered his clothing and acquiesced. After slipping into his trousers and clothing, he carried his boots to the bathroom. If she needed aid, he was only steps away and still fully capable of bringing his wrath down upon anyone wishing to harm Sarah.

* * *

For the hundredth time in a week, Sarah wished for a peephole. How had her life spun so far out of control? There was no chain latch so the two options were open the door or not. As she debated, a third option popped into her head.

"Give me your card or some sort of identification. I'm not opening the door until I see your badges, or I get some confirmation."

A long silence met her request, shuffling and then two business cards slid beneath the door, bearing Agent Jim Sykes and Agent Robert Falkner's names, badge numbers, office phone, fax and an 800 number. "Call the 800 number and give them that badge ID. Someone there can verify us to you."

Sarah felt Tanner's eyes on her as she dug her phone out from the pile on her desk. She Googled the office and number first. Finding the same 800 number as what appeared on the card, she dialed and waited. Maryland was in her time zone. She couldn't imagine anyone would personally man the phones at this hour and was surprised when a live voice picked up.

"NSA General Offices, how may I direct your call?"

"I have two men outside my door who claim to be agents. I need to verify their credentials before I let them in."

She read off the names and badge numbers, then waited. Muzak filled her ear and her heart raced. Ellie had said the FBI would want her computer, but why was the NSA here? What in the world was Candace into? And had she somehow dragged Sarah into it as well? Cold dread began to flood through her body. She'd happily relinquish the laptop. She just prayed Candace hadn't set her up somehow to take her fall.

"Thank you for holding. Director Ferguson of the NSA speaking. I can verify that both men you inquired about are indeed agents in-good-standing with the NSA. This is a matter of national security. Your cooperation with them and this agency is imperative and expected. Is there anything else?"

Sarah hated the way the director's gruff voice and sharp verbal demeanor made her feel small and chastised. She had plenty of questions. All of which had dissolved under his bossy response.

"I guess not."

"Good. Then let them in, Ms. Knight."

The connection severed—his doing, not hers—and her mind spun as she stared at the phone. She hadn't told him her name.

"What is it? Are they legitimate agents of this NSA? And what agency is it exactly?" Tanner whispered from the bathroom.

Sarah crossed to him, scared. "Yes. They were verified. NSA is the National Security Agency. It's a big government agency that basically spies on everyone for the defense of the nation. I don't know what Candace did to garner their attention, but it looks like it's spilled over."

"Are you going to let them in?" Tanner asked.

"I don't think we have a choice. But they don't need to know about you. Stay in here. Maybe they've just come for the computer, and they'll go."

Tanner took her hand in his and gave it a squeeze. "I'll be right here. Do not fear."

"Ms. Knight?" one of the agents asked through the door. "Did you get what you needed? Or do we need to call for you?"

"I got it. I need a minute to get dressed." Sarah hurriedly dressed in her discarded clothes, then gave Tanner a warning look. "Hide in the shower and don't say a word."

She crossed to the door and clicked open the deadbolt.

Agent Number One, dressed in black jeans and a dark jacket under his black overcoat, reached inside his jacket and produced a badge. "I'm Agent Sykes," he said, handing it to her for inspection.

Sarah took the badge and studied it. "And you?" she asked Agent Number Two.

He produced a duplicate badge, except for the name and photo. Despite the palpable gravity of the situation, she felt a smile creep across her face.

"BOPD?" Sarah couldn't suppress the nervous laugh that slipped out. "You work for bopped? As in Cyndi Lauper's 'She bop he bop a we bop'?"

Agent Sykes' eye twitched and the corner of his grim mouth ticked down a bit. "It's a special division of the NSA, ma'am."

"Do we have permission to enter the apartment, Ms. Knight?"

"I suppose," Sarah answered. Saying *no* would only delay the inevitable.

Seconds later, Agents Sykes and Falkner stood in her small apartment, sucking the air out of the room and making it seem much, much smaller.

Agent Falkner began to wander toward her desk, and she shifted in front of him before he could get any closer. "Why are you here at three in the morning, and what do you want? Is it about Candace and my computer? I was under the impression the FBI wanted the computer. I have no idea about anything Candace was into or has done. I understood I could turn in the computer tomorrow. Do I need a lawyer here?"

The agents exchanged a quick look. "Where's your companion, Ms. Knight?"

Sarah blanched. The unexpected question stole her bravado. Agent Falkner nodded toward the only interior door in the room, and reached into his jacket once again, this time producing a gun. He walked along the hall-side wall, then stood to the left of the bathroom door.

"Come on out here, Mr. Dawson."

CHAPTER TWENTY-FOUR

The two-hour car ride to Maryland was long and silent. The agents had confiscated her computer, all of the notes and papers littering her desk, and then stuffed her and Tanner into the backseat of a black Suburban. The doors only opened from the outside. She'd tried them. Both.

A thick piece of protective glass separated her and Tanner from the agents. At least they hadn't separated them from each other. Tanner held her hand, which did offer some comfort as she shuffled through the myriad of possibilities. The agents refused to discuss anything in her apartment but had promised full disclosure at a secured location.

They'd made it clear that refusing wasn't an option.

Sarah was afraid to discuss too much with Tanner in the car, even though she didn't have anything to hide. Or at least she didn't think she did—except Tanner's odd state of existence, which at the moment seemed ridiculous to even consider. Other than his offered explanation and that one instance of seeing him shimmer the first night they'd met, there'd been no indication he was anything other than one hundred percent solid human. His warm hand in hers was proof of that. For all she knew, that shimmer could have been a trick of the firelight, her trauma and exhaustion from the night before taking its toll.

Thinking of that led her straight down the squirrel path in her mind to their night together. Or few hours, if she wanted to get technical. She'd had the best sex of her life with a virtual stranger and was now a prisoner with her supposed ghost lover in the back of a Men-in-Black car being taken to a secret government location.

Yeah. That seemed about right.

What she wouldn't give to have Ellie here right now. She'd have this mess sorted in no time. Sarah fingered the chain around her throat. The ring bounced against her chest under her T-shirt.

Tanner leaned in against her neck and whispered. "Don't lose that ring. No matter what. If you keep the ring, I'll be near."

Sarah pursed her lips and pulled in a breath through her nose, watching the agents for any sign they'd heard. Neither made any indication.

When the car approached a Fort Knoxesque security gate, the gravity of their predicament ratcheted up. This was happening. She feared that whatever *this* was would soon get a whole lot more intense. She wondered if she'd ever see Bitly or her little apartment again.

* * *

Sarah sat in a windowless room somewhere inside the basement of the NSA offices. Agents Sykes and Falkner had led them through a labyrinth of hallways and past dozens of cube farms and walled offices, which buzzed with the beehive efficiency of busy people. The hum of hundreds, maybe thousands, of servers somewhere near permeated the air, lending to the hive atmosphere. At the last moment, the agents escorted Sarah to one room and Tanner to another. She'd never been so scared in her life. Ever.

Certain she was under electronic observation, she resisted the urge to finger the necklace. She'd already grown accustomed to sliding the ring along the chain for solace. The slight warmth it still generated against her skin spread across her chest, giving her some comfort. There had been no frisking or pat down, which was a little surprising, really. Once Tanner and Sarah passed through the gate with the two agents, the swiping of the agents' badges got them all past each additional security door, no problem.

Still, Sarah couldn't shake the feeling her every move was being watched. No need drawing attention to herself or the ring. Maybe her luck would hold as long as she held the talisman. She prayed Tanner was so fortunate. The question was—which of them was the NSA most interested in, and why?

She pressed her hands to her lap to steady their constant trembling and sat with her head bowed for maybe fifteen—or a thousand—minutes. She didn't know, not daring to retrieve her phone from her pocket to see. The sooner this was all over and she was back home, the better.

A quick rap on the door snapped her head to attention and her focus lasered onto Agent Sykes as he stepped through, two Starbucks cups balanced in one of his meaty hands and a notebook in the other. Her notebook.

"Sorry for the delay. Things don't really come alive around here until after eight a.m. Lots of paperwork to turn in." Agent Sykes sat one of the coffee cups in front of her. "There should be some pastries coming around soon. You're probably hungry."

Sarah shook her head no, but her stomach betrayed her by growling at the mere mention of food. The coffee would help fill her nervous stomach, but it probably wouldn't do much for her worried mind or trembling body.

She wrapped both hands around the cup and brought it to her lips. "Thank you."

"Sure thing." Agent Sykes attempted a casual smile that didn't quite work and eased back in the chair.

"Is this an interrogation room, Agent Sykes?" Sarah asked.

Agent Sykes laid her notebook on the table and spread his hand across its face. "Something like that. You can just call me Sykes, or Jim if you'd feel more comfortable."

"Being home would make me feel more comfortable. You have my computer. Why am I here? And where's Tanner?"

Sykes tapped the notebook. "Tell me about this."

"I'm sorry. What does my notebook have to do with Candace or Tanner or any of this?"

"None of this is about Candace. In fact, we haven't been able to determine why the FBI might want your computer. Fill us in. Save us some legwork and you'll be home by dinnertime."

Sarah took a long drink of her hot coffee and tried to untangle her thoughts as it made its way to her stomach. Nothing made any sort of sense. She wasn't accustomed to telling lies. It just wasn't in her nature, which was why calling in sick hadn't even occurred to her. It had been Ellie's suggestion. The only way out of this situation was *through* it. She jumped in with both feet and prayed for the best possible outcome.

"Candace Day is my boss at Rappahannock Reveals Web Arts. I called in sick today and my coworker told me that the FBI was at the office. Candace had been taken into custody and was being charged with cyber theft, among other things. My coworker told me the FBI wanted my computer, and I needed to turn it in. I was going to bring it by this morning. But you two showed up in the middle of the night for it instead. Except now you're telling me that's not why you came at all and now I have no idea what's going on."

Sykes nodded toward the notebook. "What is your interest in the Brothers of Peril?"

Sarah nearly spat out her next drink of coffee. "That's what this is all about? An urban legend?"

"You have quite a few pages of transcriptions in this notebook as well as on your laptop. There haven't been too many folks even interested in the BOP, let alone spend the money for the flash drive and take the initiative to attempt any real decoding. Yet you have. And quite well, I might add." He smiled again, this time a bit more convincingly than the last.

Tiny synapses fired in Sarah's exhausted brain at last. "BOP? Your badge said 'BOPD'? You're an agent of the Brothers of Peril Division? That's a thing?"

The twitch at the corner of Sykes' eye betrayed his irritation. "Yeah. It's a thing. A very important thing, as a matter of fact."

Snap. Snap. Snap. More pieces fell into place. "You spied on me with the flash drive. You turned on my webcam and literally spied on me while I worked on the code. You…"

The full gravity of the spying in question became clear. The webcam must have turned on the second she'd plugged in the flash drive and opened the files, activating the worm. The webcam was most likely on for hours. They would have seen and heard…everything.

Sykes cleared his throat and averted his eyes. Sarah felt a blush overtake her. She rose abruptly from the chair, which screeched across the floor like nails on a chalk board. "You had no right!"

"We have every right, Ms. Knight. It's what we do here. Gather intel and break codes. A rather simple mission, actually. Except this particular code is so well or oddly encrypted we haven't gotten any further than you have. Neither has anyone else. It seems your companion might have some insight into that, however. How well do you know Mr. Dawson?"

Sarah's blood pressure had to be sky high. Between the stress of being stuck in this room in some X-Files basement where no one—and she meant no one—would ever even *guess* to look for her, two spies and God only knew how many more had heard and possibly watched her have sex. She'd just inadvertently made a sex tape.

Good God.

What in the world could Tanner be telling them next door? If he was just next door. They'd taken her into a room first so she hadn't actually seen where he'd ended up. Sarah only assumed he'd been taken nearby for convenience, if nothing else.

"Again, Ms. Knight. Why the interest in the BOP?"

"I like puzzles. I write code for a living. Which you probably already know. I took a few cryptology classes in college. When I saw the book and found out about the flash, I thought, what the heck?"

"And how long have you known Mr. Dawson? How did you meet? Exactly."

"We've been corresponding for a while. He approached me first. Last night was only our second in-person meeting." Sarah paced along the side of the long rectangular table.

"I see," Sykes said, clasping his hands in his lap and steepling his index fingers in silent judgment. "We found some of your conversation with Mr. Dawson puzzling. Perhaps it lacked context. And his clothing? Can you explain his odd period dress?"

Here she was. At the corner of Truth and Crazy Talk. Even if these guys were some sort of X-Files agents, there was no way she was going to start spreading her crazy around. She had no idea what Tanner was saying to Agent Falkner or whoever was playing good-cop/bad-cop on his end of things. Generally she liked to follow the rules. It was coded in her very DNA, but this was so clearly an example of a situation where the truth would most assuredly not set her free but more likely dig her a deep, deep hole.

Ellie would believe everything she had to say on the matter. These two were not Ellie.

Sarah swallowed hard.

Lie.

Now was the time to throw Tanner under the bus and get out of here. She didn't even really know him. Except she had *known* him. Intimately. Only a few hours earlier, and every nerve and cell of her body told her there was much, much more to him than met the eye or touch so far. He needed her. He'd told her as much.

Her heart squeezed, two sizes too small in her chest, and she went for broke.

"He's an actor. He volunteers and participates in Civil War reenactments at Chatham and around the area. We...I...like the uniform." Sarah's blush confirmed what her words could not, even though her embarrassment was in the lie, not the admission of a fictional fetish.

Sykes coughed and gave her a skeptical glance before rediscovering the design on the front of her notebook. His wheels were clearly turning.

"What do you know of the Brothers of Peril, Ms. Knight?"

"Only what I've read. They were supposedly a secret sect of the Masons who manipulated supernatural elements to affect the outcomes of wars and military actions during the Civil War. Crazy, right?"

"Indeed. Except it's my job to prove otherwise. Do you know what a government could do with power like that? What a government would give to have an advantage like that in war... or peace for that matter? And it's a power we had. But that tool was lost when the key to the grimoire was lost as well. We want that key, Ms. Knight."

"Well I don't have it. The first part was pretty easy to figure out. Surely you've gotten that far."

"Of course. Your Mr. Dawson seemed to indicate he might know a bit more than that. Unfortunately, our—communication—went black before we discovered if that was indeed the case. Did Mr. Dawson give you any further indication or suggest in any way he could decode the second translation during your time or correspondence with him?"

At least this one, she could answer truthfully. He'd said he was the key all right, but they hadn't gotten around to discussing it much before things between them had ignited. At this point, she didn't know any more about the decoding situation than the agents did. Unless Tanner was singing a different tune down the hall. Something told her he was not.

"Honestly, I have no idea about any further decoding or keys. You have everything I worked on as well as my computer and frankly, my curiosity on the matter is quashed. As far as I can see, I haven't broken any laws and unless you have criminal charges to press against me, I want to go home. If you're not going to let me go home, I want a lawyer. Now."

Sarah crossed her arms to keep her hands from trembling in front of Agent Sykes. That one speech had used up her remaining courage. The only card she knew to play at this point was the lawyer card. She meant it. There was no way she'd done anything wrong. They couldn't hold her here—at least not legally. She wasn't a terrorist and this wasn't the supernatural version of Guantanamo Bay.

She hoped.

CHAPTER TWENTY-FIVE

Tanner was fading fast. In the few short hours he'd spent away from Sarah and her sustaining energy, his form had deteriorated. Agent Falkner hadn't seemed to take notice yet. The agent's preoccupation with Sarah's notebook had frustrated his negotiations with Tanner.

"This is all bullshit without the key. We want the key, Dawson." Agent Falkner punctuated his demand with a resounding pound of his fist on the table.

Amateur.

Agent Falkner had given no indication he was indeed an inducted member of the Brothers of Peril, let alone a Mason. All could have been alleviated if he were indeed a member of the Brotherhood with the stamp of his Peril ring. The agent had not even asked about the ring and didn't don one, himself. The Masons had secret handshakes and such, but the Brothers of Peril was a level beyond that.

When covered in ink and rolled along a parchment, the dragons engraved along the sides of his own ring merged to form two words—the Brotherhood's own secret code as it were.

Pericula noctis: peril of night.

To be answered with, *numerus signorum*: untold wonders.

Any true member, and certainly any member of the upper echelon worthy of further discussion, would know such a thing. Agent Falkner had failed to mention the ring or any substantiation of membership.

What Agent Falkner knew of the book was really no more than what was available to the general public. What he *did* seem to know was that the book was valuable. And it was. In righteous and worthy hands, it was the most valuable text in existence. A supernatural Holy Grail. Thus far, Tanner held no confidence that these two men or this organization were either righteous or worthy.

"We've done some checking on you, Mr. Dawson. Since you have no identification with you and you refuse to answer our questions, we've had to be…creative. Ms. Knight has been more than helpful so far. Much more so than you have been."

Agent Falkner reached for a silver case at his feet and placed it on the table between them. Two locks clicked simultaneously as he pressed them with his thumbs. The lid popped open slightly.

"A quick search of Ms. Knight's apartment by one our associates found this correspondence. Is this yours, Mr. Dawson? You do go by Tanner, yes?" Agent Falkner fanned Tanner's letters to Sarah on top of the growing pile of 'evidence' on the table. "Ms. Knight says you've been stalking her. Have to say, these letters do come off a bit stalky. And the thing is we can't seem to find you in the system anywhere. No social. No birth record. No passport. Nothing. It's like you're a ghost.

Yet here you are. Paperless and filled with mystery. Weird, huh?"

Tanner didn't answer. In his heart, he knew Agent Falkner was trying to spread misgiving and doubt to prejudice him against Sarah. She was stronger than this. He'd seen the evidence of her strength time and again over the past two weeks and was certain she could understand the gravity of the situation, if not entirely what was at stake. They'd made a connection. In a physical way, yes, but something more had sparked between them. She only needed to hold on long enough to realize it. Long enough for the curse to be broken.

Tanner sat stoic and at attention, unyielding in action or word. He'd spent an eternity locked in a black Hell. This room? This interrogation was nothing compared to that. This agent held no power over him. Not compared to what Sylvia had manifested. Agent Falkner, from every indication thus far, appeared a human with no supernatural qualities, and if he was as ignorant to the ways of the Brothers of Peril as he seemed, the agent was about to get the shock of his life.

Agent Falkner paced the room, clearly recalculating his approach. The man's demeanor was not consistent with a military discipline, seeming more athletic than militant, but with a clear ax to grind nonetheless. His physical form was his most imposing weapon, and one he'd clearly relied upon heavily in the past. When that failed, he tried to prove himself again and project respect and authority. Instead he exhibited his desperation. Tanner almost felt sorry for him.

A shiver slithered down Tanner's spine seconds before he felt his form slipping back to the ether from which he'd been cursed. Losing his corporeal form little by little, he studied his hands, rubbing at his ink-covered fingertips. A man had collected a pressing of his prints by rolling Tanner's finger pads along thick paper. For what reason, he had no idea. Tanner spread his fingers wide as he rested his hand on the table, the papers below quickly becoming visible through his flesh. He felt a slow smile stretch across his face.

The interview was over.

The look on Agent Falkner's visage when he turned to address Tanner with his latest barrage of accusations and threats slipped into shock, and then fear as Tanner faded out of corporeality. While he hadn't witnessed much of the actual decline with his back turned to him, what he had seen was just enough for Agent Falkner to have time for some serious soul searching before trying to explain what had happened.

Tanner chuckled. This development was the only bright spot of the past few hours. He passed through the closed door to go in search of Sarah. He'd thought to drain Falkner's energy to improve his condition, but keeping an eye on Sarah and working toward an escape from this facility would be much easier if no one could see him. He knew she was still nearby because his tether had yet to snap him back to its source. She wouldn't be able to see him now that he'd faded, but at least he could make sure she was safe.

And continue to protect her.

* * *

"What the hell, Falkner?" Agent Sykes jumped to his feet, gun drawn within seconds of Agent Falkner crashing through the door of Sarah's interrogation room.

Falkner's formerly cool façade was gone. He stalked across the room and pressed his face inches from Sarah's. "Where is he?"

Sarah recoiled, thankful for the steel table between them and Agent Sykes' quick hands on Falkner's shoulders, which pulled him back farther to stall his advance and increase the distance from him.

"What's wrong, Falkner?" Agent Sykes asked.

"He's gone. One second I'm talking at him, and the next he's gone. As in vanished. As in not in the goddamned room. What the hell?" Agent Falkner pointed at Sarah. "She knows something. Where is he? How he can do that? He's not in the system. Anywhere. I ran everything back the past fifty years. Even had the guys dig through microfiche. No prints in the system either. The guy doesn't exist."

Sarah's heart kicked up, and she sucked in a shuddering breath, unsure if she were more relieved or terrified that someone else had witnessed what her mind refused to process, despite the growing evidence. At least it looked as though she'd have company in the loony bin. Agent Falkner practically checked himself in with his own crazy talk.

Agent Sykes took a long look at Agent Falkner, and then turned to Sarah.

"Pericula noctis."

Sarah hesitated, sure it was a test for which she didn't have the answer. "I'm sorry. What?"

"I guess we're done here."

CHAPTER TWENTY-SIX

The drive home in the back of the same black Suburban was lonely, and Sarah's mind filled with questions. The ring blazed against her skin, but she resisted the urge to pull it from its concealment. She'd made it this far and was too close to home to reveal her hand now.

There'd been no indication as to what had happened to Tanner. Perhaps Agent Falkner's tirade had been a ruse to set her free so they could continue their surveillance and wait to learn for themselves whatever it was they thought she was hiding. They were going to be sorely disappointed.

Sarah pulled her phone from her pocket and powered it on. It had been a quarter past five when they'd walked out of the NSA headquarters. She'd spent twelve hours at the NSA office and now had yet another two-hour drive home. Six missed calls from Ellie filled her screen, as well as six voicemail messages. At least someone in her life knew how to leave a flippin' message.

Paranoia filled her. The one thing the NSA was good at was electronic surveillance, and even though she didn't have anything to hide, she was fairly certain they weren't done with her. Or Tanner.

Where was he? Would she ever see him again?

A hard lump formed in her throat, and her eyes burned. Somehow in the course of a few days, she'd been attacked by one lover, found another, temporarily lost her job, been interrogated by the government and maybe lost another lover.

How was this her life?

She blinked back the tears. No more crying. This was bullshit. As soon as she got home, she would pack a bag and head to Ellie's. No way did she trust that her apartment wasn't bugged. Her next stop would be Alex's shop. This ring could not possibly be a lucky talisman. While she didn't believe in Alex's supposed psychic powers, where else could she turn? Maybe her skepticism would be verified, but what if Alex could help her? Prove once and for all if the ring was a hex or lucky talisman?

And Tanner? She couldn't even think about him right now. Maybe she'd cracked completely. Maybe...

It didn't matter. He was gone, and she was alone to face whatever *this* was. Everything that had happened in the past two weeks was somehow tied to the damned ring that was currently burning a hole through her cleavage. She clutched her chest through her blouse and held it away from her skin as nonchalantly as she could. Two more hours until she was home.

A hundred more miles until she took control and got some answers.

* * *

Tanner sat beside Sarah in the back of the Suburban, desperate to console her. The grim line of her lips and the worry swirling in the fine wrinkles of her forehead betrayed her inner debate. He feared she might take some drastic action before he could reassure her that everything that had happened between them was real and good.

Still, he couldn't blame her for her consternation or the fear playing out across her beautiful pale face. There were no logical explanations for what he was or for the dark magic behind it. It was otherworldly. Of course she couldn't comprehend it. He was living it, and he scarcely could himself.

His one consolation was that she retained the ring. She hadn't exposed it during her interrogation and been forced to hand it over. It was his only link to her, and the one true way to reconnect with the Brothers of Peril and secure the grimoire once his body was restored. He refused to consider the probability of that not happening. Freedom dangled much too tantalizingly before him to concede now.

Sarah's energy rolled off her trembling body, but he dared not tap into it inside the car. The last thing he needed was to reappear beside her in a closed car with Agent Sykes feet away. He was thankful Agent Falkner hadn't been invited on the return visit. Not surprising, after the way he'd attacked Sarah in her interrogation room. Tanner had been witness to the entire debacle and was shocked when Agent Sykes had presented the Brothers of Peril code phrase to Sarah. Of course she didn't know the response. But Tanner did. And now knew he had at least one Brothers of Peril ally when the time came.

But there was much to be done before that moment.

They pulled up outside Sarah's home, and relief filled him. He'd have to wait until her neighbors were sleeping to reenergize, then he could come to her again and try to soothe her troubled mind. Already memories of her warm, supple body beat at him, demanding he take his fill of her as well as her energy. But that wouldn't be possible for some time. He had too much to explain. Too much to do. He had to prove to her once and for all her importance to him. Not only for his own salvation, but for the protection of the country.

His tormented heart insisted she fulfill its needs as well.

One problem at time.

His patience, however, was long gone.

Agent Sykes exited the car and walked around to Sarah's side. He opened the door for her.

"I'll walk you up," Agent Sykes said.

"No." Sarah pulled away from his offered escort. "I think you've done enough."

Agent Sykes pushed her door closed and narrowed his eyes. "If you see Tanner…"

"I'll be sure to contact you. Don't worry. I don't want any part of whatever is going on."

"Sorry for your inconvenience. We'll be in touch if anything changes."

"I have no doubt." Sarah turned and disappeared through the shared entrance and up the stairs.

Agent Sykes stood outside, watching her go. His dark eyes took in everything. "Where are you, Tanner?"

Tanner couldn't resist brushing Agent Sykes' powerful red aura. For the pure satisfaction of consternating the man, Tanner pulled the small antenna back on the rear of the car, then released it abruptly so it whipped back and forth. Agent Sykes twisted around, gun drawn before the antenna stopped bouncing. His aura transformed to a dark blue as uncertainty crossed his face. Sykes raised his face toward Sarah's upstairs apartment, watching as she pulled her drapes closed, and Tanner's taut leash snapped him home.

CHAPTER TWENTY-SEVEN

What is he waiting for?

Sarah peeked from the corner of her drapes as Agent Sykes remained by his car, staring at her apartment, looking perplexed. He'd actually drawn his weapon briefly, much to her dismay, nearly activating a panic attack in her. Her heart pounded in her chest as Bitly wound through her legs, pressing his vibrating body against her calves, purring his greeting and chastisement for her absence.

She wanted to call Ellie, tell her the plan she'd formulated on the car ride home and everything that had transpired in the past few days, but she wasn't doing that until Agent Sykes was out of sight. There was no way to be certain of visual surveillance in her apartment, but she had little doubt they'd planted some sort of listening devices. Since the laptop was now at the NSA office, she didn't have to worry about the webcam, but she was fairly certain the NSA had access to all manner of James Bond style spying devices. Her imagination was on overload.

Her cell phone rang, and she jumped back from the window, nearly ripping the drape from its rod and peeing her pants in the process. God, she was coiled like a Jack in the Box. She wasn't sure her heart could take it. Or her bladder.

She hated to do it, but she hit decline. Missed call number seven from Ellie.

She peeked again and finally Agent Sykes holstered the weapon and walked purposefully back around to the driver's side. The breath she'd been holding puffed out of her in one long exhale, and she leaned against the glass.

Pack.

Careful not to stumble over a very needy Bitly, she pulled her overnight bag from beneath her bed and hurriedly stuffed in clothes and God only knew what else. In her panic, her mind was not tracking. She scavenged in the back of her small bathroom linen pantry for her toiletry bag and filled it with her toothbrush, paste, and the handful of makeup products she used. Ellie would have everything else she needed, and she could borrow whatever she may have forgotten.

The ring blazed against her skin, reminding her of the urgency of her escape. She reached for the chain and spun it around, unlatching the clasp. The ring and chain pooled in her palm, searing her hand. Sarah grabbed her purse and dropped the ring inside, not wanting contact with the cursed object any longer.

Finding that damned ring had been the beginning of this entire mess.

Bitly meowed his disapproval loudly, reminding her to drag his crate from beneath the bed as well. He'd hate the trip, but she couldn't leave him here alone in the apartment. It wasn't fair to involve Adam or anyone else by asking them to feed him. She stuffed him into the crate, despite his protests. Bitly loved her unconditionally. He'd forgive her. Besides, she needed his company.

One last look around the apartment. She grabbed her phone charger and headed out the door, not knowing when she could come home again.

* * *

Tanner's concern was great and his heart filled with dread. Sarah's reaction was completely unexpected. She'd packed and fled her home. On foot. Mercifully, it hadn't been but ten or twelve blocks, but now he worried about his need to reenergize and the complete lack of able bodies with which to do so. From the photos around the home they'd entered, he'd surmised they'd taken refuge at her friend Ellie's house. Ellie apparently lived alone, quite a distance away from the nearest neighbor. Certainly farther than his tether would reach, hindering his ability to seek out potential energy donors.

Sarah freed Bitly from his carrier, and the cat began curiously sniffing every corner of the house. Sarah curled herself within a quilted blanket in a guest room and sobbed. It was soul crushing. He'd tested the tether boundary in every conceivable direction, yet had not succeeded. In her current state, he didn't dare draw from her own energy. Even if he had, it wouldn't have been enough. His efforts would only have weakened her further and added to his own frustrations. The end result was not justified by the effort.

And so he spent several long hours in quiet observation, his heart breaking a little more with each passing moment until he could scarcely stand it any longer. Yet he couldn't bring himself to leave her side. He curled himself against her and held her even though she couldn't feel his touch. Sarah didn't seem to sense his presence at all.

Even more troublesome was the fact she'd removed the ring, which now sat in the bottom of her dark and cluttered purse. Helpless to remedy the situation, all he could do was wait to see what she would do next, wait for an opportunity to reenergize and hope for another chance to win her acceptance. And her heart.

He prayed it wasn't already too late.

* * *

She'd cried long enough.

Sarah wiped her tears and went to the bathroom to splash some cold water on her face. She hadn't even called Ellie yet to tell her she'd broken into her house. Not that Ellie would mind. She'd planted the key under the toad just for her and would have loved it if Sarah would have just moved in with her in the first place. But she hadn't. She'd wanted her own home. And now she'd lost it. At least temporarily.

Her body shuddered as she pulled in a deep cleansing breath, the last trembles of the ugly cry. The return call to Ellie would not be a FaceTime call.

She scrolled down her recent calls list and hit Ellie's number, having no idea where to even start the impending conversation.

"Oh. My. God. Why haven't you called me back all day? I've been worried sick. I was about to call the police because I was afraid Jason had gotten to you. Adam came over a dozen times today looking for you. What the hell is going on? Talk to me. Sarah? Why aren't you talking? Are you locked in Jason's trunk somewhere? Oh. My. God. I'm calling the police. Do *not* hang up your phone. We'll track you—"

"Ellie!"

"I'm dialing the landline now, calling the police, I—"

"Ellie, shut up for a minute."

"Okay."

"I'm not locked in Jason's trunk. I'm fine. Mostly. I wasn't talking because I couldn't get a word in edgewise there."

Ellie exhaled a long sigh of relief. "Thank God. What. The. Fuck? Where are you?"

"I'm at your house. I brought Bitly. I hope that's okay. I couldn't leave him at my apartment."

Ellie held silent for way too long, and Sarah dreaded the inevitable explanation.

"Things must be really bad if you left your apartment. Is it Jason? No, is it this new guy, Tanner? What happened, Sarah? I'm about to come unglued over here."

Sarah paced through the house, finding herself in the kitchen, and sat at the table.

"Ellie, I…I don't even know where to begin. Everything is crazy. There's so much I haven't been able to tell you and now the NSA has my house bugged. Maybe even this phone. Crap, I should have called you from your phone instead." Sarah's hand began to shake, and she pressed her cell phone closer to her face to stay the trembling.

"Do it, Sarah. Hang up. I'll call you on the landline."

Sarah complied and, even though she was expecting it, jumped when the home phone rang. Ellie's landline was a twisty corded number, which hung on the wall in all its retro glory. She removed the receiver and pressed her back against the wall to steady herself when she answered.

"Sarah, start talking, or I'm getting on a plane tonight to come home. I'll rent a car. I can be home in four and a half hours."

"No. Don't do that. I'm fine."

"Then tell me. Everything. From the beginning."

"Oh, Ellie. Do you believe in ghosts? Really believe?"

Sarah spent the next two hours filling Ellie in on every detail of the past two weeks, and especially of the past few days they'd been apart. Somehow Ellie had even managed to make her laugh a few times. Bitly curled in her lap and kneaded her thigh, almost as a sign of reassurance and encouragement.

When Ellie had been silent too long on the other end of the line, Sarah's courage failed again.

"I'm going to call Alex, Sarah. I'll call her tonight. I'll be home day after tomorrow. If you will stay at my place and lay low, we'll take that damned ring to Alex and figure out a way to unhex you or whatever the hell has happened. I'm sorry I ever dragged you to Chatham. We'll fix this."

"It wasn't all bad." Sarah smiled, hoping it came through in her tone, although it didn't feel that way.

"One night of good sex doesn't make this all okay. I can't believe those words just came out of my mouth. We're clearly in uncharted territory here. Do you feel safe now? At the house? You don't think anyone...or...thing...followed you?"

"I feel safe."

"Where's the ring now?"

"In my purse."

"Good. Don't put it back on until we have Alex take a look. I'm so sorry, Sarah. I hate that I'm not there for you."

"You're here *and* there for me. You're helping to save my job."

"Yeah, what a mess. You don't even want to know about it now. We're going to be okay. Just hang on until Thursday."

"Okay. Thanks, Ellie. For letting me stay here. For believing me. Believing in me." A lump formed in Sarah's throat, and she couldn't go on.

"Always. Day after tomorrow. Promise."

* * *

Tanner had done his best to listen in on the conversation, but he'd only heard Sarah's side clearly. The gist of their plan was evident. Sarah was prepared to jettison the ring and him along with it. He had until Thursday to accomplish his mission. One day until Ellie would return, and they would take the ring to some mystic.

What fresh hell would she employ upon him?

Without access to energy, he was helpless. He'd tried for hours and couldn't even manipulate a piece of paper, let alone materialize enough to speak with her. Time was running out. Sarah's exhaustion beat at him. Tanner was torn. If she'd never found the ring, he'd have never been freed from his prison, never gotten to know her in her quiet hours alone. The real Sarah. She was strong and smart and clever. And he couldn't fault her for the fear and uncertainty in her eyes.

While people had faith in the unseen, the unknown, there was a line some minds couldn't cross. The unseen needed to remain unseen for faith to continue. Cross the line of a person's known reality for a glimpse to the other side and all bets were off. The human mind couldn't process it. Perhaps it was a failsafe in itself, built into humankind's very essence to keep man from prying beyond the curtain, getting too close to the other side.

Sylvia and the witches employed by the Brothers of Peril had a foot in both realms, manipulating both the natural and unnatural worlds for their personal gain and indulgence. Were Brothers of Peril any better? While they professed to be working toward a worthy cause, Tanner now knew the true price of the power they had wielded. Perhaps it was best that the code had died with him.

Perhaps some things were best not resurrected.

Tanner walked the house, peering out the front windows from time to time, while Sarah showered and dressed for bed. Respecting her privacy was what his gentlemanly upbringing required, although every cell in his dematerialized body demanded another look, another touch, another taste. The memory made the physical loss of her all the sharper.

His heart soared briefly when she pulled the ring up by the chain from the depths of her purse. Holding it to the light, she inspected her reflection in the shining black stone. Hesitantly, she lowered it into her palm and closed it around the ring. The downward curl of the corner of her mouth and the worry swirl between her brows quashed the hopeful flutter in his chest. Her free hand fisted around the ring, knuckles turning white with the effort, and then she dropped it back into the dark cavern.

She'd made a choice.

* * *

Dreams and an unfamiliar bed had left Sarah with fitful sleep. Once she'd startled herself awake, thinking Tanner had slipped in beside her. Her heart hammering against her sternum, she'd rolled over to find Bitly curled against her. No one else.

Perhaps she'd imagined the entire thing. Maybe she'd been under more stress than she'd thought. Had a psychotic break of some sort. If not for Ellie, she could have made herself believe all that. Instead, she'd felt better, if only briefly, after spilling the entire truth to Ellie and been validated by her friend's supportive response.

Hours after she'd fallen into a deep and dreamless sleep, the sound of breaking glass stirred her. Bitly rose, arched and hissed beside her, staring at the guest room doorway.

Fear rose inside her as she came to full alertness, her eyes adjusting in the darkness enough to make out someone moving through the house. She slid out of the bed silently, dragging Bitly off the bed beside her, stroking him to ease his low growling. Searching the room, she looked for something she could use as a weapon. There was really nowhere to hide except for the side of the bed not facing the door where she already crouched, which offered no real coverage.

A quick glance showed her the window behind her was locked, and she couldn't unlock it without drawing attention. The intruder made his way through the main bedroom, and she heard his footsteps on the hardwood floor.

The doorway filled with torso and shadow, and she cowered further, half crawling under the bed. His heavy breathing sounded in her ears like ocean in a seashell, drowning out even the pounding of her own heart.

"I knew I'd find you here."

Jason.

Relief and dread battled within her. At least this was a devil she knew. But this was a devil she *knew*. She drew herself up from the floor and stood, keeping the bed between them.

"What are you doing here, Jason? I have a restraining order."

He flipped on the bedroom light, and her eyes squinted against the harshness as they adjusted. Several days of unshaved beard covered his lower jaw, his hair hung limp and stringy without his usual array of products to keep it erect and in place. She'd never seen the thrift store quality clothes he wore. The gloves on his hands worried her most. They weren't winter gloves. They were rubber gloves, the sort used for dirty labor.

"Right. Fifty feet from your home. This isn't your home or work. And when you weren't at either of those places, I knew you'd come here."

"It's also fifty feet from me. You understand contracts. Do you want to go back to jail?"

"You've already ruined my career."

Sarah started to protest, but the look in his eye told her he wasn't interested in rebuttals. He took one step toward her, and she pressed her back against the wall. His second step brought him to the opposite edge of the bed. She sidestepped to the right, and he lunged, catching the end of her T-shirt and yanking her across the bed. The shirt ripped from her shoulder and hung across her, barely attached by the reinforced collar.

His second lunge had her by the hair. Jason dragged her as she scrambled for her footing on the slick hardwoods. Struggling, she lashed above her head, trying to make contact, to inflict damage, to force him to release her. Jason pushed his knee into her back and pinned her face to the floor. An unusual tearing sound caused goosebumps to creep across her flesh. Her flailing arms were caught and twisted behind her back. Wide sticky tape bound her wrists against one another and her fear rose like bile.

"Jason! What are you doing? This isn't you. Stop before…"

A piece of tape pressed against her mouth, silencing her. Only Ellie knew where she was, and she wouldn't be back until Thursday. Sarah wondered if she'd even make it through the night, let alone until Thursday. She hadn't screamed. Not that it would have done any good.

Ellie's neighborhood was along the highway, just on the outskirts of town. On the edge of the historic district. Her father had bought the house ostensibly as an investment, letting Ellie live rent-free. The homes were each on a half-acre lot. No one would have heard her. And now?

Sounds emitted from her, unbidden. She couldn't stop the pathetic whimper leaking out. There was no Adam or Tanner to save her this time. The sound of more tape tearing spurred her to action. Sarah rolled beneath him and pulled her knees up, then kicked him hard in the groin. Jason doubled over, and she struggled to her feet.

Out of the house!

She raced to the front door as Jason squirmed on the floor, cradling his damaged jewels. Desperate, she forced herself to slow and concentrate as she worked the door knob behind her back with her entrapped hands. The door clicked, and she pulled it open. Sarah pushed out of the screen door, and it slammed back against the house with her effort. She scanned up and down the empty street, but found no passing cars this early. She turned right, back toward town. There were twenty-four hour gas stations and a McDonald's if she could make it there before Jason recovered enough to take chase.

Hands on her shoulders nearly stopped her heart as she spun around.

"Shhh." Agent Sykes peeled the tape from her mouth in one quick effort, the removal stinging as it pulled her skin. A knife slid between her skin and the tape around her wrists, freeing her arms.

"He's inside. My ex. He…he…"

"Go to the Suburban, a block down. Lock yourself in and wait for me. Don't come out until I come for you. Use the OnStar and call the police." Agent Sykes pressed the key fob in her hand. "Go!" He turned and raced back to Ellie's house. His drawn weapon flashed in the street light.

She didn't ask any questions. She ran. Straight to the Suburban and did what he told her, trembling nearly beyond control as she waited for some sign of help.

CHAPTER TWENTY-EIGHT

Agent Sykes entered the home to find Sarah's assailant gathering his supplies into a duffle bag and preparing to make a hasty exit. When the man saw him, he turned for the back door.

"NSA. Stop or I'll shoot!"

The man turned, raising a 9mm from his side. Agent Sykes shot him once in his upper chest and the man fell to his knees, dropping the duffle bag. Sykes kept his gun trained on the assailant and waited. He'd shoot him again if he had to. Seconds later, the man fell forward, his face turned to the side, eyes wide. His head cracked upon impact against the hardwood floor and blood oozed from his open mouth, the result of the last beats of his ruined heart.

Sirens wailed, distant at first then growing louder as they approached.

Good girl.

It wasn't the first man Agent Sykes had shot in the line of duty, but it didn't get easier. Normally, his quarry sat behind thick eye glasses and a computer screen.

Geeks and hackers. He used the barrel of his weapon to part the unzipped duffle bag, revealing a roll of duct tape, two hunting knives and a box of heavy duty trash bags. If he hadn't been surveilling the girl after dropping her off at her house, Sarah Knight would, from all appearances, have ended up a victim of a violent crime. Nothing in the duffle said *romantic interlude*.

Some days, a guy got lucky.

Officers arrived outside. Agent Sykes holstered his weapon and held his badge high above his head, both hands showing. The next six to twelve hours would be filled with questions and paperwork, first at the local precinct then at his own, despite the fact the kill was clean. The assailant faced him on the floor, his weapon still in his hand.

This girl was in a mess the depth of which he had yet to determine, and he wondered if the attack was related to the Brothers of Peril.

The dragon scar on the palm of the dead assailant's hand said it was.

* * *

Tanner drew as much energy from the investigating officers as he could while Sarah sat inside the ambulance, covered in a blanket. Shock, the paramedics had said. He wasn't surprised. Tanner had experienced quite a fright himself. Helpless to come to her aid, he'd watched in horror as Jason subdued her. A shudder passed through him. The fresh thought of Sarah coming to harm further enraged him. He needed to be careful he didn't materialize, rather store enough energy so he could reveal himself to Sarah when they were alone again. God only knew how long that might be now. At least she was safe, in police hands. And Jason…would no longer be a threat to her.

What the hell was the man thinking?

Obviously, Tanner hadn't known Jason prior to meeting Sarah, but the man's apparent decline in the past few weeks had been rapid. He'd gathered that while he'd always been a bully, he'd been respected in his professional circles.

The most puzzling aspect now, as the technicians rolled the body into a black zipper bag, was the dragon scar Tanner had spied on Jason's hand. When Jason had attacked Sarah the first time, he'd been burned by the ring. Could that interaction have somehow transferred the contagion of his hex? There were such laws of magic, like the Law of Contagion, which might account for such a thing. An object, once hexed, could in theory continue to project its magic onto any and all who came into contact with it.

His mind churned.

Police personnel gathered Sarah's personal belongings and presented her purse and phone to her upon her request. They insisted she ride to the hospital for a more thorough evaluation. Much to his relief, she agreed to the checkup, but refused to let them call anyone on her behalf.

Tanner took his place inside the emergency vehicle and worried at Sarah's vacant stare. He gathered her hand in his, and let her draw energy from him, although she wasn't aware of the exchange.

Ten minutes later, she was being put through an entire battery of tests and given a light sedative so she would sleep. A few hours of rest—the most healing and restorative medicine. Tanner used the time to roam the hospital halls and reenergize completely from the host of visitors. Sometime in the early afternoon, he caught a young maintenance worker alone in a supply closet and took his fill to fully materialize, then made his way back through the labyrinth of hallways to Sarah's room. Her puffy, red-rimmed eyes focused on him with recognition and relief as he entered.

"Tanner? Where have you been?"

Tanner approached her cautiously, uncertain.

"I'm so sorry. I told you I might not be able to stay. When my energy faded, so did I. I've been with you though. The entire time. I saw…everything."

Sarah covered her face with her hands. "Jason is dead. I don't know how this has happened. Or what happened to him. He has disintegrated these past few weeks. Like something had hold of him. Changed him."

Tanner crossed to the side of her bed and tentatively reached for her hand. "I think it's the hex. I think the black magic of the ring has affected us all somehow. That first time he touched the ring. Do you remember?"

"It…burned him. His hand."

"Yes, I think the hex affected him after that. It may well have been the reason behind some of his actions."

"Poor Jason."

"It wasn't the reason behind his first attack on you. That was solely the responsibility of his own heart. Regardless, it's time to end this before anyone else gets hurt. Before you get hurt."

"How?" Sarah's eyes filled with tears.

"I'll tell you how," Ellie said, standing just inside the doorway of Sarah's room, surprising them both. "Alex. We're going to destroy that ring and whatever bullshit voodoo is attached to it."

"Ellie? How did you know? What are you doing here so early?"

Ellie's eyes bored into Tanner, her distrust and anger evident. "Tanner, I presume?"

"Yes. It is my honor to make your acquaintance, Ellie." Tanner extended a hand in greeting, which was rebuffed.

"I'm not feeling real warm and fuzzy about you yet, Tanner. I'm not sure if you're the cause or the cure for this fiasco." Ellie closed the distance to the bed and gave Sarah a thorough appraisal. "So he's dead?"

"Yes. NSA Agent Sykes killed him after Jason drew a gun on him. Ellie, he broke into your house. He was trying to abduct me...or worse. I 'kicked him and ran. If Agent Sykes hadn't been there..."

Ellie hugged Sarah to her. "Shhh. For all that's happened, you're still a lucky, lucky girl. Where's that damned ring?"

"It's in my purse," Sarah offered.

"Alex is expecting us. Let's end this thing." Ellie gave Tanner a hard look.

Tanner slid his hand from Sarah's. "Yes."

Sarah's concerned gaze met his own. "What will happen to you? If we manage to destroy the magic of the ring?"

"I'm ready to find out," Tanner said. "You've been through enough."

CHAPTER TWENTY-NINE

Alex Cayce worked out of the psychic shop only a few blocks from Sarah's apartment. The street-level shop windows were filled with candles, stone and ceramic angels, fat Buddhas, live plants, and flowers. An oval-shaped neon blue sign flashed PSYCHIC READING with a red neon hand glowing within its center. A sunburst wind chime hung from the doorway and tinkled as Sarah followed Ellie through the already partially opened door.

It was after five and most of the shops along the street were locked up for the night. Weekday hours were short in the winter, with the exception of First Fridays. Ellie led the way, a longtime customer of Alex's.

Alex peered around the door frame between two floor-to-ceiling curtains, and then crossed to the door to shut and lock it behind them. "This way."

She led them through the shop. Clear bottles lined the back wall, bright yellow, hand-lettered labels describing the contents: oils, powders, herbs and more.

Books, tarot cards and CDs lined the other walls and displays of jewelry, stones, crystals, candles and wands filled the center display tables. In front of the apothecary wall ran a long glass counter filled with an array of ritual knives. A rack of T-shirts and tie-dyed dresses hung in the center. One black shirt with a colorful third eye stared at them, pinned to the wall by the video surveillance camera declaring, "I have my eye on you." An impressive crystal chandelier hung from the ceiling, casting prisms around the room.

"Thank you for seeing us on such short notice. I—"

"Stop." Alex held her spread palm toward Sarah. "Don't tell me anything else. I understand you have questions about a hex? The less I know, the more accurately I can determine if a hex exists. That's all I need to know for now. I'll ask more when the need arises."

Alex continued into a back room, which was, in contrast to the shop itself, homey and ordinary. Sarah realized she'd imagined more Romanian gypsy than shabby chic.

Alex sat in an overstuffed red chair—lace doilies covering each of the piece's threadbare arms—and motioned to the small chair that circled a rather large wooden coffee table.

Ellie grasped Sarah's hand and led her to the loveseat, leaving Tanner to sit alone in a single, hardback chair.

"Before we begin, you're probably wondering about my fee. I charge a flat fee for an hour of service— seventy five dollars—regardless of how long it actually takes. If a hex or curse is determined to exist, I'll gladly assist with its removal for no additional cost. No one likes a hex. Now, which of you is afflicted?"

As usual, Ellie took charge and pointed an accusatory finger at Tanner. "It's him. And this. Show her, Sarah."

Sarah pulled the ring by the chain from her purse.

"Lay the object on the table, please. And then sit back away from it." Alex let the object settle on the table, and then turned her attention to Tanner. "Your name, please."

Tanner cleared his throat. "James 'Tanner' Dawson, ma'am."

"Mr. Dawson, have you been out of the country recently? Or do you have any enemies proficient in any magical systems?

"No, I have not been out of the country. Yes, I have encountered a woman quite capable with magical systems."

"Your hands, please. Palms up."

Holding her own hands forward and palms up, she waited while Tanner leaned in and placed the backs of his hands in her palms. At the instant of contact, Alex's hands closed tightly around Tanner's and her head snapped back, eyes rolling up behind her open lids. Sarah pitched forward, uncertain whether or not an intervention needed to be made on either's behalf, but Ellie quietly held her in place with a hand on her thigh and shook her head 'no.'

After several long moments, Alex came out of her trance-like state and focused, once again, on Tanner's face. Her gaze slid down his torso, taking him in—his dress, his form, his essence—and settled on his palms.

"Your aura is darkly mottled and thin. The energy you have is not your own. You are an incubus of some sort, a psychic vampire somehow incarnate. You are something I haven't seen." The skin of her brow, between her eyes, furrowed in a grim swirl.

"This star." She pointed to a starburst of lines on his hand, which looked like an asterisk. "This is the Star of David, sitting directly upon your lifeline. Run through by your lifeline, if you want to be exact. See how it stops just at the right, outside edge of the star? This indicates life before the hex, the hex, and then…nothing."

Sarah's nails bit into her palms as she sat silent, listening. Normally she would have discounted Ellie's psychic, but now? She hung on her every word. Jason was dead because of her. Somehow she was sure of it.

And Tanner?

Her heart squeezed painfully. Despite everything, she had to admit she had feelings for him. As crazy as it was. As quickly as everything had happened. Something drew her to him, and she didn't want to lose him or anyone else.

Alex continued, "This line here." She traced her finger along a faint line a bit below the first, which had been speared by the asterisk. "This is a dual lifeline. See how it picks up and runs just beneath the star, and then angles upward toward your mount and beyond the star? Sometimes it means a dual career, but for you? I'm not sure. Your aura is not manufactured by your own energy at all. In fact, I see no signs that you can even produce your own aura. I don't want to know how or why. Not yet."

She glanced down to the ring on the table and pulled a pale blue crystal with a silver chain from her pocket. After grasping the pendulum between her thumb and forefinger, she draped it across the back of her hand and fingers. Lifting her pinkie finger so the crystal hung down, she allowed the pendulum to swing freely over the ring. Her eyes closed, and the air sizzled in Sarah's ears. Alex breathed audibly, her bare feet pressed firmly against the hardwood floor beneath her. Growing very still, Alex finally opened her eyes, her steady hand still held the pendulum above the ring.

"Show me what 'yes' looks like," she said, apparently to the pendulum.

Immediately the pendulum began a gentle sway, rounding in a clockwise circle.

"Thank you," Alex said. "Show me what 'no' looks like."

The crystal took up a slow, rhythmic pattern left and right, like a Newton's Cradle, pinging against an unseen force.

"Thank you," Alex said once again. The pendulum stilled.

Her gaze passed over the three of them, one at a time. "Is this ring under the influence of malicious magic, a curse or a hex?"

From a dead stop, the pendulum began to swing in a clockwise circle indicating 'yes.'

"All right then. Spill it, you three. What are we up against here? Clearly the ring." She turned, directing her gaze to Tanner. "And you, sir, are hexed. It feels like some sort of old, black magic. Honestly, I've never come up against anything like this before."

Tanner leaned forward, elbows on his knees and his hands clasped. "Can you destroy it? The hex?"

"Every hex that is cast can be undone. Tell me everything you know about who hexed you and how you discovered it. Then we'll work on the cure."

Sarah sat in rapt attention, barely able to endure the torturous squeezing of Ellie's hand around her own as Tanner recounted his tale, or as much as he could relay to Ellie and Alex, concerning the Brothers of Peril, the General's insistence on dealing with the witch, Sylvia's fury and the resulting hex.

"Holy shit, this has been going on the entire time?" Ellie blurted. "For weeks? And Jason? The ring actually burned the engraving into his skin?" She aimed her amazed look at Sarah. "This doesn't excuse everything that happened before he held the ring. You know that, right?"

Sarah did. Mostly, but still.

"Right?" Ellie pressed. "This was not your fault. Or even Tanner's, now that I hear the entire story. This Sylvia chick was bad news."

Alex blanched. "Sylvia. Did you happen to know a last name?" she asked Tanner.

Tanner ran a hand through his hair and leaned against the slatted back of the chair, tilting his head upward and concentrating on the antique ceiling.

"DeWitt," he finally said. "Sylvia DeWitt."

"And you say she was a known witch whom you worked with personally? As in, in the flesh?" Alex asked.

Tanner hesitated, clearly trying to puzzle together her odd question. "Yes, she was very much in the flesh. That, it turns out, was the main problem and why she hexed me. She wanted…" Tanner's look cut to Sarah and a blush colored his face. "She had unrequited feelings for me of a sexual nature."

"There was a long line of witches named DeWitt. Some perished in the Salem debacle. Others escaped to Virginia. One you may know from the very grounds of Chatham as The Lady in White. Ring any bells?"

"Ellie, the ghost hunt?" Sarah turned to her friend, and the color had gone from her face.

"The night Sarah found the ring we were at Chatham for a ghost hunt," Ellie said. "The Lady in White had been seen, or at least some supposed activity had been seen on the grounds. We didn't see anything. But Sarah found that damned ring, and then started having all of this great luck. We thought it was a lucky talisman. But then things with Jason kept escalating. What's going on, Alex?"

Alex picked up the Brothers of Peril ring by its chain and held it like she had the pendulum, holding it up toward the light for a more thorough examination. "The stone is interesting. Onyx is actually used to keep energy vampires at bay. It resists the draining of energy and has been used as a protection against black magic. It's curious how she turned it against its nature. It's mounted in silver, which normally restores desire to live but, no, it's not a talisman or an amulet. This object, this ring, had great importance to you, Tanner?"

"Yes, it's my Brothers of Peril ring. I never took it off. I was, as I told you, the supernatural liaison for them. I cannot tell you any more of their affairs, only of the final result."

Alex nodded. "It is a fetter then. Sylvia cast a hex on the ring and tricked you into sacrificing yourself by leading that charge. She was denied once before and forced to marry another. She died more than seventy years before you met her at Chatham. Reincarnated perhaps? Somehow she cheated death once at least, and when she thought she was about to lose at love again, she clearly snapped. I'd say there's a very good chance that whatever magic bound you to this ring also entrapped her to Chatham. Breaking the hex may free you both."

"What does that mean for Tanner?" Sarah asked. "Will he…die? Again?"

"That's a chance Tanner has to decide if he's willing to take. I can't predict the outcome of breaking the curse. But it's already killed one man by the Law of Association and Contagion, it would seem."

"What does that mean?" Sarah asked.

Alex leaned in. "The Law of Association makes it possible to easily deliver a hex to a person through an object. The ring was hexed and it carried the curse to its intended target—Tanner. Unfortunately the Law of Contagion makes cursed objects dangerous to others as well, whether they are the intended target or not."

Ellie stood, then began to pace. "I touched the ring, same as Jason. Why did it affect him and not me? Or the jeweler Sarah took it to a few weeks back?"

"A cursed object can continue to plague a person who has touched it if his or her personal energy, their chi, is drained or diminished by chronic ungrounding. It can lead to insomnia, irritability, mood swings, paranoia, irrational thoughts."

"You can check all of those boxes for Jason well before we ever came across that ring," Ellie offered. "He was ripe for the taking."

Alex returned the ring to the table. "Yes, and if he were that susceptible, his rapid decline would likely continue to feed on itself. If the ring actually burned him, reacting with its inherent energy? His decline is understandable. Regrettable, but understandable. The only way to make sure nothing like this happens again is to remove the hex and destroy the cursed object. Then live with the results." She looked at Tanner. "Whatever they may be."

"Agreed," Tanner said. "Let's put this to rest once and for all."

"When can you perform the ritual?" Ellie asked.

"The moon begins to wane tomorrow night," Alex said. "The fetter must be exorcised first. That will remove the curse. Then the ring must be destroyed. The results should be immediate. A hex cannot renew itself without the energy of the maker who created it. Since Sylvia is clearly a ghost again and has no energy of her own, she and Tanner should both be released."

Sarah slid her hand into Tanner's and a visible flicker of energy sparked between them.

"So tonight could be your last night on Earth? Are you sure this is what you want?" Sarah asked Tanner.

"Dear one, it is the only way to keep you and your loved ones safe. What I want no longer matters. This is what we need. Let it be done."

"Sarah, I'll settle up with Alex and make sure things are ready for tomorrow. Why don't you go home?"

Sarah cringed. Were there still cameras, bugs, surveillance at her home? Did she care? After tomorrow, Tanner would be gone and no amount of surveillance or questioning would bring him back. Not from the other side. Not this time.

Her mind grappled with all that had happened and had now been explained. She couldn't deny the evidence before her. Or the man.

"Okay." Sarah gave Ellie a long hug. "Thank you," she whispered.

"No problem. It's what friends are for, right? Breaking hexes, kicking ass. Typical day, really."

Sarah turned to Alex and offered her hand. Alex shook it.

"Thank you, Alex." She reached down to retrieve the ring and slipped it back into her purse.

"You don't want to take that ring with you. You've been exposed to it enough. It's been proven unsafe," Alex said.

"Tanner goes with the ring, and he's coming with me," Sarah replied.

"At least let me store it more safely then, until tomorrow night."

Alex returned with two gallon-sized Ziplock bags full of what looked like fresh earth, a can of salt and a small pine box. She filled the box half full of salt, then picked the ring up by the chain and lowered it into the salt, letting the chain fall around it in a pile. When the ring was covered to the rim, she closed it and flipped the little latch down snuggly. Alex opened one of the Ziplock bags, then placed the sealed box inside. She added more earth from the other bag, filling it until the bag barely zipped.

She presented the bag to Sarah. "That should keep it safe until we can unhex it."

"Thank you." Sarah smiled up at Tanner and took his hand back into hers.

"Let's go home."

CHAPTER THIRTY

Tanner was emotionally drained but still very corporeal, having maintained his overindulgence of hospital energy.

A psychic vampire, Alex had called him. *Yes, that seemed about right.*

He was not good for Sarah. Made even more apparent after Jason's disintegration and death. Yet another dead soul he counted himself responsible for. He deserved to pass into the beyond, to face whatever was to come on the other side.

Sarah busied herself about the apartment, overturning sofa cushions, dumping drawers, swiping behind photo frames and furniture edges in search of listening or tracking devices—in search of s*py works*, she'd said. When she found none, she escaped to the shower for nearly an hour, hot steam leaking from beneath the bathroom door and rising like a cloud into her living/bedroom. Finally she allowed herself to collapse on to the couch. Bitly remained at Ellie's for the night, having been unable to accompany her to the hospital, and Sarah had not wanted to return to Ellie's so soon after Jason had passed. His blood still pooled on the floor, no doubt. Someone would have to clean that up.

Tanner was amazed Sarah even wanted to be near him after all that had happened. He kept his physical distance all the same, unsure of what she needed or wanted from him, if anything.

"Come. Sit by the fire beside me, Tanner," she said, her invitation sparking something within him. Hope, he realized. Maybe they could end as friends. He'd thought she was his salvation when she'd freed him from the ring, but now he realized he didn't deserve salvation, and no longer expected it. Still, an ember of that hope burned inside him like a hot coal. What could he give her? He had nothing.

Tanner sat beside her, more than a foot away from her so they wouldn't touch, not presuming her invitation to be anything more than an offer of friendship to a dying man.

Not long for this world, he thought and almost laughed aloud at the irony of it.

Not long indeed.

Sarah closed the space between them and snuggled up against him, the heat of her body warming him more deeply than the fire ever could. His heart cleaved in two when she laid her head against his shoulder.

"I am sorry for your loss, Sarah. If I had never been released, he would still be alive."

"And I'd still be with him. And eventually, he would likely reach a similar end. It's not your fault. The hex may have exacerbated the circumstances, but deep down, I think it would have all eventually played out. The difference is you were there to save me. More than once."

Tanner stiffened. "I didn't save you this time. Agent Sykes saved you."

"Only because he was still looking for you so he could interrogate the Brothers of Peril key from you. Which you'll take to your grave, once again?"

"I think, after everything, Agent Sykes can be trusted with the key, but I'm not sure the rest of the government can. Not if Agent Falkner is any representation. The question Agent Sykes asked you, before he released you?"

"Something Latin? About the peril of night?"

"Yes, that was a code itself. A greeting of sorts. He is indeed a Brother of Peril, of the most recent incarnation, at least. I don't know that it's wise to continue in the Brothers of Peril mission, considering my outcome."

"Maybe that's not your decision to make. Maybe you should pass along the code and let your brothers take up the fight. You could die a hero. Again."

"Yes. Would that ease your suffering, if I were to do that? Write out the key for you to hand over to Agent Sykes after I am gone? If so, I will do it. For you."

"Tanner, do it for your country and for your own peace of mind if that is what you think is right. I wouldn't ask you to give anything of yourself that you didn't want to."

"And that, dear Sarah, is why I fell in love with you these past weeks," Tanner said.

"You've been with me through everything. The entire time I've had the ring."

"Yes."

"Tanner, I..." Her eyes locked with his and he stilled, held by her gaze alone. In the firelight, he memorized her face to take with him for however long the next Purgatory might be.

Sarah stretched up and brushed her lips across his, her hands searching to find access beneath his jacket. His ridiculous Union jacket. His body simmered beneath her touch, and he savored every moment, knowing with mortal certainty it would be his last.

His pulse quickened, pounding against his ears and urgency ratcheted his adrenaline, sending it spiking through his body in response.

More. Now. Forever.

When he could resist his heart's demands no more, he eased her back onto the couch and stretched out across her, pressing her into the cushions, her face illuminating, angelic in the firelight. She reached to unfasten the many fat buttons of his coat, and he peeled it off and over his head instead, saving them time, because time was as precious as ever.

This night. This one more night they would have together, and then he would be gone, unable to even watch her from afar through the veil. Once the ring was destroyed, his tether to it would be severed, and he had no doubt he'd plunge into whatever dark afterlife awaited him.

But it was the right thing to do. The only thing to do.

What he would do.

For Sarah.

Her hands wove through his too long hair. Kissing her lips, her chin, her throat, Tanner worked at her shirt with his hands, and she arched for him, making it easier to strip the blouse up her torso, shoulders, and finally off. The sight of no undergarments to discard brought a smile to his face.

Cupping her breasts, he bent and took her nipple into his mouth, rolling his curious tongue around its pink and roughened skin until it stood high at attention. He slid a hand beneath the curve of her lower back and pulled her to him, fit her against him as they were meant to be joined and ground against her through his trousers.

"Enough," Sarah ordered. "Clothes off. All of them. Now."

"You first," Tanner countered and pulled the drawstring on her pants. Once loosened, her trousers slid down her body easily, revealing her smooth, bare beauty. "You are different."

"Where?" Sarah asked, her doe eyes black in the light.

"Here," Tanner answered. He lowered his mouth to her core and drew his tongue through her folds. "When did you do this?"

Sarah gasped in a sharp breath. "In the shower. Shaved. All of it. It was a bitch, but so far…totally worth it."

"Yes. It is."

Tanner couldn't keep his eyes, or his mouth, from her now and planted his hands beneath her hips to raise her to his face and satiate his desire.

"Still clothed, soldier. Let's see more naked, please."

A growl of frustration escaped him, surprising himself with his base animal urges. He hurriedly dispatched of the remainder of his clothing.

"If Sykes still has eyes and ears here, he's about to get a show," Sarah said.

"I don't care." Tanner resumed his previous position, raising her hips from the couch and burrowing his face between her legs.

"Oh, God. Me either. Don't stop doing that. Ever."

Ever was a long time. A time they would never have.

He pushed the thought away and refused to address it. He had the here and the now and that would have to sustain him for what was ahead.

Skin against skin created a delicious friction that demanded action. He climbed up her body and settled his erection between her legs, nestled within reach of her sweet heat. The pulsing head of his cock pushed against her folds, sliding inside just enough to take his breath away with the agonizing pleasure. Sarah's urgent restlessness and slight movements only increased the torture until her fingernails bit into his buttocks as she grasped him, raising her own hips and pulling her body up to meet his. Undone, he acquiesced and slammed his shaft into her, eliciting a moan, which consumed him and spurred him onward in the hopes of earning more of her sweet affirmations.

Maintaining his rhythm, he stroked in and out of her slick heat, the pressure building down low as the rest of his body tensed in anticipation of the impending consummation. Before he could climax, Sarah's walls wrenched around his shaft, stopping his progress with the powerful contraction.

"Wait," Sarah demanded. "Sit up, on the couch."

Reluctant, Tanner obeyed, pressing his bare back and ass against the soft upholstery, the head of his cock pulsing and weeping in protest as he worked mentally to stave off the inevitable. Sarah stood before him, in relief with the firelight illuminating her from behind so that a yellow/orange glow radiated and flickered around her like an aura.

Surprising him, she crawled onto his lap and straddled him, grasping the couch back with her hands, her breasts swinging enticingly within easy reach of his eager mouth. He licked one nipple, and she arched closer to him, encouraging him to continue. His hands slid along the curves between her ribs and hips—a perfect fit—but he wanted more and he continued downward to grasp her buttocks. Purposefully, she positioned her folds *just so* against the back of his shaft and slowly punished him by working herself down the outside of his erection, obstinately avoiding his sensitive head.

Tanner's head snapped back against the couch at the acute agony. His hands stilled their roaming, finding hard purchase, his thumbs burrowing into the hollows of her hips when her folds finally parted and she impaled herself upon him.

She rode him like a slowing carousel horse, up and down in the slowest, most punishing of paces. Helpless to do much more than continue to be the willing recipient of her ministrations, he did finally unclench one hand from her hip and massage his thumb across her nub on each uptick of her canter.

Soon her rampant breathing matched his own. Their pleasure culminated, first hers, and her walls constricted around his member one final time, and then he reached his own terminus. Sarah collapsed against him, settling her slight weight within his lap, her breasts crushing against his chest, and he settled his face against her damp neck. Tightening his arms around her, he clung to her, refusing to allow any separation between them for as long as he could maintain his hold.

Ever, it seemed, was a much shorter time than one would expect.

CHAPTER THIRTY-ONE

Sarah wasn't surprised to see several missed calls from Agent Sykes the next morning. His messages indicated he was still trapped in paperwork and bureaucracies of his Maryland office after Jason's shooting, but promised a personal visit soon. She was actually touched with his concern, although she knew his ultimate goal was to sleuth out more concerning Tanner and the Brothers of Peril. She was also thankful no other officers had shown up at her door for follow-up.

She and Tanner had made love several times during a long and lazy day together. As the sun set, Tanner became more distant and had spent the past few hours bent over a fresh notebook, reconstructing the code key for the grimoire. Neither of them knew if it was the right thing to do, but it was a secret too important to take to the grave…again.

The thought of Tanner vanishing—for good this time—turned her stomach cold. The short time she'd spent with him, despite the tumultuous events, had filled a void in her she hadn't known existed. Leave it to her to finally find Mr. Right and he wasn't even human. Anymore.

Miraculously, Tanner's corporeality had held, and he was very much real. Very much alive. And very much one hundred percent male, sitting at her desk, filling a notebook with secrets that could change the future course of history.

There was that.

Ellie had called several times earlier in the day to check in, and Sarah had reassured her they would be at Chatham in a few hours to complete the ritual. The longer she sat in her living room watching Tanner work, the less she wanted to make the short drive. It felt like a death march. She could only imagine what it felt like to Tanner, yet he'd not expressed any uncertainty or regret. Still, the ritual sat between them almost like a physical thing in the room.

Restless, she called ahead to the café a block down from her apartment and placed their takeout order. Tanner was so engrossed in his work, he didn't even notice.

"Tanner," she said, squeezing his shoulder and breaking the spell he'd fallen under.

His head snapped around and his bloodshot eyes shot up to meet her own. "Is it time? Already?"

"Not yet. I ordered us some food. I'm going to run down and get it. I'll be back in fifteen minutes."

"Thank you, dear one. That would be lovely."

She leaned down and brushed a kiss across his forehead.

When she stepped outside, she noticed Adam walking to his apartment

"Sarah, I'm so sorry to hear about Jason. Ellie told me everything. I'm glad you're okay," Adam said.

Sarah doubted Ellie had told Adam *everything,* but appreciated the sentiment. "Thank you, Adam."

"Is there anything I can do for you?"

Sarah pulled the door closed behind her, so Adam wouldn't see Tanner working. "Um, I ordered food. Any chance you could run down to the café and pick it up for me?"

"Sure."

She handed him her cash, and he hustled out. As she waited outside the door for him to return, she marveled that she'd forgotten about the tether's boundary already. This was not the time to risk Tanner's corporeality by testing his limits.

Minutes later, Adam returned with two bags.

"That's a lot of food," he said, handing her the change.

"I missed a few meals. Making up for lost food." She laughed.

He reached over and hugged her. "Okay. Be careful. I'm right down the hall if you need me."

"There's nothing to fear anymore, right?"

"Let's hope not."

Sarah pushed through her apartment door to find Tanner unmoved from where she'd left him. Relief coursed through her, and she released a breath she hadn't realized she was holding.

That ridiculous tether. What would she give to free him so he could stay with her? *Everything*, she realized. The ring lay buried in earth and salt still in the Ziplock on her bedside table, just where she'd left it.

That damned ring.

They ate in silence. She wondered if Tanner even tasted the food.

"How much longer?" she asked, then quickly clarified. "On the code?"

"It's finished."

"Oh."

A small smile turned up one corner of his mouth. "We still have an hour? Before we need to go to Chatham?"

Sarah ducked her head, needlessly embarrassed at his implication. "Yes. We should spend it well."

"Indeed."

* * *

The best two weeks of Tanner's life had come a hundred and fifty years after his death. He had little hope that the next stage of his existence—or in this case, nonexistence—would be nearly as lovely.

The code was broken. The complete key lay within the pages of Sarah's notebook now. It would be up to Agent Sykes to wield its power with integrity. He wished he could present it to Sykes in person, but he didn't want Sykes or anyone else interfering in what needed to be done tonight. Too many innocent souls had already been affected by Sylvia's dark magic. Against Brothers of Peril protocol, he had shared the necessary reply to Agent Sykes' earlier inquiry with Sarah. It would be enough to convince Sykes of the notebook's authenticity. If Sarah made the reply, Sykes would understand the implications.

He'd done all he could do.

It was time to move on.

CHAPTER THIRTY-TWO

They followed the bright and waning moon across the Kings Highway Bridge to Chatham. Ellie and Alex were waiting in the ancient Mustang in the Chatham parking lot when Sarah and Tanner arrived. The enormity of what they were about to undertake pressed against Sarah's chest, making it difficult to breathe.

Was this the wrong thing to do?

Tanner didn't seem to have any doubts. Or at least he hadn't voiced them. Of course, they hadn't spent much time talking during their last day together.

The notebook and the earth-covered ring weighed heavy in her purse. She was afraid to leave the notebook at the apartment. She didn't want any chance of it falling into the wrong hands. Together, she and Tanner decided she would text Agent Sykes as soon as Tanner was gone and wait here for him to meet her. Regardless of his current situation, she knew Sykes would drop everything as soon as he learned what she had for him.

She was counting on it.

"Hey," Ellie said, exiting her car.

"Hey," Sarah replied, curling her hand into Tanner's.

Ellie frowned down at Sarah's hand, enclosed around his. "Are you sure about this? Maybe there's another way." She glanced at Tanner.

"No," Tanner said. "This is the only way. Break the curse, and Sarah will be free from its effects. You all will."

Ellie nodded. "You're a hell of a guy, Tanner. I'm sorry things didn't work out differently. Sarah deserves a good man in her life."

Silence filled the space between them until Alex broke it. "Where did you find the ring, Sarah?"

Sarah pulled Tanner behind her, walking across the lot to where Ellie had parked the night of the ghost hunt. She pulled her peacoat tighter around her and momentarily released Tanner's hand to button it against the biting cold wind.

"There." She pointed.

Tanner surveyed the landscape in respect to the house, the walls and grounds. "I must have dropped the ring then, because I was shot and killed over there." He indicated the front side of the manor, overlooking the Rappahannock River.

"Let's do the ritual there, then. It will hold the most residual magic," Alex said.

They followed a flagstone walkway and gathered on the lawn in front of the manor, near the stone wall. Even in darkness, the grounds were impressive and the manor rose like a beast behind them. A shiver ran through Sarah. Memories of their day together heated her cheeks, and she was thankful for the cover of night.

Alex slipped a backpack from her shoulder and lowered it to the ground. She unzipped the pack, then pulled a canister of flour from it.

"I'm going to cast a circle. We all need to stay within it until the ritual is complete. I'm going to mark it with flour so you'll see it," Alex said.

Silently, Alex walked three paces from their little gathered group, then continued in a circle, pouring a thin line of flour across the grass. When it was complete, she returned to its center and stood, eyes closed, with her palms up and open, for several long minutes before finally opening her eyes again.

"Do you have the ring?" Alex asked.

"Yes." Sarah pulled it from her purse, then held the bag out to Alex.

Alex removed a piece of white linen from the backpack and snapped it out across the grass. She smoothed the wrinkles. Next, she removed a velvet pouch and a hammer. She unearthed the ring from the bag, unlatched the wooden box, and spilled the salt in a separate pile until the ring fell free.

"Wait," Sarah said, suddenly filled with dread. "Tanner, this is your last chance. Surely there's another way. I can't let you go. I...I..."

"What, dear one? Tell me."

"I love you."

Tanner's arms closed around her and his forehead pressed to hers, his eyes closed. "I love you too, Sarah Knight. I always shall. Thank you. Thank you for saving me from that black Hell I was cast into. Even if it was only for these few precious days, I'll carry them with me to whatever my fate is to be. Carry out our business with Agent Sykes. Live your life. And one day, perhaps we'll find one another again."

His lips pressed to hers and tears leaked from the corners of both of her eyes.

"Continue, please." Tanner addressed Alex but continued to hold Sarah, his eyes seeing only her and his hold firm.

Alex fished the ring out by the chain, then lowered it into the velvet pouch. She pulled a pair of safety glasses from the pack and put them on.

"Just in case," Alex said. "I'm going to pop out the stone with the hammer, and then crush it in this bag." She hammered away until a clear crack sounded, and shook out the contents. The stone was indeed released from its setting and freed from the silver. Using the velvet bag as a glove, she let the stone fall inside it, then pulled the drawstring tightly, placing it on the flat stone of the walkway.

"Because we don't know exactly how the hex was placed or have access to the same materials that were used, we're destroying the ring. The stone I'll physically destroy by crushing the onyx to dust, and then we'll scatter it in the running waters of the Rappahannock. The silver we'll bury once again. We'll remove the curse." Alex looked at Tanner. "That will be the end, Tanner."

Tanner nodded, keeping his eyes on Sarah.

The repeated striking of the hammer echoed into the darkness, and Sarah was thankful Chatham Manor was still surrounded by rural landscape. Explaining what the four of them were doing trespassing on the grounds in the middle of the night was the last thing she wanted to do.

On Alex's last strike of the hammer, movement at the edge of Sarah's peripheral vision caught her attention. Turning, she blinked twice, trying to clear her sight, unsure of what she was seeing. A figure seemed to be moving toward them from the curved steps of Chatham. A gasp escaped her and the others turned to follow her gaze.

"The Lady in White," Ellie said, confirming what was forming in Sarah's own mind.

"Sylvia," Tanner said.

The ghostly form floated toward them across the lawn, her hair whipping as the wind picked up its bluster and her dress, clean and gauzy, swirled behind her. The closer she came, the more transparent she appeared.

"Don't be afraid. She's drawn to the energy we've raised with the circle. Even if she's like Tanner, she won't be able to manifest to human form without drawing from our personal energy. She can't reach us inside the circle. I doubt even magic could make her corporeal again now."

"How do you know?" Sarah asked.

"Because if she could have, she'd have attacked us when we first arrived with the ring," Alex answered.

"That's reassuring," Ellie offered.

Alex clutched the bag with the crushed stone. Sarah held her breath and waited to see if the apparition would attempt to pass the circle of protection. When the ghost hovered outside the circle instead, Alex reached into her pack and withdrew a small spade. She dug a deep hole in the ground and emptied the salt from the box at the hole's base. She then placed the now stoneless ring into the hole.

"Once the hex is removed, the silver will corrode quickly in the wet ground and the salt will speed the process," Alex said.

After covering the stone in salt, she filled in the hole with the displaced earth and scattered the remaining soil.

"Let us form a circle and pray the curse be lifted." Alex reached out to Sarah, and they all held hands and completed the circle.

Alex closed her eyes and the rest followed her lead, despite Sylvia's animated but silent protests behind them.

"Hail, Spirit. You are true, fair and generous. I praise you. Thank you for removing any hex, curse or negative energy from this ring immediately, with harm to none, and for the highest good of all. So may it be. In return, I offer you gratitude, love, devotion and ask your will be done concerning Tanner's fate. Blessed be," Alex said.

"Blessed be," Ellie echoed.

The gale diminished immediately and the air warmed around them. Sarah turned quickly, looking back to where the apparition had floated only moments before. Nothing. She completed a circle, along with the others. The Lady in White was gone.

She stared down in disbelief at Tanner's hand, warm and firm in her own. Tears welled in her eyes as she dragged her gaze up his torso to his face.

Tanner remained. Whole and real.

"That's it? It's that easy? What does this mean for Tanner, Alex?" Ellie asked.

Sarah stood in silent awe, unwilling to believe what she prayed was true. What she saw and felt was too good to be trusted after all that had happened to them both. Had the ring given her one last gift of good luck?

"I don't know. The results are immediate. Sylvia is released. The hex is broken. All that's left is to scatter the stone in the river," Alex said.

"So Tanner is freed?" Sarah asked. "Returned?"

"It would appear so," Alex said.

"Holy shit," Ellie offered.

* * *

Tanner pulled Sarah close and held her hard to him in the parking lot under the moonlight to stay the trembling of his own body. Alex and Ellie cleaned up the evidence of their ritual. He couldn't yet believe it. Doubt lingered. Sylvia had gone much too easily. Her mouthed protest hadn't gone unnoticed. She was clearly angry. At him. Yet she'd vanished, and Alex assured them there were no lingering traces of her or any sort of magic as soon as the circle was broken.

It was too good to be true, yet it was all he'd ever hoped for from the very moment he'd awakened in Sarah's apartment. Sarah sobbed softly into his chest, the wool of his Union jacket impermeable to her tears. God, he hated that jacket.

"Are you ready?" Ellie asked, placing a tentative hand on Sarah's back.

Sarah sniffed and wiped at her face. "Yes. I can't believe that worked. Alex, are you sure he gets to stay?"

"You'll know for certain if he can leave the Chatham grounds...and the ring behind. The hex is broken. Only one way to test it now."

"Are you sure you can drive? Do you want to ride with me? We can get your car tomorrow."

"No. I don't want to ever come back here," Sarah said.

"Agreed," Tanner said.

"We're stopping on the shoulder on the bridge so Alex can scatter the stones in the river. And that's the end of it," Ellie said.

"No," Tanner said. "It's a beginning."

"I like him," Ellie said. "Let's keep him."

CHAPTER THIRTY-THREE

Tanner and Sarah sat at the all-night diner in the wee hours of the morning. Sarah had texted Agent Sykes as soon as she'd parked the car back in the garage. There was no need prolonging the inevitable. Sarah wanted any surveillance the agent still had in place terminated, and Tanner was ready to hand over the notebook. They were both a little shaky. The ring was destroyed, part of it buried at Chatham. The rest was scattered somewhere downriver. Tanner remained, alive and very much in the flesh three miles from the hexed ring and was currently drinking a cup of coffee. That fact alone chased their remaining concerns into the shadows. Mostly.

With this one loose end wrapped up, Tanner would be truly free from the Brothers of Peril and all that it had unleashed upon him. Sarah was more than willing to spend the rest of her days helping him forget his past and make a new future together. She hadn't even asked to see the code key. The less she knew about it, the better they both would be. A clean break and they would be out. Everyone would be free to live their lives. Everyone except Jason, but there was no undoing what was done. What *he* had done. She knew Tanner held guilt about what had happened with Jason, but it wasn't his fault.

"Penny for your thoughts?" Sarah asked.

"I'm afraid my thoughts are much too muddled to be worth anywhere close to a penny." Tanner smiled.

Sarah pulled one of his hands from the coffee cup and held it in her own. "Perhaps we can achieve some clarification as soon as we're finished with Agent Sykes."

Tanner stroked his thumb across her hand in a suggestive way. "That would be lovely."

"Ahem." Agent Sykes appeared beside their table like a specter. They hadn't even noticed him come through the door. Had the entry bell chimed? "May I?"

Sykes pulled up a chair at the end of the booth and pressed his palms flat on the table. "Mr. Dawson. I have to say I'm a bit surprised to see you here. See Agent Falkner went ahead, after my strong suggestion and conducted a much more in depth search for James Tanner Dawson. I suggested he go back further into the archives. Much further. Which, of course, he did and found this." Sykes handed Tanner a photo, a reproduction of one he'd had made when he joined the service. "And this." Sykes laid another piece of paper on the table between them. "A death record from Chatham. See, the thing is, it's from 1862. So this tells me something very important about you, Mr. Dawson. Either you're a liar, and you're using a stolen identity, just happening to look very, very much like this soldier in the photo, right down to your coat, I might add, or you're something...other. Considering how you managed to vanish right before Falkner's eyes—he's pretty shook up about that still, by the way—I'm betting on 'other.' We'll work that out later, I suppose. For now, Sarah said you two had something for me?"

Tanner looked up from the photo and the death certificate, meeting Agent Sykes' curious gaze. *"Pericula noctis."*

Sykes stilled, his breathing stopped, and he took a quick survey around the diner before leaning in and responding. *"Numerus signorum,* Mr. Dawson."

Tanner reached inside his coat and produced the notebook. He laid it on the table between them, his palm pressed tightly against it. "Power like this can change more than our future, Agent Sykes. The key to the grimoire is here. With this last contribution, I submit my resignation from the Brothers of Peril and demand release from my service. Do not contact me further. Remove your eyes and ears from Sarah's home, from her life and leave us be. That is the price for this gift."

Sykes grimaced, his hand curled and his thumb and forefinger rubbed together. "The Grand Inspector General will want to know where this came from. He'll have follow-up questions."

"And you'll craft answers sufficient to appease his inquiries, leaving Sarah and me out of it hence forward. I have given all to the Brothers of Peril, including my life. I won't do it again."

Tanner pushed the notebook toward Sykes and sat back against the hard booth.

"Done. I suppose this means those questions I have about you are off the table as well?" Sykes asked.

"You'll have enough answers within these pages to keep you busy for a good long time, Agent Sykes, I've no doubt."

Agent Sykes' lips pressed into a grim line. "I'll send an agent over in a few hours to remove the surveillance. Sarah, there will still be questions concerning Jason I'm afraid you'll have to answer. The sooner the better."

Sarah nodded. "Thank you, Agent Sykes. For everything."

"I think I'm the one who should be thanking you two. You've done a great service to your country with this. To the Brothers of Peril as well, Tanner."

"Use it wisely," Tanner warned.

"Of course."

EPILOGUE

"Hurry up, Sarah! We'll miss the first band."

Sarah flipped the brass cover and peeked through her new peephole to see Adam and Ellie on the other side. "We're coming," she said.

Tanner's arms slid around Sarah from behind, eliciting a squeak that she hoped Ellie didn't hear through the door. She spun around in his arms.

"Are you certain you can walk in those shoes all night?" Real concern sent crow's feet fanning from the corners of his eyes.

"No, but it will give us an excuse to come home early."

"You are a clever, clever woman, dear one." Tanner pressed his lips to hers, and for a moment the entire evening plan was forgotten.

"The car is parked in the fire zone. Seriously, we need to go. Now," Ellie implored.

Sarah sighed. She'd been excited about WZRK's Rocking New Year's party when she'd won the tickets last month, but now? She wanted to burrow in and enjoy every second alone with Tanner. With Ellie all but moved in next door with Adam, she'd barely had a moment's peace. Ellie was constant with the pop-overs. Still, life was settling into something that felt right despite their unusual start. This party would be the first night out they would enjoy together as a foursome. And Tanner was in for a huge culture shock.

Now that they were free to move about together unfettered, Sarah had taken Tanner up and down every street of Fredericksburg. They'd learned the history since 1862 together and Tanner still marveled at the changes and modern conveniences. None of which surprised him more than to discover the country was currently led by a black president. His childlike amazement and thirst for knowledge endeared him to her even more. Still, he wrote daily love notes and left them for her to find. She kept them all in a box under her bed. She was enamored.

And Bitly? Bitly seemed to love Tanner even more than Sarah. The cat slept on his shoulder every night, and Tanner patiently tolerated the attention.

Sarah opened the door, catching Ellie in a full-on pout.

"About time," Ellie said, racing ahead of them down the stairs.

Ellie got into the driver's seat, and Tanner opened the back door of the new Ford Fusion for Sarah. Despite Ellie's protests, Sarah had followed through on her gift. The prize car was now Ellie's. In return, Ellie had sold her Mustang and given Sarah the money, which helped fund a new wardrobe for Tanner, among other things.

The past two weeks had been a whirlwind of police investigations, FBI questions concerning Candace and helping Tanner acclimate to life in the twenty-first century.

Ellie hit her cell phone's 80s playlist, and it started playing across the Fusion's Bluetooth. "I thought you two might like this one. Full circle and all," she said, smiling into the rearview mirror.

Pat Benatar's "Love is a Battlefield" filled the car.

Tanner turned to Sarah, confusion written on his face. "It's a song about war?"

"It's a song about love. That sometimes you have to fight for it."

Tanner's eyes searched her face and his hand wound around hers.

"Indeed."

The End

ABOUT THE AUTHOR

Lisa adores beasties of all sorts, fictional as well as real, and has a farm full of them in her Southwest Missouri home, including: one child, one husband, two dogs, two cats, a dozen hens, thousands of Italian bees and a guinea pig.

She may or may not keep a complete zombie apocalypse bug-out bag in her trunk at all times, including a machete. Just. In. Case.

Keep in touch here:

Website: http://lisa-medley.com/books/
Facebook: /lisamedleyauthor
Twitter: @lisamedley
Google+: +lisamedley
Pinterest: medley3
Amazon: http://amzn.to/1axwex7

Don't miss a thing! Sign up for my New Release Newsletter http://eepurl.com/9Zhcz

Other Books by Lisa Medley

Reap & Repent
(Book I of The Reaper Series) - March 2015

Reap & Redeem
(Book II of The Reaper Series) - May 2015

Reap & Reveal
(Book III of The Reaper Series) - July 2015

Reap & Reckon
(Book IV of The Reaper Series) - September 2015

The Reaper Series:

A small group of reapers and supernatural beings in Meridian, Arkansas are all that stands between humanity and the apocalypse when a fallen angel stages a demonic invasion. In their battle to save the world, each will meet his or her match, discovering the power of love...and the importance of risking everything to protect it.

The only thing worse than having nothing to live for...is having everything to live for.